Adapted for the Screen

LM Foster

This is a work of fiction. Names, characters, places and incidents are products of the author's imagination. Any resemblance to actual events, locales, organizations, or persons, either living or dead, is entirely coincidental.

ISBN-13: 978-0692735046
ISBN-10: 0692735046

9th Street Press
www.9thstreetpress.com

There is only one plot – things are not what they seem.

— Jim Thompson

.

Carolyn Adyon Speaks

How's that for ego?

Like anyone would ever listen, retorts my Realistic Sense of Self-Worth.

Ya never know, counters Ego again.

It's not entirely out of the realm of possibility. Someday, people might want to hear my thoughts. After all, I'm credited as co-screenwriter on *Dorian and Henry,* and even though Wilde purists were not amused, it nonetheless enjoyed a modest success. And the original idea for critically (if not financially) acclaimed *Kinship* was mine: it even says, *From a story by Carolyn Adyon* in the opening credits. Maurice Claremount, writer and director of mega-hit *Cheyenne Sundown,* turned a little tale I made up into a movie that was praised by *Time Magazine.* He wrote the script for it, because I wasn't entirely comfortable with screenwriting at the time.

Maybe you'll never be comfortable with screenwriting, pipes up my Realistic Sense of Self-Worth.

Pish posh, returns my Ego. I'm a storyteller, a *raconteuse,* as Maury says; I've been one since childhood. And a screenplay's just another way to tell a story. So what if I tend to want to put in a little too much description?

"It's a *movie,* Carol!" Maury always tells me. "We're going to *see* what's going on! You don't have to *describe* it!"

At least I've finally gotten the formatting down right.

And he's always there to check me, to imperiously correct me, with total disregard for the ol' ego. He's made me tough, reinforced that Realistic Sense of Self-Worth. I'm really just a nobody, an Inland Empire girl who got very lucky. Any and all other aspiring screenwriters should be so lucky.

Maybe my next effort will stand on its own.

My next effort hasn't been too forthcoming, but I found my two green keys yesterday, and it's prompted me to start this new journal. At least I'm writing *something*.

Finding those two pistachio-colored keys on their little ring brought to mind my last journal, and remembering that ponderous epistle and the dark wonders it recounts might've planted the seed for another tale between the folds of my brain. At least I'm putting words to blinking cursor, filling in that accusingly blank space. Goodbye, writer's block!

So, thus.

My last journal is still under lock and key in a safe deposit box in Riverside. After finding my two green keys, I scared up the computer file of that journal, buried on some external hard drive. I skimmed it, resisted the urge to edit, to rewrite. It should stand untouched, a paranoid testament to my disbelief at all the supernatural things happening in my life at the time. It's another chapter in that tale as old as time: when all of hometown girl's dreams come true, she's still too dumb to realize how good she's got it. She's doubtful, suspicious.

I wrote down the catalogue of events, the tragedies and joys. Then in true cinematic style, I hid it away, and left a sealed envelope for my former boss, an attorney. *Open in the event of Carolyn Adyon's death or incapacity,* it says on the outside. Inside lurks the key to the safe deposit box, the location of the bank.

I took all these precautions because I was worried that my life might be in danger then, and if something happened to me, I wanted the world to know why. If I woke up dead, I'd left instructions for my former employer to publish my true Hollywood story.

Briefly:

It was 2013, and my best friend Ruthanne had a crush on a movie star named Franck O'Day. She always preferred actors from the Golden Age of Hollywood to more modern thespians, and Franck was her very favorite. Unfortunately, he'd died in a plane crash in 1968, two decades before she and I had been born.

But Ruthie, God love her, *just knew* Franck wasn't dead.

On the way home from work one afternoon, I noticed two pistachio-colored keys hanging from her keychain, and asked her about them.

And so the saga began. Ruthie told me that the keys were a good luck charm, that they represented a lost movie that would've starred this matinee idol, had it ever been completed. The symbolism was not overly complicated: the movie had been entitled *Two Green Keys.*

Ruthie explained. "It's something that Franck's fans can share. Nobody's ever heard of the movie, unless they've heard of him, so it's a little way that we can identify each other, so to speak. Almost like a secret handshake."

I had certainly never heard of the guy, so Ruthanne showed me his fan site on the interwebs. Without a whole lot of originality, it was called *TwoGreenKeys.com.* Ruthie read aloud from it: *"Keep sending all your good wishes and love energies to Franck. While his health had been faltering a little lately, your healing energies have once again put him on the road to recovery. Keep sending in those keys! Watch this space for news of a personal appearance in the not too distant future!"* Ruthanne blinked solemnly. "See, I told you he wasn't dead."

"What was that about love energies? And keys?"

"There's a belief that people can send healing energies to others. It works like this. You find two keys. Any two will do. You meditate on them – fill them with your good wishes, your love for Franck – then you send them with a self-addressed stamped envelope to the fan club. Franck receives the energy and love from them – and infuses each with a little of his own grateful energy. They're painted green to complete the symbolism of the movie title, and mailed back to you.

"I own something that he actually touched, Carol! Something that's imbued with a little of his energy, a little of him. What better good luck charm is there than that?"

I had no response. Ruthanne sighed, smiled a little sheepishly. "I know you don't believe any of this. But Franck's life, not to mention his beliefs on healing energies – it would all make a great book."

Ruthie, my childhood friend, knew how much I'd always aspired to be a writer, and with very little effort, she soon talked me into penning her beloved Franck's biography. Emails with the webmaster of *TwoGreenKeys.com* were exchanged; I even joined the fan club myself, received my own two green keys in the mail.

All that claptrap about healing energies – I wouldn't believe any of it, right up until I knew beyond a shadow of a doubt that it was all true; until I began to benefit from it. But I'm getting ahead of myself.

Damned if Ruthanne and I didn't get to actually meet Franck O'Day.

Not only wasn't he dead, he looked great. He had a few wrinkles, and his once black hair was now an iron gray. But on the other hand, he was eighty. No one would've guessed it. He didn't look a day over fifty.

Ruthanne was charmed, as she couldn't help but be charmed, what with finding out that her favorite old-timey actor wasn't dead. What with getting to actually meet him and all. Finding out that he looked great. If you were a fan of Marlon Brando, it would've been like getting to meet him and discovering that he looked just a few years older than he did in *On The Waterfront,* instead of the wreck he'd become by *The Island of Doctor Moreau.* Not to mention finding out that he wasn't dead at all.

Ruthie was thrilled. She was ecstatic. She was in love.

After our first visit, we drove back to Beverly Hills again the following weekend, and lo and behold, Franck's iron gray, old man's hair color was gone. He'd dyed it, restored it once again to the inky black of his decades-passed youth. Now he looked forty.

I listened to Franck tell his life story – it was a doozy, full of sex and love and death and betrayal and success in old-Hollywood. It goes without saying that the oddest chapter was about the energy. The energy, Franck revealed, was the reason he'd stayed in Japan so many years after the plane crash that had not in actuality killed anyone but the unfortunate pilot.

At some stripe of monastery in the wilds of Japan, Franck related, he and his fellow Hollywood refugee, director Robert Ecksmith *(Who?* I'd thought) had learned to harness this mystery of the universe. Much later, Franck would explain the phenomenon to me in detail: "When you love something, you give off a special kind of energy. The things you love, they soak it up – who looks happier and healthier than a beloved child, or a pampered house pet? Even plants respond to love. It's a force of nature. In Japan, I learned to recognize this energy – to harness it, to assimilate it."

He claimed that it wasn't plastic surgery that made him seem so well preserved for his age. It wasn't dye from a box or salon that had changed his locks back to their glossy, youthful black. It was the admiration of his fans, come to him via emails and keys. And it was Ruthie's admiration in person.

Franck told me that after he'd returned to the States, unannounced, in 2006, he'd often go to midnight showings of his one hit movie, *High Times in Manhattan.* Incognito (but who would've recognized him, anyway?) he'd sit in the back row, and, "all that adoration directed at my character on the screen would bounce off and come back to me in waves. It keeps me young."

At first, of course, I didn't buy any of it. It was unbelievable. It was insane.

Franck decided it was time for his comeback, so Ruthie and the webmaster of *TwoGreenKeys.com* organized and promoted a fan club meeting, a semi-private screening of *High Times in Manhattan.* Franck chose a tiny venue for the historic event: an old, creaky, Veterans of Foreign Wars Hall in

5

godawful Las Vegas. He didn't want to announce his reappearance to the whole world, he said. He only wanted to see his *real fans.*

Just a handful of people had arrived for the event when Franck tried to send Ruthie back to our hotel to fetch the guestbook that he'd forgotten there. She refused to go. She was having too much fun meeting and greeting Franck's *real fans,* most of whom she'd recruited herself for the event, in Riverside and LA.

So Franck asked me to go, called me a cab, gave me a wad of money for the fare. Forgetting the guestbook – I thought perhaps his eighty-year-old mind wasn't what it used to be, no matter how good he looked otherwise.

It should've only taken a few minutes, a half-hour at the most. But the always-killer Vegas traffic was atrocious that night; the cabbie hopped on the freeway and was immediately confronted with a jackknifed big rig. I was gone almost two hours.

When I got back, red and yellow flames were devouring the VFW hall.

Ruthanne Midley, my very best friend in the whole world, died in the fire, along with Franck himself, as well as seventy-three others. I was the only one attending the event, in fact, to survive, because I had been off running Franck's errand when the place caught.

I went back home to Riverside and grieved. I missed Ruthie terribly, and I even missed Franck, despite the fact that I'd considered him to be quite full of himself, always entirely aware of his movie star's good-looks and the effect they'd had on his fans. I'd found him to be shrewd, crafty, old-Hollywood-dangerous. But his undeniable charm was inescapable, and after he died, I discovered that I missed him, too, almost as much as I missed Ruthie.

A year passed, then a year and a half. I began to put my life back together, to move on. Then I heard Franck's voice come out of my television. It was a trailer for some new western, no faces, just voices, and a shot of a steam locomotive exploding. I recognized Ryan Gosling's voice, his name, at the end of the trailer. The other actor's name was unknown to me: *Alvee Smith-Killem.* But he had Franck's voice.

It just couldn't be. Franck was dead. I did a little research online, found a picture of this Alvee Smith-Killem of the ridiculous name, this unknown. Sometimes you'll see a young actor, and you'll think that he looks just like an older actor, from back in the day, when he was young. Sometimes, the resemblance is amazing, uncanny. So much so, that you wonder if this young one could be the old one's son, from some yesteryear's dalliance with an original fan, perhaps. And at first glance, this was what I thought of Alvee Smith-Killem: that he could be Franck O'Day's son – no, he'd have to be a grandson – any son of Franck's would be in at least his fifties, if not his sixties.

I'd found this Alvee person's picture on *IMDb,* a promotional shot from his very first feature, some English flick called *Downpour,* that I'd never heard of, just like I'd never heard of him. He looked like he was maybe twenty-three or twenty-five.

I knew of no extant photos of Ruthanne's idol at twenty-five – but if there had been a photo of Franck at that age, looking just as wild and sexy as he wanted to be, then this would've been it. I felt like I was losing my mind, because not only did Alvee Smith-Killem resemble Franck a great deal, as if they could be related. *Alvee Smith-Killem was Franck O'Day.*

It was nuts, but I couldn't get it out of my head. I rented a car, journeyed to LA, to the secluded Beverly Hills manse where we'd first met the old actor, where Ruthie had fallen in love with him in person, just like she'd fallen in love with his character from *High Times in Manhattan.* Where I'd interviewed him.

I felt silly pushing the intercom button in front of the gate. Franck O'Day was dead. Some other rich and famous personage owned this grand house now. What was I going to say?

A man's voice came through the intercom's grill. "Yes?"

Seriously, what was I gonna say? *I know you're in there, I know you're not dead?* I knew nothing of the kind.

Then inspiration struck. During our interviews, telegrams had often been the *deus ex machina* that had moved the old actor's story to the next scene, so I said, "I've got a telegram for Franck O'Day."

The same voice, muffled. "What?"

"I said, I've got a telegram for Franck O'Day."

I counted to ten before the gate rattled open.

(I'll just cut and paste a little here, from my original journal.)

When I drove up the curving driveway, I beheld Alvee Smith-Killem standing halfway down the steps, looking curiously in my direction. He was wearing a light-blue, short-sleeved shirt, unbuttoned, thrown carelessly over a wife-beater. He wore jeans and black, high-topped Converse. I couldn't gauge the sum of his expression, because he was wearing a pair of Ray-Bans, as perfectly black as the curly hair that reached nearly to his shoulders.

I pulled up in front of the old stone staircase, got out of the car, and looked up over its roof at him.

Alvee Smith-Killem smiled, and Franck's mellifluous voice exclaimed, "Carol!"

The man that walked down the steps was not wearing an impeccably tailored, slate gray suit, as befitted an actor in his waning years. No. Alvee was dressed perfectly for someone his age, but he still had Franck's gait.

He took off his sunglasses as he trotted around the car and enveloped me in a bear hug, picked me up off my feet. Then he released me, set his shades on the roof of the car, and held me by the hands. The blue eyes smiling out of Alvee's twenty-five-year-old face were Franck's.

Ruthanne had once typed up a description of her idol for me, which was to have been included in the biography that, because she and Franck had died, would now never be. The lengthy paragraph had been a fan's paean to her favorite star's beauty. Part of it had read: *His teeth, just ever so slightly, endearingly crooked, lend an everyman, boy-next-door quality to his otherwise flawless face.*

In the year and a half since I had seen him last, Franck had gotten his teeth straightened. They were now perfect, like Bradley Cooper's teeth. Movie stars couldn't have crooked teeth in the era of HD. But they were still *his teeth.* There could be no doubt.

"How nice of you to come!" Franck's voice said, and Alvee hugged me again.

How nice of you to come? Like I'd just dropped in unexpectedly for a little visit. *How nice of you to come?* Really? Not like he had returned from the grave, again, younger, more devastatingly attractive than ever. Not like that at all.

A million things to say flew through my mind. At last I chose the simplest. "What happened, Franck?"

"It was the energy, Carol."

He smiled humorlessly at my familiar look of disbelief. He retrieved his sunglasses from the roof of my rented car, folded them, put them into his pocket. He took me by the hand and led me up the staircase to where he'd been standing. We sat on the step.

He spoke of the VFW Hall, of all his *real fans.* "I just sat there with my eyes closed, feeling the energy channel through me, feeling it wash away all the years. I knew that I'd wake up the next day, feeling alive and refreshed, as if I'd had some incredible spa treatment. Except no spa can do what that adoring energy can do, Carol, if you know how to assimilate it. I knew I would wake up the next day feeling alive and refreshed, but I also knew that I'd look younger. I would *be* younger.

"But then something went wrong. There was just too much! All those people, my biggest, most loyal fans! Suddenly, the projector on the ceiling exploded, and dropped onto the podium, sending sparks and shards of plastic everywhere. The room was plunged into darkness. Flames raced across the ceiling. The podium was on fire. It was the only light in the room. People were screaming and backing up, overturning chairs, getting tangled in them, all to escape the heat.

"I wasn't holding Ruthie's hand anymore. The screen was on fire. The place was filling up with smoke. Everybody was trying to get to the door, but the flames – people were screaming, crying. I kept looking for Ruthie, calling her name."

Franck buried his face in his hands and sobbed. I put my arm around his shoulders. He cried, but I remained curiously dry-eyed. His story wasn't quite finished yet.

"I don't remember getting out, don't remember running to the pizza place at the end of the plaza. But I remember trying to get in, banging on the window. The door was locked and the pizza guy was sitting at a table, reading. I remember him not even looking up, saying, 'We're closed!' I remember pounding on the window, remember screaming at him, telling him to call someone, telling him that the VFW Hall was on fire. I remember him looking in that direction, scrambling back around the counter, yanking the phone off the hook . . ."

Franck drew a deep, shuddering breath, then let it out again. "There was only one thing for me to do then. I staggered around the corner of the building . . . I took my phone out of my pocket and called Bobby."

"Bobby? Bobby Ecksmith?"

But really, was it so impossible to believe? Eighty-two-year-old Franck O'Day was twenty-five again, standing here in front of me, just as fine as he wanted to be. Why shouldn't Robert Ecksmith – Franck's friend, his director – still be alive, too? They had been in that plane crash in Japan together, after all.

"Of course." Franck swiped at the tears on his face. "Who else would I call?

"Bobby told me to start walking down Las Vegas Boulevard. I'd barely made it under the 515 before a cab picked me up and took me to the airport. A man with an English accent met me there. 'I'm Dr. Urstig, Mr. O'Day,' he said. 'Do you have your passport with you?'

10

"My passport was in my pocket. That was something that Bobby had taught me. Always carry your passport. You never know when you might have to leave the country."

From his estate in England, the once-famed director had made all the arrangements, pulled the necessary strings. "We got on a little plane, and Dr. Feelgood gave me some kind of a sedative. The next thing I knew, I was disembarking at Heathrow, still smelling like smoke. I'm sure we changed planes somewhere, but I don't remember it."

For a year and a half, I'd been probably the only person in the US that had known that matinee idol Franck O'Day had not perished when his plane disappeared in Japan in 1968. For a year and a half, I'd believed that he'd burned to death in a little VFW Hall in Vegas. Yet here he was, not only alive, but young again.

The rest of my first journal chronicles how I, for lack of a better expression, *took up* with Franck and Bobby. Except, of course, Franck was now Alvee and Robert Ecksmith was Maurice Claremount.

Maury answered all the dreams I'd had of becoming a writer, those dreams I'd had since I was a little girl. Many years before, after attending my cousin's wedding, I'd made up a story, had the ego to call it a screenplay. Maury made a film out of it, called it *Kinship,* and while his spin was quite a bit more outré than the original manuscript, that's what made it great.

And Alvee made my other dreams come true, more grown up ones, ones I'd begun to (guiltily) have, once Ruthanne and I started hanging out with charming, good-looking Franck O'Day. Alvee and I became lovers.

Surely, I felt ashamed when I fell for Ruthanne's man. It just wasn't right, and I tried mightily to resist him, but as with the Borg, it was futile. My friend was gone, and once Alvee turned his incredible blue eyes toward me in invitation, I immediately lost myself in them.

He is everything I've ever dreamt a man could be; everything all girls dream of. Tall and spare, with the mouth of

11

a god – ah, the way he smiles at me! Just the faintest grin, arrogant, cocksure – *I know you want me, Carol. Why should you be different from everybody else?*

To look into his eyes is to ken supreme confidence. His is an expression that has never known the ache of unrequited longing, nor have even the mildest disappointments yet occurred in perfect Alvee's stellar new life. Not one incident that might give pause to his faith in himself. The tragedies weathered by Franck O'Day have been forgotten by Alvee Smith-Killem. No trace of their shadows ever cross his flawless face.

His eyes are the dark-blue of a summer sky just before twilight; his hair is as black as the soul of a demon. He can be poetically complimentary, deviously clever; bitingly, cruelly sarcastic. Although I've never been the object of the knife's edge of his wit, I've seen him duel with Maury frequently enough. I've seen blood drawn between them, metaphorically, of course. Yet they remain the staunchest friends.

In my opinion, Alvee is beyond a doubt the best actor ever to strut and fret his hour upon the stage. He has only demonstrated the realities of love and affection and passion to me – he's never shown me anger or discontent. But I've seen him pretend these emotions effortlessly onscreen, as well as innocence and heartbreak and regret.

He is mysterious, sexy; infinitely fascinating, utterly charming. He is mine. I love him.

At the start of our romance, regarding the universal energy, Alvee said to me, "Sometimes, two people can attain a sort of equilibrium. Just between the two of them. It takes a great deal of study and meditation. And it also takes a damn near superhuman melding of love and respect and understanding between two people."

He explained that this was the reason why his director had also attained the fountain of youth. While in Japan, Maury had formed a relationship with the leader of the monastery. I would meet the distinguished monk. His name was Maki, and like

Maury, he seemed to be in his late forties. He lived there in Beverly Hills with them. He spoke no English at all.

Alvee continued, "Maury loves me, Carol, and I love him. I've known him for so many decades . . . We're like brothers. Simpatico. But Maury and Maki? *They are Zen.* They are halves to the same whole.

"Sometimes two people can attain that balance, and then it's akin to all the pop iconography borrowed from the East, all the stuff people see and think they understand. Yin and Yang. That's Maki and Maury. The energy flows back and forth between them like magnetic poles.

"The energy that I received in Vegas was much stronger than what Maury and Maki share, much more concentrated, because it came from all those people at once. It was like an inundation, a baptism. That's why I look so much younger than Maury now – I actually am younger than Maury, by eight years. But I look so much younger now because I was fortunate to receive all that energy in one dose. But Maury and Maki keep each other young."

And that was when Alvee asked me if I would like to attempt such an arrangement with him. He was sure he loved me, was sure I loved him. We would keep each other young.

How could I refuse?

But still I wrote that first journal, had it put away under lock and key in case something should happen to me. I can laugh at it all now, of course. But at the time, I wasn't sure that I loved Alvee with the entirety that was required to attain *that damn near superhuman melding of love and respect and understanding between two people.*

The reason for all my doubt and suspicion was this: I had a dream.

From the original journal file, slightly edited for brevity:

The hall of VFW Post 864 was dark. There was only a little reflected sheen on the floor from the screen, where *High Times in Manhattan* had reached its climactic scene.

Franck stepped in front of the screen. It was like I was standing right there next to him. He held up his hands at shoulder level, palms out, like a preacher before his flock. His face was in shadow. All I could see clearly were the palms of his hands, the white cuffs of his shirt, bright against the blackness of his suit.

Inexplicably, a blue bolt that looked like lightning shot out of his right palm. It zigzagged through the crowd, striking everyone in the eyes and mouths and chests like that scene from *Raiders of the Lost Ark,* where the wrath of God kills all the Nazis. The bolt passed through everyone, gathering speed, turning yellow as it went. At last it struck the back wall, blasting the commendations and proclamations and pictures of dead veterans to smithereens. Pieces of glass and frames clattered to the floor, followed by charred scraps of photographs, drifting down slowly. The bolt bounced up, hit the ceiling, then shot earthward again. Franck held up his left hand and caught it, like an outfielder snaring a fly ball. I watched as the power of the concentrated energy burnt a quarter-sized whole in the palm of his hand.

I looked at the crowd. Every single one of them was dead. Nothing was left except ashes in the shapes of Franck's fans, like they were all vampires who'd been exposed to the sun. The wall and ceiling where the energy bolt had bounced off were ablaze, blue and yellow flames greedily consuming the old building, lighting up the room.

"I'm sorry about Ruthie," Franck's voice said to me. But he wasn't standing beside me anymore. Somehow, he'd crossed the room, and in the dim light coming through the doorway, his face was indistinct, just a silhouette – as it'd been when he stood before the movie screen.

"I loved Ruthie," he said. "I didn't want to take her, too, Carol, but when she wouldn't go back to the hotel . . ." His silhouette shrugged, noncommittal, then disappeared through the doorway. I heard his footsteps as he walked down the hall – the only way in or out of the building.

I watched, enveloped in the protection of dream, as VFW Post 864 burned around me. The fire moved so fast – it sped across the entire ceiling. It spread out from the back wall toward the adjacent walls. The convection of the rising heat stirred the ashes of the dead like a breeze, scouring them away like unseen water, leaving behind only grinning skulls and exposed bones.

Franck had held the event here, so he could do this. The little VFW Hall was old, isolated, probably not up to modern fire code. A fire at a hotel on the Strip would've been discovered, put out. The people would've been saved. After the MGM tragedy, there were probably fire sprinklers every other foot at modern hotels. Franck had staged his comeback here, so he could kill all these people in private. So he'd never be found out.

The ceiling started to collapse and I raised my dream hand in defense, and snapped awake. I didn't scream.

The dream had told me that Franck had sacrificed his biggest fans on the altar of fame – it sounded ridiculously cinematic, even to me. But it could be put no other way. Their energy had made him young again.

****

I never told Alvee about this horrible dream, this product of my imagination. But I did ask him about the very real scar on his palm. He laughed, off-handedly spoke of a clumsiness that I knew he didn't encompass: no one was more graceful than Alvee. He said that he'd tripped over a rake and then landed on it, years ago. I searched my mind, but couldn't say for sure if I'd seen the scar there or not, when he was Franck, before the fire.

So I could never, ever know for sure. Tragic paranormal accident, or calculated, self-serving mass-murder? What my mind had shown me had just been a silly dream, after all, and all my other silly dreams were coming true. I was living the lavish high life in Hollywood, collaborating on screenplays with a famous director. I had beautiful, black-haired, blue-eyed Alvee as my very own. We were going to keep each other young. Why worry about a dream in my head when dreams in real life were becoming concrete?

15

But still, I wrote that journal and locked it away, just in case my nightmare-induced fears were true. Just in case Alvee started to suck the very life out of me, just like I'd seen him do to all those people in my dream of Las Vegas.

I doubted his motives for a long time, because I was a little tired at first. The shoot for *Kinship* was a nightmare in and of itself, and after that, Maury was a slave driver. He made me work like a dog assisting him on the screenplay for *Dorian and Henry,* day in and day out, sun up to sundown. Any whiny cliché about overwork you'd like. When it was finally completed, I relaxed, at last perceived my life for the paradise it had become. Before that, I was just tired; paranoid, anxious, suspicious.

It's been years since the catastrophic fire, since Alvee and I entered into the mystical covenant of sharing the universal energy. I'm not worried that he might be out to sap my life force anymore, that he might be out to take more than he gives, that he might therefore be aging me before my time, *unto death.*

Nothing could be farther from the truth. Alvee loves me, and I love him. He and I seem to have aged hardly a day. As Maury and Maki do, we look pretty much the same. I feel great. I'm confident that sharing the universal energy with the man I love is indeed working its incomprehensible magic.

I'm even beginning to feel the inklings of a new story, maybe even a new screenplay. I can't see any reason why I would have to lock *this* journal away

A Screenwriter Remembers: My First Movie Shoot

The idea for the new project is still only a foggy cloud in my head, however. I've got a beginning and a middle, and even one tangent, going off at a right angle from the rest. Maury'll probably raise an eyebrow at that part. He likes stories to be linear, to follow the three act structure. He says that they make for a better movie that way, don't confuse the simple, ticket-buying populace. Exposition, confrontation, resolution. Arty movies are shunned by the average nuclear family; they aren't profitable.

And of course, he's right. He's the director, after all. But this new one – I've got the exposition and the confrontation, but the resolution . . . It kinda starts a whole 'nother story.

I can hear him now: "Then make it another story, and end this one with something else. Sequels make money."

Sigh. I don't really want to listen to that, so I'm not gonna bring it up to him until I can put it into three acts, instead of five. Or six.

Kinship was a three act story. The exposition was lengthy: two people have a relationship; woman cheats, man catches her, punches other man (his best friend), leaves town. Woman comes up pregnant – does she know whose baby it is? Daughter is born, and the audience knows whose baby it is: the woman's first lover. Her new lover believes the child to be his.

The conflict was short, brutal: first lover returns to town, discovers daughter grown up, now a standard, rebellious teen. He aims to corrupt her. He knows she's actually his, but he doesn't care. All he wants is to hurt her mother and his former best friend, and what better way to do so than to destroy their daughter?

The resolution was lightning quick, the moral of the story explicit. Daughter discovers the truth – her shady older boyfriend is really her father – she flees in horror, dies in a car wreck. Everyone is sad. *Revenge is a dish best served cold.*

The story as I wrote it was about the lengths to which a person will go to fight back against betrayal. It was about evil, about revenge. In the manuscript, I'd only hinted at the possibility of an incestuous relationship between the jilted lover and his daughter. I'd been afraid to actually go there. I had dear old Dad feeding his own daughter all manner of illicit substances in a twisted bid for revenge. Hollywood Fun Fact: the original title to the manuscript that would become *Kinship* was *The Eyes of the Drug Dealer.*

The drug angle was evil enough, corrupt enough, for me. Anything else would've been a little too outré, out of my comfort zone. I was not that edgy.

But Maurice Claremount was edgy. He was outré, he reveled in making people uncomfortable. He warned me that the public would not be able to see the forest for the trees regarding *Kinship.* He told me that they would miss the vindictive retribution aspect, zero in on the salaciousness of the entirely icky idea of the father-daughter angle, because he'd shot it that way.

"They're going to call it *The Incest Movie,*" he'd said.

And so they had.

In the later scenes, when his daughter is grown, the make-up team had to old Alvee up somewhat to play the incestuous father. The effects were realistic enough to please those that cared about effects; no reviewers thought that Alvee was too young for the role.

The Los Angeles Times said, *"Mr. Killem's performance will be long remembered in the annals of the anti-hero. Never before has malevolent, unrepentant evil been so convincingly portrayed by such a pretty face."*

Maurice Claremount's controversial vision of my tame little tale was not to everyone's tastes, however. They didn't *love it in Pomona;* the subject matter, as it was perceived in the reviews, turned the simple, ticket-buying populace away in oft-mentioned droves. *Kinship* didn't make a lot of money, but it was critically acclaimed.

Alvee bemoaned the poor box office take, but he was only kidding. Between the two of them, Alvee and Maury had more money than God. They'd already had successful Hollywood careers many years before, under forgotten names. And their profits had remained mostly untouched, gathering interest for decades, whilst they'd been learning the secrets of eternal youth in the Far East.

That was another bitchin' aspect of my new Hollywood life. I had a skilled auteur for a good friend, a flawlessly beautiful actor for a lover, and I'd never, ever again have to worry about there being too much month left over at the end of the money. In day to day life, as well as in business, *price* and *cost* were not words in Alvee and Maury's vocabulary. They made movies for fun.

The shoot for *Kinship* had not been fun for me, however. It was my first time on a movie set, my very first (and hopefully only) time in England. I found the weather to be awful, the people incomprehensible. The chronology of the shoot was confusing, and the cast and crew didn't believe that I'd written the original story. They considered me simply as the American lead's on-set squeeze, and treated me with UK-style rudeness and barely disguised derision.

And I came smack up against the fact that, when they were filming, Maurice Claremount and Alvee Smith-Killem were no-nonsense professionals.

The frisky, deviously off-color gentleman that I knew from poolside at Alvee's house became awesome, unapproachable in his director-ness. He was everything I thought a filmmaker should be, actually – terse, sarcastic, impatient, loud. A sardonic, unimpressed, unamused auteur.

As the shoot proceeded, I discovered that my darling Alvee was something of a Method actor. If I got a rare chance to talk to him between takes, he remained in character as the scheming baddie – he was cold and distracted, as if he really was tormented by betrayal and plans for revenge.

Neither of these pros had a whole lot of time to hold my hand, to ask how my day was going. I pouted, I felt sorry for myself. I typed my dark musings about Alvee's dark gifts in my journal file – was he using the incredible things he'd learned in Japan to drain off my life energy? Was that the reason why being on a movie set for the very first time wasn't turning out to be as much fun as I'd always dreamed? Was it why I was feeling particularly lonely and ignored and unloved?

Once we returned to the States, when they were off the clock, so to speak, my director and my leading man, again became (respectively), my friend and my lover. Once *Kinship* was in the can, I had their attention and affection once again.

But still I didn't relax completely, because our next project was to be a rewrite of Oscar Wilde's *The Picture of Dorian Gray*. The creation of the screenplay was, as my grandpa used to say, *a bitch*-kitty for me. Maury was a stern and pitiless Simon Legree; he worked me like a dog. I re-typed and rewrote from dusk til dawn. His red pen was like a bleeding sword.

When the screenplay at last met his perfectionist's impossible standards, when he at last proclaimed it *fini*, I finally looked around me and said, *"Well, I've made the big time at last."*

Life had become a bowl of cherries; compared to *Kinship,* the shoot for *Dorian and Henry* was a breeze.

.

The Love That Dare Not Speak Its Name, Updated

What is it about a gay man?

Despite my meager contributions to the filmmaking industry so far, I do live and work in Hollywood, so I've known *of* quite a few, heard those whispered speculations at parties, and chatted at those same parties with brilliant, beautiful men that don't give a damn who knows. I've heard stories about past industry giants.

But the only gay man that I've ever had the pleasure to call my close personal friend is Maury. There's been something about him that I've liked from the moment we met.

"Avoid those clichés, Carol," he tells me all the time, when he reads my stuff. But I must use one here: It's just some indefinable *je ne sais quoi* about my director that I like, a turn of phrase, an expression, a crafty wink. All of which never fail to tickle and amuse me in a way that would elicit no such response coming from a heterosexual man.

The worst dismissal one can receive from the haughty filmmaker is summed up in three simple words: *It's been done.* I heard it frequently, and on one occasion, after he'd savaged some treatment I'd thought up, I playfully asked him why I loved him so much, regardless.

"It's trust, Carol. Honesty. A rare commodity in this town. Whatever I tell you, you know it has no basis in an ulterior motive. You know I'm not trying to get in your pants, so whatever I say, whether praise or insult, you know it comes from heart or mind, and not from some fleeting desire that it might make you decide you want to sleep with me." Maury grinned, a mischievous, schoolboy's expression.

Yeah, all that was true. But there had to be more to my affection for him than trust and honesty alone.

"And there's also the fact that we have the same taste in men." The director's smile turned into a delightfully evil leer when he nodded at Alvee, down by the pool, out of earshot.

Maury had Maki, of course, and what they shared was eternal. *Zen.* The love and respect and understanding that they had for each other, augmented by the intervention of the universal energy, kept them young.

The feelings the auteur had for his blue-eyed leading man, however . . .

"Ah, my darling Alvee. I can't remember my life before I saw Alvee, do you know that, Carol?

"I fell in love with him the very moment I saw him. It was the 1950s. A colleague had told me about a good-looking young hopeful named Francis Joseph O'Day, had gotten my hopes up with a story about him possessing a certain . . . *affability.* Franck was indeed affable, but not in the way I'd been led to believe. He let me go on just far enough to make a fool out of myself – but not a fool out of him. He wasn't angry or offended or even amused. He wasn't scared. He just wasn't interested."

My British director has of course been blessed with the benefits of a classical education, so he's always dropping pithy, obscure quotations upon me, most of which I have to Google if I want to know the source and the original context. Such was the case when, speaking further of Alvee, Maury cited Violet Trefusis, an English aristocrat who, according to ever-handy Wikipedia, had carried on a stormy, decades' long affair with another woman, at a time when such things were not even to be discussed, nonetheless accomplished.

As Violet spoke of her beloved Vita, so did Maury *yearn* to be able to say of Alvee: *You are my lover and I am your mistress and kingdoms and empires and governments have tottered and succumbed before now to that mighty combination.*

But it was not to be.

"An unkind God chose to curse me and make Alvee heterosexual. And not even remotely curious." Maury held his thumb and forefinger close together. "Not even the tiniest bit.

"But there's still an element of fate between us, one that goes beyond mere fleeting fleshly pursuits. I wouldn't kick Alvee out of bed for eating watermelon, Carol." Maury leered at me. "But the idea of the impossibility of anything physical between us has fused in my mind with the impossibility of his incredible beauty. He's more perfect to me than he could ever remain if we were to become lovers.

"Don't think I wouldn't sacrifice all this philosophical platonic bullshit in a heartbeat if he were to reconsider, but in the long, dark night of the meantime, he'll always be my muse. Any fragment of plot line that comes to my mind – it stars him. He's an archetype to me. I can make him into anything, any icon – saint or sinner, cop or criminal, butcher, baker, candlestick maker. Whatever character I create, he's always Alvee at the center, gorgeous, eternally fascinating."

You can make him into anything except that one thing which he refuses to be, I thought. Thus, the agony of art.

Except in *Dorian and Henry,* Maury succeeded in his eternal quest, cinematically, at least.

Alvee had never had any trouble with the inescapable fact that certain men were attracted to him, as much as were his legions of female fans. When he was still octogenarian Franck O'Day, he'd told me his opinion of the phenomenon.

"You can't be a homophobe in Hollywood, Carol. There's no profit in it. Attention is attention. Love, adoration. It's all the same. You just acknowledge it, say, 'I'm flattered, but, unfortunately for you, I don't swing that way.' They're usually okay with that."

****

In *High Times in Manhattan,* Franck O'Day's sole memorable film, he'd played Perry Calibri, a wealthy bon vivant. Alvee had told me once, "A million years ago, a million women in a million theatres fell in love with Perry. He was suave, rich, handsome, single."

The film was a love story, and Franck had played the lover, the good guy. And the characters he'd portrayed in his new incarnation had been much the same. Alvee had been the lover-who-almost-loses-the-girl in his first feature, the critically overlooked, English-made, straight to video, *Downpour*. He was the lover-who-gets-the-girl-then-loses-her-to-the-better-man, in the mega-hit western *Cheyenne Sundown* (costarring Ryan Gosling as the better man).

Both films had been directed by Maurice Claremount, and a gloriously well-lit, pluperfectly understated love scene in the latter had put enchanting Alvee Smith-Killem on the map. Ryan who?

But after the financial success of *Cheyenne Sundown,* Hollywood's newest heartthrob wanted to take his career in other directions. When Maury was considering putting *The Eyes of The Drug Dealer* on film, Alvee had jumped at the chance to play the lead.

"I'm ready for my close-up, Mr. DeMille. I'm good at being bad." That deviously subtle, cunning smile. "Now we'll finally get it on film."

(Once upon a time, I'd had a dream that matinee idol Franck O'Day, irresistible to both men and women, had been, in fact, a very bad man indeed. In my first journal, I'd compared my affections for the actor who now called himself Alvee Smith-Killem to my fondness for his director: *Truth be told, you might actually even like Maury a little bit more than sweet, sexy Alvee, eh? You certainly trust him a little bit more. He did not, after all, miraculously escape a fire that killed seventy-five people. You did not dream that he'd started the fire in the first place, while robbing those people of their very life energy, in order to make himself young again. Maury didn't say to you in that dream that he was sorry that he'd had to take Ruthanne. That had all been the pretty boy. He's got the bluest eyes, and perhaps – just perhaps – the blackest heart imaginable.*

Of course, I don't believe any of that anymore.)

Because his favorite leading man had a yen to play the bad guy for a change, Maury turned my little tale with the lumpy title into *Kinship,* and pretty face Alvee Smith-Killem drew kudos from *The Los Angeles Times* for his ability to play the heavy. So thrilled was he with the reviews, that he spoke of continuing in the bad guy vein for his next project, waxed poetic, even, suggested that perhaps he should do a classical turn, play Richard III.

Maury sighed, as only a successful filmmaker can. "I'd like to make another profitable picture in this decade, my darling. You are definitely unrepentantly evil enough, but you're too young, too pretty for that role.

"Deformed, unfinish'd, sent before my time into this breathing world, scarce half made up – nobody's going to buy you as Richard, Alvee. No one's more finished than you."

And that statement brings me back to gay men. How I do love a good segue!

Perhaps that elusive *je ne sais quoi* about them that I like so much is just that quality. Maury, and the other ones I've met – they've always seemed so *finished* to me. Always devastatingly witty, always flawlessly turned out, not a hair out of place. Maury is by no means an attractive man: even at the hale and healthy fiftyish he seems to be, instead of the century plus that he really is – he's too regal, too spare and bony and English for me, even if he wasn't gay. But look at someone like Matt Dallas – not only is he *finished,* he's also as hot as the Fourth of July. Hot damn, gay Matt Dallas is almost as cute as Alvee!

Before my luck turned golden – before I *took up* with Alvee and Maury and began living the awesome Hollywood high life – I'd been just another troglodyte, slaving my life away as a legal secretary in a ten by ten cubical in good ol' Riverside, California. I'd been just a regular gal, and as such, I'd known perhaps more than my share of regular guys.

Some of them had been attractive – not Alvee Smith-Killem, movie star attractive, of course – but not bad for regular guys. In retrospect, however, I must say that the quality I remember the most about them is that, unlike Alvee, they slouched. They wore sweats and ragged T-shirts. They went unshaven when the grizzled look did nothing but smack ten years onto their appearance, made them slovenly, accentuated their jowly-ness. They snored. They chewed with their mouths open, slurped their noodles.

Alvee does none of those things. He's always on, always superlative. He has a walk-in closet that would astound Kylie Jenner. He's the definition of a clothes horse – an aspect of a man's personality that has always delighted me, if he has good taste. Alvee's taste is impeccable; once every couple of months, he discards anything that might have grown even remotely out of style. Yet classics endure – he still has the tuxedo that he wore to the premier of *High Times in Manhattan.* Although he never actually dons it anymore, the cut is still timely. He has perhaps four or five more trendy tuxedos. Clothes do make the man, and Alvee certainly knows to dress.

He isn't gay, but he's *finished,* as I've always found gay men to be.

With *Kinship,* he'd discovered that he liked playing bad guys, so when Maury suggested an update on Oscar Wilde's *The Picture of Dorian Gray* as his next film, Alvee was thrilled. There can be no more quintessential part for a pretty face who wants to explore evil than the degenerate, eternal youth.

(*Alvee* is *Dorian Gray,* that still watchful part of my mind whispered, at the time. *And he doesn't even need a painting in the attic.)*

****

On once-famous, now forgotten Robert Ecksmith's page, Wikipedia tells us that he helmed twenty-five films, starting with *Miami Moonglow* in 1953. Several of his productions were nominated for Academy Awards and/or BAFTAs.

(Franck O'Day had once confided to me that the only flop Bobby'd ever made was the one in which he'd starred.)

26

The short piece on Wikipedia goes on to state that his cinematic style was *often marked by a subtle, yet controversial eroticism.* After seeing Maurice Claremount's blockbuster, *Cheyenne Sundown,* I knew that the "new" director's style had not changed.

There had definitely been a little something extra there in the fight scene between Ryan and Alvee's characters. They were at odds over a woman – the standard, romantic movie trope – but were they really? Was there something else in this fistfight, something akin to that love that dare not speak its name? It was *extremely* subtle, just the merest whiff – something about how Maury had shot their shifts in dominant and submissive positions, the way the grunting sounded more like some kind of rough lovemaking than a fight.

It was superb.

His reimagining of *The Picture of Dorian Gray* would not be as subtle.

The novel had been written in a vastly different era, so Wilde's classic merely hints at the true quality of artist Basil Hallward's devotion for the subject of his portrait. And Oscar had not even attempted to paint roué Henry Wotton, Dorian's tempter, as gay at all. He was just clever, worldly, debauched. He revels in pointing out the ideas of fleshly pleasures to the innocent Dorian, but the two of them don't participate in them together.

Maury's screenplay for *Dorian and Henry* (with my nominal help) changed all that.

Dorian starts out, as in the book, as an innocent. But Basil is *just as queer as a three dollar bill,* as my grandpa used to say. His motives toward the subject of his painting are plain to all, but he doesn't quite have the nerve to act upon them.

In Maury's retelling, Lord Henry Wotton has no such compunctions. He uses Wilde's words to seduce Dorian: *The only way to get rid of a temptation is to yield to it. Resist it, and your soul grows sick with longing for the things it has forbidden to itself, with desire for what its monstrous laws have made monstrous and unlawful.*

They embark on a happy (though secret) love affair, but Dorian's cravings turn darker. In the novel, Wilde tells us that both men and women would leave the room when Dorian entered it; he mentions suicides, alludes to young men's lives destroyed by their association with him. Maury's screenplay spelled out the whys to all these occurrences.

Toward the end of the timeless tale, Dorian feels that he'll be able to redeem himself, because he spares a simple soul from the ravages of his influence. In the novel, it's a farm girl named Hetty. In *Dorian and Henry,* it's a young footballer named Jason.

Inexorably, Dorian realizes that he did not spare Jason because of some new decency dawning in him. *In hypocrisy he had worn the mask of goodness. For curiosity's sake he had tried the denial of self. He recognized that now.*

Maury's update ends as the original: Dorian would *kill this monstrous soul-life, and without its hideous warnings, he would be at peace.*

The director offered the screenplay to his favorite leading man as a challenge. Alvee had discovered that he liked playing baddies, and Dorian Gray (especially as Maury had reimagined him) was the epitome. And as Alvee was not fazed by either gay men themselves, or their affection for him, here was an opportunity to portray one.

Alvee Smith-Killem was nothing if not a great actor. I knew it; Maury knew it. *The Los Angeles Times* knew it. But no one knew it more than Alvee himself. He had no trouble whatsoever pretending to be that which he was not. Challenge accepted.

Preproduction: *Dorian and Henry*

Maurice Claremount preferred making his pictures in the States, yet he had no time to argue dollars and cents with American studios, because he had quite more than enough dollars and cents. So he owned his own movie-making machine, based in England, called Title XVII Productions. Little Title XVII could remake *The Ten Commandments, Titanic,* and *Pirates of the Caribbean,* and promote them as thoroughly as a big studio, and it would barely make a dent in the vast amount of funds Maury had socked away in various financial institutions around the globe. Employed under Title XVII's masthead were writers and producers and other directors; lawyers and a marketing team. They turned out a few films a year, *over there.*

On *Dorian and Henry,* therefore, Maury would produce as well as direct (not to mention having pretty much written the entire screenplay.)

He sent to Europe for Hans Baumhauer, his trusted director of photography, snatched him right out of preproduction on a lower-paying project. Maurice Claremount called this brilliant cinematographer *Mr. 8 Millimeter,* because Hans always claimed that, regardless of the picture, he could shoot the whole thing on a handheld and save millions. It was a joke that never got old to Maury.

The screenplay finished, the crew hired, the next part of preproduction was casting. Heavy is the head that wears the crown, and here did micromanager Maury fit himself with yet another hat. Not only did he usually write, always direct, and most times produce, he also always cast his own movies.

To play the part of Lord Henry Wotton, Dorian's foil, Maury chose his fellow Englishman, Armand Hambrick. The blonde actor, like Alvee, was somewhat of a newcomer, having only starred in a couple of modestly successful films *over there*. Still, he had quite the following of birds and lassies, frauleins, mademoiselles and senoritas in Europe, shōjos in Japan. *Dorian and Henry* would be his first picture for Title XVII; it would be his first American picture.

Maury related that he had made the young actor's acquaintance whilst filming *Downpour* in London with Alvee. Armand had not yet broken into film, then, but Maury had loved his portrayal of Brick in some little company's attempted revival of *Cat on a Hot Tin Roof.*

"The accents were atrocious," Maury sniffed. "But darling *Rubio* was excellent."

The fair-haired thespian kept in touch with the director, trading emails about the state of theatre in London, about their respective movie projects. Maury called him a *chancer,* down for any part, however miscast he might've been in it. Armand had even volunteered for the Ryan Gosling role in *Cheyenne Sundown.*

"As if anyone would believe a blonde Englishmen as a cowboy," Maury snorted.

"The believed a blonde Canadian," Alvee pointed out.

Maury turned his laptop around and showed us a publicity still of Armand Hambrick. "Ryan's a touch more masculine than *Rubio*. I wasn't trying to do an all-twink remake of *Butch Cassidy and the Sundance Kid.* "

Maury grinned at Alvee, who rolled his eyes at being included in the somewhat disparaging appellation. He was certainly pretty, but he wasn't hardly a twink.

My leading man considered Armand's publicity photo and sighed. "I suppose he's gonna make a pass at me?"

"Oh, most definitely."

Maury said something in Japanese, and Maki, sitting beside him, blushed. It was my director's favorite means of communicating blue commentary without endangering my delicate sensibilities. It worked admirably: whatever he'd said might not have actually been overly dirty to me, but Maki's blush and my own imagination made it filthy indeed. Maurice Claremount performed such clever tricks in his filmmaking, also. The things that he left unshown, unspoken, always played infinitely better in the viewers' imaginations than if Maury had put them onscreen.

Alvee pretended not to know what Maury had said in the foreign tongue. It was his standard response.

"I'm sure Carol will protect you from this beautifully commanding British sodomite." Maury leered at me, and I couldn't help but smile.

"Alvee can protect himself," I replied.

Altogether unconcerned, Alvee laughed. "It just takes one word. *No.*"

Maurice Claremount gestured at his countryman's picture. "He's big in Japan, as the saying goes. He's lovely. You should be more polite."

"All right. I'll say, *No, thank you.*"

A Historic Meeting

Alvee's palatial Beverly Hills estate featured a terrace, where a table that sat four overlooked an enormous swimming pool. (When Alvee had declared his love for me, when he had invited me to join with him in the sharing of the universal energy, I'd begun to think of the grand old house as my place, too, after a fashion. Like Maury and Maki, I considered myself to be Alvee's permanent guest.)

It was on this terrace, at this familiar table, that I sat with my director, whilst Kimura, silent and dutiful, set out the service for brunch. As neither Alvee nor Maki had yet emerged from the house, he was more carefully methodical than usual.

What can be said about Kimura? He was the other dignified Japanese man that shared Alvee's digs. Similar to Maki, who never spoke English, Kimura rarely did. He was Alvee's . . . what was Kimura, anyway? Alvee's concierge? His valet? His chef?

He was all those things and more. He'd been steward of this opulent and very private household before I'd taken up residence, since at least the time when my leading man called himself Franck O'Day. The thought struck me, not for the first time, that perhaps Franck had brought Kimura back with him from the Far East. Perhaps he also knew about the youth-giving properties of the universal energy.

Kimura certainly received a part of the requisite admiration from me. I thought he was the best factotum a person could ever have. He was a Michelin-caliber chef, and his direction of the maids and gardeners was spot-on: house and grounds were perennially immaculate. Just the right outfit for meeting or premiere was always set out for me, in gentle suggestion. I always praised his efforts effusively. I think it embarrassed him a little bit.

Maki appeared, and Kimura bowed his respect to his peer in age (if not in status) and went back into the house. Maki was garbed traditionally, as was his wont, although he seemed a trifle more dressed up, more formal than usual. I glanced questioningly at Maury.

"Papa-san's a big fan. He's got all three of Armand's films on tape."

Not literally, I thought with amusement. *Nothing's* on tape *anymore.*

In Japanese, the director spoke to his soulmate, and Maki nodded, smiled shyly. Maury had no doubt asked if he was eager to meet the good-looking blonde actor.

Maury had told us that Armand Hambrick had arrived in town the night before, but it had slipped my mind that he was coming for brunch. I thought with further amusement that this had to be the reason why Alvee was late: my gorgeous actor-friend wanted to make an entrance. It was certainly his prerogative.

Moments later, Kimura announced the British thespian. He was attired in an impeccably tailored, white linen suit, turned casual by the fact that he wore only a wife-beater beneath the jacket, and was shod in a pair of pricey Italian sandals. He wore a pair of large, round, Jackie O-style shades, and his striking blonde hair was done up in a top-knot.

He removed his sunglasses and smiled at Maury. As he crossed the terrace, the director said to me, sotto voce, "I do so love how foreigners dress in LA."

The two Brits embraced. Maury introduced me as *the screenwriter for our little update,* and Armand shook my hand, said it was nice to meet me, as if he really believed that I had written Maury's faultless screenplay.

Dorian and Henry's actual screenwriter-helmsman-producer-casting director then introduced his star to one of his biggest fans.

Armand bowed deeply. *"Ohayō gozaimasu, Maki-san,"* quoth the Brit. *"Ogenki desu ka?"*

A smile of surprised pleasure crossed the monk's face. *"Hai, genki desu."*

Maki said something else and Armand shook his head with a shade of regret. These few words were apparently the sum total of his Japanese. Still, it was more than I knew.

"He says, *Welcome to our home,"* Maury translated.

"Domo arrigato," Armand replied and bowed again. That one I did know. It meant *Thanks.*

We took our seats, and for a few minutes, Armand and Maury chatted about the *auld sod,* about the service on the traveler's interminable flight across the pond. Not feeling it necessary to contribute to these pleasantries, it gave me the opportunity to study the actor, to silently applaud Maury's genius in casting.

Armand's fair excellence was the ultimate foil to Alvee's dark-haired perfection. Surely, Ryan Gosling wasn't hard to look at, and he had paired well with Alvee in the dusty, rustic oater that had been *Cheyenne Sundown.* But *Dorian and Henry* was to be a different kind of period piece, a tale of the sins of the gentry, and no one resembled a decadent young lord more than Armand Hambrick.

He had the accent. (I wondered if Alvee was going to attempt one, or just allow the honeyed cadence of his incredible voice, American though it was, give life to Wilde's dialogue.)

Armand was pale, yet with just enough color to broadcast a robust vitality. His chin was perfect; his mouth: wide, inescapably sensual. His nose was large, but not overly so, aquiline. His cheekbones were high, sculpted, cruelly beautiful.

I remembered Wilde's description of Dorian Gray – *his finely curved scarlet lips, his frank blue eyes, his crisp gold hair. All the candor of youth was there, as well as all youth's passionate purity* – and for the briefest of seconds, a traitorous thought crossed my mind. It occurred to me that Maury

34

should've cast blonde Armand as the doomed innocent, instead of dark-haired Alvee.

But my doubt at the director's decision evaporated as I watched Armand Hambrick. Dark brows arched above mantis-green eyes, and the expression in them, when he would glance briefly at me, politely including me in the conversation, was utterly smug, haughty. *Not conceited,* as my dear friend Ruthie used to say, *but convinced.*

Am I not a vision? The be-all and end-all, the very personification of your dreams, American girl?

Not hardly, Blondie. His confidence amused me. *You are surely cute, but you ain't no Alvee Smith-Killem.*

Oscar Wilde had said of Dorian: *One felt that he had kept himself unspotted from the world.* This ultimately important detail of characterization was not in any way my impression of the elegant Brit. His face reflected Dorian's highborn, blonde beauty, true, but not Dorian's innocence.

Armand was sly, seductive; he was amused by the effects his splendor elicited. There was not one thing *unspotted* about him, and I reckoned that his arrogance was intrinsic to his charm. It was the very basis of his real-life persona, but unless he was a much better actor than I imagined him to be, I didn't think he could pull off the purity necessary to make the main character, and his subsequent downfall, believable.

But Alvee could. Alvee was not a blonde, but I knew he could be anyone he wanted to be. He could effortlessly portray Dorian's initial virtue, while Armand Hambrick embodied all of Henry Wotton's superior, worldly decadence. I chided myself for doubting the casting choices of the inestimable Maurice Claremount.

Kimura brought another chair to the table. This, and a lull in the conversation, was Alvee's cue. He sauntered across the terrace, and I saw immediately that Alvee had, with a seemingly studied indifference, out Southern California-casualed the British actor.

Before Alvee's entrance, Armand's white linen suit and fabulous shades had seemed to be *just some old thing* that he'd carelessly thrown on; perhaps he intended to take a stroll on the beach after this meeting with his director and costar.

But now . . .

Alvee, a nearly-native of very, *very* many decades, had donned a pair of black board shorts, which intimated that he wouldn't just be strolling on the beach like a tourist, maybe-later; he would be actually going in the water. To this he'd added a loud yellow Hawaiian shirt, a pork pie hat, his Ray-Bans, and a pair of not-expensive-at-all flip-flops.

I recognized the get-up as the one Alvee had worn, what seemed like a million years ago, when he'd taken me, thus incognito, to a matinee showing of *Cheyenne Sundown.* Even though Ryan Gosling was the star and Alvee the unknown in the picture, the disguise hadn't worked. The ticket girl had recognized him on his way out of the theatre, had asked for his autograph.

And it surely wouldn't work now. After his sexy introduction in *Cheyenne Sundown* and his actor-in-a-serious role in *Kinship,* if Alvee Smith-Killem stepped out on the mean streets of LA these days, he'd be mobbed. There was no way he'd actually be going to the beach, unless it was a private one. All that was how an actor spelled *success*, and it suited Alvee just fine.

Beside his native's nonchalance, Armand was transformed from a hip, ambiguously androgynous foreigner to an *Am I gay, or what?* tourist.

I shared a glance with Maury. *Actors,* his return expression said. *Aren't they cute?*

Score one for Alvee, I thought.

Now Armand raised his perfect eyebrows at his countryman, offering a very British smirk at Alvee's very American (and perhaps somewhat childish) sartorial one-upmanship. *Are we English not the makers of fashion?*

Maury shrugged.

But as Alvee got within smiling range, as he extended his hand to shake Armand's, I noticed a change pass across the Brit's face. It was only there for the briefest of eye blinks, and then it was gone. He was then all bland politeness, all *So glad to meet you, Alvee, loved you in Cheyenne Sundown, I'm so looking forward to working with you, and of course, Maury, too.*

Funny that the British thespian hadn't said he'd loved Alvee in *Kinship,* the more serious picture. *Cheyenne Sundown* had been romantic fluff, a money-maker, but soon forgotten. Alvee's sexiness in it had set screens ablaze, however, the whole world 'round, and it was this aspect of the film that had beyond a doubt appealed to Armand.

Franck O'Day's words suddenly came back to me, as if I'd heard them only yesterday. *(Thus with imagined wing our swift scene flies.)* It was during our initial interview; he was talking about when he'd first arrived in the movie capitol of the universe. He'd only been thirteen at the time. His stepfather's brother had been "what we called a theatrical agent. He fell in love with me at first sight.

"I didn't mind that Uncle Jesse had a crush on me. It's not like he ever acted on it. They were a little more apt to hide it in those days, you see, and I was just a kid. But I could tell, nonetheless. It was just the way he looked at me, the way his hand would linger that extra second when he would pat me on the shoulder."

And then Franck had told me about the first time he'd met famous English director Robert Ecksmith, an episode to which Maury himself had only vaguely alluded. Something about Franck's *affability.*

With a smile in his voice, Franck had related the tale in detail.

"Bobby said, 'I've been working on a historical piece, and now that I've met you, I think you'd be perfect for the lead.'

"Now I smiled slightly at him. 'Is that a fact?'

"'Indeed. I have a script in the house, if you'd like to take a look at it.'

"Bobby led me to a little office. I stood in front of a convenient couch and watched him lock the door behind us. Then he turned and looked at me, in the same way that Uncle

Jesse did. Only on Bobby, that look was deeper – there was an additional hunger there.

"I sipped my drink, and smiled in slight surprise when he started to unbutton his shirt. I really wasn't surprised at all. I watched him take off his shirt, fling it on the desk, his eyes never leaving mine, that hungry look only increasing. He took of few steps closer to me.

"I waited. As he reached out to touch my face, I said, 'I don't know what you've been told about me, Mr. Ecksmith. But I'm just interested in being in your picture. Didn't you say something about a script?'

"Bobby's hand froze in mid-air, inches from my face. He narrowed his eyes, paused. That hungry look never dimmed, even as he realized just how uninterested I was. Then he burst out laughing. He turned and retrieved his shirt from the desk, and threw it on.

"'I'm Robert Ecksmith, kid,' he said as he buttoned up his shirt. 'I don't carry scripts around. I thought you looked smarter than that.'

"'I'm Francis Joseph O'Day, Mr. Ecksmith,' I replied, 'and I *am* smarter than that.' I sipped my drink and smiled at him again. 'But I still bet I'd be perfect for the lead in your picture.'

"Bobby considered me, then smiled wryly. He said, 'That you would, Mr. O'Day. That you would.' He took a pen from the desk and scribbled something on the blotter, then tore it off and held it out to me. 'Call this number on Monday. Tell them I said to make you an appointment for a screen test.'

"I took the paper from him and stuck it in my pocket without looking at it. 'I will certainly do that. Thank you very much, Mr. Ecksmith.'

"He waved absently and stepped to the door. He put his hand on the knob, then turned back. 'Are you sure that you don't want to . . .'' I shook my head. 'But I've heard . . .'

"I sighed. 'I think we'd both regret it, Mr. Ecksmith.' I walked past him and unlocked the door, opened it. I stepped out into the hall, then turned back and smiled at him again. 'After all, we've just met.'

"Bobby smiled at me, then slapped me on the shoulder. 'We're going to be great friends, Francis Joseph O'Day. I just know it.'"

In the rest of my interviews with Franck, all for that biography that would never be, he frequently mentioned that *hungry* look. Almost *ad nauseam*, in fact, did Franck mention it. Uncle Jesse, Bobby and other gay directors; his female costars (one in particular, and emphatically). Extras on-set, his fans, tourists from Topeka, *Ruthie*. All these people stared at Franck O'Day with undisguised, *hungry* desire. He'd beheld the expression so often, he told me, that he'd come to immediately recognize it.

I mention Franck O'Day and his insufferable ego, his complete, instantaneous comprehension of those that wanted him, because Armand Hambrick couldn't hide that same look, the one with which Franck had been so familiar: dumbstruck, wondering awe at the incomparable beauty of the raven-aired vision come swaggering across the veranda in a loud shirt. Desire, uncontrollable, sprung fully formed, like Athene from the forehead of Zeus, for the young actor in the black shades.

Armand's cool British composure returned, and we all sat back down to chat about *Dorian and Henry*. That ravenous need was there only for a heartbeat, but Alvee caught it, nonetheless.

He and I were partners in the eternal energies, and when he wasn't acting (and when he permitted it), I could read him as lucidly as black upon white. He placed a finger on the corner of his sunglasses, and winked at me over them, a la Sonny Crockett in *Miami Vice*.

Well, what d'ya know, Carol? Seems I have another fan.

Franck O'Day was forgotten, lost and presumed dead on a snowy Japanese mountainside, more than half a century before. But his towering ego was alive and well, and it peeped out at me with faux innocence from the eyes of Alvee Smith-Killem. Of all things, I had to admit that he had come by this sense of his own attractiveness honestly: he was indeed irresistible. His inimitable charm had certainly worked on me.

The beginning had been a startling interlude in a bar in Las Vegas, a few hours before the show at the VFW Hall was slated to commence. Franck O'Day had pretended to make a pass at me. He'd suggested that the two of us should go up to my room . . .

His charisma, concentrated instead of merely ambient, channeled directly at me, had been difficult to resist. Instead of his usual polite interest, his eyes held a different kind of interest, explicit, just for me.

I knew then what Ruthanne meant when she'd said, "He made me feel as if he'd never wanted anyone like he wanted me. It was . . . *unbelievable.*" Franck was communicating that he wanted me, with only his stunning blue eyes and that breathtaking, silky voice. It wasn't what he said, it was how he said it. We were friends, after all, and no one, not even Ruthie, would suspect anything shady if they saw us going into my room. But I knew what he meant, because he wanted me to have no doubt.

I was dumbstruck at his proposition; then after a heartbeat of speechlessness, I perceived that all the simmering lust in his eyes, there just for me – it wasn't real at all. Franck was just acting. As breathtaking as it was, it was a sham. *Damn, he's good.* Franck wasn't actually propositioning me at all. He was threatening me.

I'd found out some fairly shocking information that he needed me to keep to myself until after the show at the VFW Hall. He was saying that if I told Ruthanne about it, before he had a chance to, then he was going to hurt me.

He was telling me that if I spilled the beans to Ruthie, he'd hurt me in the only way he could. He'd hurt my friend, break her heart, as effortlessly as walking out and riding up on the elevator with me. But it wouldn't be me, it would be someone else. By this show of seduction, he was demonstrating precisely how effortless it would be. Any woman wandering around in the casino would do.

If I opened my big mouth, then he'd break Ruthanne's heart, and it would be my fault. He'd hurt me by hurting her.

"So, Carol. Should we go up to your room?"

"No, Franck," I'd replied evenly. "I can keep a secret, but I'm not inclined to want to have to keep that one."

Even though, had our situation been different, had there not been him and Ruthie, I knew I'd have taken him up on it in a heartbeat. If the suggestion had been real, and if circumstances had been different . . .

I would forgive him for his threat to break Ruthie's heart; he was actually trying to protect her by shutting me up. What I'd discovered would've had an impact on their relationship, and she needed to hear about it from him and not me. I decided to take the high road and give Franck the benefit of the doubt. I decided to believe that he was trying to shield Ruthie's feelings until he got a chance to explain, and that made me think that he really cared for her.

I still thought he was a son of a bitch for the way he'd gone about it, but I couldn't find it in my heart to seriously dislike him. Anyone that was good to Ruthie and made her happy, couldn't be all bad to me.

It had been fake, just acting, that knowing, confident invitation. Franck didn't want me, or anyone else but Ruthie. She loved him. Yet his proposition, sham though it had been, kept playing through my mind. In that instant, I began to think have impure thoughts about my best friend's man. I could no longer deny that I found him to be one sexy old beast.

If Franck O'Day wasn't Ruthie's lover – what would it be like if he was mine?

That night, I believed that Franck died, right there beside Ruthie. He never got to tell her about the things that I'd uncovered.

Eventually, after I discovered Franck living back in Beverly Hills, young again, calling himself Alvee Smith-Killem, I got to find out about all the things of which I'd guiltily mused that afternoon in Vegas. Ruthie was gone, and who would she rather see with the man she'd loved so completely? If it couldn't be her, wouldn't she be glad that it was me?

Alvee is everything that I'd imagined Franck O'Day could be, and so much more. There will never be another man in all the world for me. No one is more cognizant of this truth than he is: he is quite aware of the inescapable power of his charm.

Now, as we chatted with Maury and Armand, a lesser man might've put his arm around me, used a PDA with his woman to let his newest admirer know which he *swung*, as the old saying went. But not Alvee. He would wait for Armand's inevitable pass before stating his preferences.

Let the blonde Englishman ruminate upon his desire. Until he marshalled his nerve enough to speak, let him hope, let him dream. All that admiration was positive energy. Such things kept Alvee young.

The Shoot

Director Maurice Claremount, he of the many hats, had underlings for costume design, but he mostly made all the hands-on decisions regarding that aspect of the production, too.

As in his casting, his brilliance also shined through here. He set *Dorian and Henry* in the 1890s, the era in which the novel had been published. Being a period piece, it allowed Maury to array Alvee in waistcoats and trousers of dark blues that accentuated his incredible eyes; top hats and lined capes, mourning coats in sable that contrasted with the brilliant whites of bow ties, while pointing up the inky blackness of his hair.

He draped Armand in sunny yellows and understated beiges that complimented his immaculate blondness, and pale greens that sung odes to his predatory, mantis-colored eyes. Maury's costume choices made Alvee's Dorian breathtaking, Armand's Henry, stunning. He was starting out with exceptionally attractive actors, but the clothes made both of them supernal.

As was the purpose, the magic of cinema, neither of them could ever look as good in real life.

As credited co-screenwriter, I had a legitimate interest in the shoot; unlike on *Kinship,* none of the crew or other cast members shot me *Who the hell do you think you are?* hard looks. I wouldn't have noticed, anyway. I was too absorbed by Alvee and Armand's phenomenal onscreen chemistry.

In the initial scenes, Alvee played the innocent perfectly, as I knew he would. He refused to directly acknowledge Basil's besotted praise of his splendor, letting it simply pass him by.

Then Armand's Henry arrives, droll, dangerously witty. Dorian is as captivated with the things he says as he is by his beauty.

With only his eyes, Alvee communicated Dorian's awe, his amazement at Lord Henry's words, words that *had touched some secret chord that had never been touched before, but that he felt was now vibrating and throbbing to curious pulses. Yes; there had been things in his boyhood that he had not understood. He understood them now. Life suddenly became fiery-colored to him. It seemed to him that he had been walking in fire. Why had he not known it?*

Armand's faint return smile also revealed Henry's thoughts: *He had merely shot an arrow into the air. Had it hit the mark? How fascinating the lad was!*

Alvee's Dorian and Armand's Henry stared at each other for another heartbeat. Basil Hallward's next line to Dorian spoke to the ethereal congruence of their attraction, in case anyone missed it: "I don't know what Harry has been saying to you, but he has certainly made you have the most wonderful expression."

I didn't see how anyone could miss it. As if it was stage direction, Alvee wordlessly communicated Dorian's impression of Henry: *There was something in his low languid voice that was absolutely fascinating. His cool, white, flowerlike hands, even, had a curious charm. They moved, as he spoke, like music, and seemed to have a language of their own. But he felt afraid of him, and ashamed of being afraid. Why had it been left for a stranger to reveal him to himself? He had known Basil Hallward for months, but the friendship between them had never altered him. Suddenly there had come someone across his life who seemed to have disclosed to him life's mystery. And, yet, what was there to be afraid of? He was not a schoolboy or a girl. It was absurd to be frightened.*

The scene was absolutely spellbinding. As Alvee gazed at Armand, I completely believed that he peered into the abyss of sin and liked what he saw there; Armand was utterly convincing as the provocateur who knew he had found another acolyte.

"Cut!" the director yelled, making me jump, shattering the magic of Dorian and Henry's moment. I successfully resisted the entirely unprofessional urge to applaud. The applause would come later.

I watched Alvee's expression of just-awakened, half-frightened desire blink out. It was replaced with a simple smile of camaraderie. He stepped forward and clapped his costar on the shoulder. "Goddamn, we're good!"

Armand smiled acknowledgement. The two of them, together, especially in this scene, were *extraordinarily* good. A trace of Lord Henry's confident lust for the *fascinating lad* that Alvee portrayed remained in his expression, then also faded.

I stole a glance at Maury. He shrugged, as if to say, *kingdoms and empires and governments have tottered and succumbed before now to this mighty combination.*

My darling Alvee caught my eye, winked at me. He was nothing if not a great actor.

The shoot proceeded swimmingly; there were very few retakes. That meant that the whole production could just possibly come in *under budget,* two words which Maury claimed were among his favorites in the English language.

Alvee and Armand's chemistry continued to smoke, and regardless if Wilde's story had been filmed before, I thought Maury's version had Academy Award potential. The director was not moved by my praise. Who was I, but a kinda screenwriter and former regular gal from the Inland Empire?

"Oscar doesn't care for Oscar, Carol," he said, and giggled at his own wit. "Not to mention that our little adaptation of the evils that men do is a trifle explicit for the Academy. Remember *Brokeback Mountain?* It won Best Director, Best Adapted Screenplay, Best Score . . . but not Best Picture. Neither that, nor *Capote,* although they did give Hoffman Best Actor.

"Even that couldn't save him from his demons. So much talent . . ." Maury frowned, flapped his hand to dispel the futility.

"The Academy is conservative, Carol. Our take on the famous Dubliner's work depicts his characters and their debaucheries quite literally, as he could not depict them himself, owing to the times."

Watching that day's shooting, I disagreed. It was true that Maury's Dorian and Henry were gay, but it wasn't like he was showing their physical relationship onscreen. It was Wilde's words, and Alvee and Armand's expressive acting that showed the depth of their connection.

In fact, they were only in any kind of intimate proximity in one scene. Henry leans in to whisper something into Dorian's ear, then draws back, pauses, as if he might kiss him. The camera freezes, and like the audience to come, I waited in anticipation, cliff-hanger stylie, savoring the desire that crackled between them.

But then Maury again yelled, "Cut!" and Alvee again smiled playfully at his costar. I thought Armand glowered at the director; but again, his annoyance lasted for only a fraction of a second.

I seemed to recall . . . I checked the script, and yes, it was indicated that Dorian and Henry were supposed to actually kiss here, followed by the customary fade to black.

But Maurice Claremount had changed his mind. Alvee and Armand had communicated their desires perfectly in this scene, and throughout the shoot; there was no need to show any actual consummation. It would play so much better if the viewer was left to imagine what came next.

****

After most days' shooting, the movie's (nominal) screenwriter, its director, and its stars dined at LA's more exclusive restaurants. Paparazzi often waited outside, and while Maury and I would take a back exit – he hated to be photographed – Alvee and Armand would dutifully go out the front door. Sometimes they climbed into a waiting limo, and later appeared together at the trendiest nightspots, all for publicity's sake. The still-in-production buzz was stupendous, rife with not-so-veiled inferences that perhaps Alvee Smith-Killem was not quite the lady-killer that he'd portrayed in *Cheyenne Sundown.*

"A famous showman said, *There's no such thing as bad publicity,"* quoth the blue-eyed heartthrob to us with a grin. Alvee was who he was, and whomever the ticket-buying populace thought he was, whether it was western womanizer or 19th century homosexual, he couldn't possibly care less, as long as they kept buying those tickets.

Nobody knew the real Alvee, except for Maury, his best (and only) friend for decades. And me, of course. I knew him.

The evening after the filming of the almost-kiss scene, Armand had other obligations, so he bid us farewell and disappeared from the set. The three of us had dinner that night on the terrace with Maki. For our homecoming, Kimura presented some ambrosial Far East confabulation; I thought it beat *Matsuhisa's* fare, hands down. It was good to dine in private for a change, with my favorite people. My family.

Maury and Maki spoke for a moment, then I saw cash American change hands, dead presidents even more famous than my movie business dinner companions. Alvee rolled his eyes: he understood more Japanese than he let on. He had spent decades among its people, after all.

I had not a clue, so my ever-accommodating translator explained, as he neatly stacked the money on the table in front of him. "Papa-san lost the bet. He was sure that Armand would just go right ahead and buss our enticing Alvee, after the cameras stopped rolling."

"The man is a professional," Alvee countered. "Why did nobody include me in this bet?"

"It was just pillow talk." Maury dismissed the wager with a wave of his hand, then wiggled his blonde eyebrows at Alvee. "But you must tell me, as Maki is dying to hear. Has our darling Armand yet made you an offer which you will so disappointingly refuse?"

Alvee smirked, shook his head. "Contrary to what *TMZ* reports, we're just friends."

"Buddies," I threw in. "Just two young actors, blowing off steam after an intense day of shooting the next GLAAD Media Award contender, prowling the hotspots for *women.*"

Maury giggled. "Whilst you're left at home, all dressed up with no place to go."

It was another joke that never got old to the director, the fact that my relationship with Alvee was a boring non-secret in Hollywood. That the talented, good-looking, successful actor shared his palatial home with a lowly screenwriter was not unknown, simply ignored. Except for premieres and the odd awards show, we never appeared in public together. Alvee rarely appeared in public, period.

We weren't married after all, and when interviewed, Alvee never spoke of me. Among the gossip-mongers and purveyors of true Hollywood stories, Alvee's status was therefore single. It made for better copy on the rare occasions when he was out and about, like these recent appearances on the boulevard with Armand Hambrick, and the idea that I was universally ignored by everyone tickled the hell out of Maury.

It was just as amusing to me, because I knew the truth, as he did. Alvee was mine. He and I were partners in the universal energy, halves to a youth-preserving whole, and this precluded any worries I could ever have about his suddenly developing a wandering eye.

After *Cheyenne Sundown* topped the box office, Alvee had been photographed dancing with his co-star, *vaporous* British ingénue Camellia Swanson. The week *Kinship* premiered, he'd been seen at *Spago* with Alyson Rushtin, the gorgeous, dark-haired, (also British) beauty who'd played his daughter.

All of Alvee's very public, seeming-dalliances with his costars were simply for publicity. He was Camellia Swanson's beard whilst she was in the States: she was an in-the-closet lesbian. Like Maury, Alvee found Alyson Rushtin to be an insufferable twit. They both faded back to the UK, after other movies took center-stage in the public mind. And so it would be with Armand Hambrick, after *Dorian and Henry* was released. Alvee was simply showing another Englishman around LA to promote the movie.

Still, Maury wheedled, "He hasn't made a pass at you?"

"Not even the merest suggestion. Perhaps Carol has warned him off." Alvee squeezed my hand.

It was not the case, even if I'd felt the need to do so. Those that thought they loved Alvee were none of my business. I knew where his loyalties lodged, and besides, Armand had not spoken more than perfunctory pleasantries to me since the moment we'd met.

Maury speculated, "Perhaps he's said something subtle, and your American sensibilities missed it."

Alvee again shook his head. He missed nothing when it came to bids for his affection.

"Our delightful *Rubio* is indeed a professional, then." Maury snapped a linen napkin, and daubed at the corner of his manicured moustache with hardly any daintiness at all. "I, on the other hand, have heard all about the height and depth and breadth of Armand's yen for you."

The hopes that his fellow Brit shared with Maury as compatriot and gay man did not qualify as confidences to the director. He'd loved Alvee for more than half a century. Some young actor's amorous confessions about his own yearnings were just amusements to Maury, repeatable to all.

He said something in Japanese and Maki glanced up from his plate at Alvee. Alvee shrugged. *Don't hate me because I'm beautiful.* Maki smiled.

"Armand waxes poetical about your –"

"Spare me the details," Alvee requested, and tucked into his sashimi.

It's A Wrap

Armand hosted the end of shoot party at the modest house he'd rented at the beach. There was drinking and hilarity, back-slapping congratulations on the success everyone was sure was to come. Armand's little place was crowded, with revelers actually spilling out onto the beach.

Hans Baumhauer asked his director why he hadn't thrown the party at his own palace in Beverly Hills. *Mr. 8 Millimeter* commented in his gruff Teutonic accent, "I hear you live in some famous actress's house. Surely, it must be bigger than this shack. Jessika Yerdlay's place, *korrekt?*"

Maury nodded, and at the mention of the forgotten 1960s starlet, I choked on my drink, coughed. I'd heard all about Jessika Yerdlay, her house, her daughter, once upon a lifetime ago, when I'd been interviewing also forgotten matinee idol Francis Joseph O'Day for a biography that would never get written. I was quite aware of where I lived, and of those that had lived there before me.

Jessika had been Franck's costar in his one famous movie, *High Times in Manhattan.* They'd had an intense, on-again, off-again love affair, and then he'd finally left her and flew to Japan with Bobby Ecksmith. She'd lived out the rest of her days shut away in her mansion, Miss Havisham-stylie, believing that he'd died in that plane crash in 1968.

After Jessika had passed on, Franck purchased the actress's house, reunited there with her daughter. I'd met the woman. She was Franck's biggest fan, the webmaster of *TwoGreenKeys.com.* She was the person who'd requested that his other fans send in their keys and healing energies to him.

She would contribute quite a different spin to *The Life and Times of Franck O'Day* than he had, insights into those reflected energies that kept him young. Like my best friend Ruthanne, she had perished in the fire in Vegas.

In my estimation, mention of where Maury resided was dangerous, his possible connections to old-Hollywood history not to be pointed up. There were very few extant pictures of Robert Ecksmith, but there was at least one on his Wikipedia page. Hollywood's attention span, not to mention its memory, was not lengthy, but Maury lived with Alvee in Jessika's house, and Alvee resembled Franck O'Day a great deal (because he *was* Franck O'Day), and Franck had once been involved with Jessika . . .

A memory played through my mind, of the day I'd first beheld Franck, after the fire, returned from the dead – no longer Franck O'Day at all, but now young, stunning Alvee Smith-Killem. After he'd told me the story about how he'd lost control of the universal energy, he'd said, "There's someone inside I'd like you to meet."

The table on the terrace was already familiar. It was there that Franck had related his life story to me. Sitting at it now was a thin, blonde man wearing a pair of half-specs, reading a copy of *Variety*.

He glanced up as we approached, but didn't smile.

Franck – Alvee – said, "Carolyn Adyon, I'd like you to meet Maurice Claremount."

The man took off his glasses and rose. He kissed my hand. "I've heard so much about you, Miss Adyon." His accent was clipped, veddy British. "You're not here for further research on your book, I hope?" His expression was expectant. He still didn't smile.

With dawning astonishment, I realized who I was looking at. I noted a small scar over his right eye, the aftermath of the injury that Franck had told me his friend had sustained in the plane crash.

"Franck O'Day is dead, Mr. Ecksmith," I said. "I won't be writing anything about him. Or you."

"In that case," he'd declared with a brilliant smile, "Welcome to our home."

And we've been the closest of friends ever since.

But as I stood there in Armand's cramped, rented beach house, at the wrap party for *Dorian and Henry,* the little scar over Maury's eye put me in mind of a horror story I'd read once. It centered around some dead soldier come miraculously, malevolently back to life. "You could still see the holes where the bullets had taken him out," some other character had declared.

It wasn't that Maury had ever been dead, nor that he was malevolent – except maybe in his opinions of critics who panned his movies. It just occurred to me that if anyone ever connected that little scar over Maury's eye with the injury Robert Ecksmith had sustained . . .

Then I realized that the champagne was going to my head.

No one knew about the injuries Robert Ecksmith had sustained, because no bodies had ever been recovered, because no one (except for the pilot) had died. The wreckage hadn't even been located until 1982, and to this day, no one is completely sure if it's the right plane.

The world had mourned Robert Ecksmith's loss for a second, then had forgotten his existence. It hadn't been Bobby who'd directed Franck O'Day in his star turn as Perry Calibri in *High Times in Manhattan,* after all. The one picture Bobby and Franck had made together had been a flop. It had been Donald Sunnerfeld, now just as dead, just as forgotten as Bobby, who had made Franck O'Day a household name.

For a couple of years. Now Franck was also forgotten.

Maury pounded me rather roughly on the back to relieve my sudden cough, but otherwise ignored me. He said to his cinematographer, "I never invite the rank and file to my home. Then they might get it into their empty little heads that we were all friends. *Compagnons d'armes. Gleich.* " Maury nodded at Sylvia, the homely script girl, as she passed. "Such is not the case, now is it?"

Hans smiled, and the subject was dropped. The cinematographer wandered off to talk to someone else, and Maury said to me, *"Your face, my thane, is as a book where men may read strange matters."*

I laughed self-consciously, set my glass down on an end table. I was done drinking for the evening. The alcohol intake and *Mr. 8 Millimeter's* offhand remark about Jessika Yerdlay had summoned an uncomfortable reiteration of secrets that only I knew.

Maury grinned at me, and for a moment my apprehension persisted. Franck had once described Robert Ecksmith to me, long before I'd ever met him, when I was still under the quite mistaken impression that he was dead. He'd called him a "skinny, blonde Englishman with stereotypically bad teeth."

Like Alvee, Maury had gotten his teeth straightened, but he was still a skinny, blonde Englishman, and though styles and haircuts had certainly changed since the still they used on Wikipedia had been taken, I thought that if the suggestion had been voiced to anyone who had ever known Bobby Ecksmith, they couldn't help but see a startling resemblance between the lost director and Maury Claremount. He probably didn't look too much different now from the forty-two he'd been when he'd disappeared in 1968.

But then a calm voice in my head reminded me that I was probably the only person still alive (who was not some dedicated, old-Hollywood archivist) that remembered Robert Ecksmith, or what he'd looked like. And like that archivist, I didn't personally remember him at all. I'd just heard stories about him, seen one or two photos.

As if reading my mind, Maury said softly, "Relax, Carol. You can't be having a coronary anytime somebody mentions that we live in Jessika Yerdlay's house. No one will ever make the connections."

As he was the director, I took his advice and relaxed. He was correct, as always. Bobby and Maury, Bobby and Franck, Franck and Alvee, Alvee and Maury, even together in Jessika's house – Hollywood's memory was short, and it would take an awful lot of concerted digging for anyone to ever *make the connections.*

And even if someone took the time and the effort, the results gleaned by making the connections were impossible. There wasn't a jury in the world that would believe that Maurice Claremount and Alvee Smith-Killem were in fact Robert Ecksmith and Franck O'Day, not dead at all, but somehow miraculously reborn.

Someone put *LA Woman* on Armand's sound system; I was familiar with the ancient tune, because my friend Ruthanne had liked old music almost as much as she'd liked old movies. I reminded myself to ask the Brit what he'd thought of the City of Light during his stay here.

(Maury's voice in my head: *"Paris* is the City of Light, Carol, not Los Angeles. You mustn't be misled by that failed film student's misappropriated lyrics.")

But sometimes it seemed that Jim was speaking directly to me: *Are you a lucky little lady in the City of Light?*

Because – what was I before I came to live here in the entertainment capital of the universe? The personalities, the egos with which I'd dealt had been small time, plain; perhaps the occasional big fish in a little pond, and a few tin-pot dictators in the workaday world. But Alvee and Maury (and Armand, too) were players on the world stage, recognized by strangers; they had *fans.* I lived in the reflected light of their fame, and the egos that accompanied it.

I had known *of* wealth – I had recognized it upon my first visit to Jessika's house. But since these kinds of fabulously expensive things could never be mine on a legal secretary's salary . . . *meh. So what?* I was not impressed by the opulence. Now . . . it's hard to describe. Maury and Alvee had taught me an appreciation of the finer things that money could buy without in any way making a lesson of it. In other words, no one pointed out to me which fork to use. The furnishings, the food; the clothes, the limos – after a while, I just came to accept that all these things were indeed . . . *better.*

54

Watching Maury and Alvee, I learned how to treat servants. Pleasant, interested chatter, but not too much. Gratitude when it was appropriate, but not a *thank you* for every single action. Kimura smiled as I slowly caught on.

Maury threw poetry and Shakespeare at me, mythology; speculations on the motivations of my fellow man, cause and effect to their actions. He allowed me to pick and choose that which I liked. He taught be about the business, and about the art of filmmaking; he gave me an appreciation for old cinema from a director's point of view. It was more enjoyable, more thought-provoking than the abject fandom of long-dead stars to which Ruthanne had once subjected me. More than just that so-and-so was attractive, Maury pointed out the subtleties of mood and characterization that the old stars and films encompassed; and I could see it, too, in Alvee's performances.

The Lizard King's lyrics again: *Or just another lost angel? City of Night* . . . The night, *the morality,* if you will, had also changed for me since I'd come to Hollywood. Where once I'd thought that maybe someday I might get married, might have a baby – I didn't want any of *that* anymore. Maury and I, coming up with vehicles in which to star his muse – that was my life now. As long as I had that, and them . . . Alvee and I didn't have to be married. My mother might still think of it as living in sin, but I didn't really talk to her too much anymore. I was busy – I called her once or twice a month. I didn't have to have family or girlfriends or children to occupy my time, anymore. Maury and Alvee and the world of the movie business were all I needed.

I can't quite put my finger on it – but living in the magnificent old mansion with my matchless lover and his imperious friend had not only reconfigured my own ambitions, it had also changed how I thought. My sudden freak-out at the secrets I knew was a perfect example. My beloved actor and director were not what they seemed, and once upon a time, that fact and its many and varied ramifications had *disconcerted* the little nobody-girl from Riverside. It had prompted me to write all my fears in that journal, led me to lock it safely away.

But nowadays, what my companions are, and more importantly (in Alvee's case, anyway), how they came to be this way, seems to bother me not at all. And myself – what I used to be, and what I've become – I sometimes examine my life, but not too thoroughly. What's past is past, and what is now . . . it's all a dream come true. It's strange, it's wonderful; it's a secret. But there's certainly nothing *wrong* about it. Maybe I feel this way because I've become a part of the secret.)

Alvee breezed up, put his arm around my waist, kissed me on the cheek. "Are we about ready to blow this pop stand?"

Again the director smiled, with his straight, white, perfect teeth. "As always, my darling, you're right on cue."

****

Maurice Claremount disappeared to oversee post production, but he made it a point to be home to catch Alvee and Armand's appearance on Jimmy Kimmel. The comedian made light of their opposite coloring, comparing them to Betty and Veronica, and other hair contrast duos of the past.

Maury was unamused, said that the bit was reaching – who'd ever heard of any of the cop dramas mentioned, staring light and dark-haired actors: *Starsky and Hutch* or *CHiPs* or *Simon and Simon?*

"Seriously?" the famous director sniffed. "Does he really think anyone remembers Xena and Gabrielle? He might as well have dug up Apollo and Starbuck from *Battlestar Galactica.*"

I consulted my phone. "You are *so old,* Maury."

The director gestured at the television. "As are Jimmy Kimmel's writers."

****

I was on the arm of *Dorian and Henry's* helmsman at the premiere, and the lady from *Entertainment Tonight* – I have some lesion on my brain which prevents me from remembering her name – interviewed us together. Maury included me by speaking of *our* challenges in making Wilde's material more transparent, of bringing modern nuances to a picture set in the 19th century. I mostly just nodded.

Alvee and Armand took a separate limo. "We can't all show up together like the Brady Bunch, now can we?" Maury had said. It further reinforced the leads' camaraderie, the idea that perhaps they were indeed more than just friends, which was exactly the way the director had wanted it to appear, to fire the prurient imaginations of the ticket-buying populace. Art imitates life, and all. There's no such thing as bad publicity.

When the sleek black car carrying the stars of *Dorian and Henry* arrived, the camera that had been trained on its director and screenwriter winked out like a candle in the wind, and our interviewer disappeared as if by magic. Maury grinned in satisfaction. He offered me his arm and we strolled on into the theater.

Under the heading of *A Picture is Worth a Thousand Words*, or whatever might be the journal equivalent, I must file the following vignette.

At the onset of shooting, some cog in the wheel of marketing at Title XVII had come up with the idea of a fan contest: *Why I Should Get to Meet Dorian and Henry*. I thought the whole suggestion was somewhat of a throwback, essentially an essay contest; not really the kind of thing to stir the short attention spans of the Facebook generation.

I underestimated the draw of Armand Hambrick, the devastating Brit, however. I even underestimated the allure of my own gorgeous Alvee. There were thousands of entries. One contestant was chosen whose words adequately expressed their desire to meet Alvee, and one for Armand, with the lucky winners getting an all-expenses-paid trip to Hollywood to worship their idols in person. They would also get to enjoy the premiere. They would get to snap a few invaluable selfies with the stars.

A handler with the customary wire in his ear had the winners standing a little off to one side in the lobby, where they wouldn't be underfoot. They gazed toward the doors with awestruck, shining eyes, waiting for Alvee and Armand to leave the crowds and the cameras behind on the red carpet and grant them a true fan's dearest wish: a semi-private moment with their best-loved celebrities.

The contestants were a man and a woman, probably in their early twenties. The girl wore a lovely white gown, and the man, a well-fitted (though undoubtedly rented) tux. As we passed, the young man actually recognized the film's director. He called him *Mr. Claremount, sir,* clasped Maury's hand in both of his, said it was an honor to meet him.

The fan complimented the director on the grit of *Kinship,* said it was in great contrast to the fun whimsy of *Cheyenne Sundown,* which he thereby declared was a testament to Maury's flexibility and genius as a filmmaker. He even praised the little-seen *Downpour.*

Maury was indeed flexible, and I, too considered him a genius (despite *Downpour's* maudlin, overwrought sentimentality). And *Kinship* had been gritty, I supposed. But I wouldn't have called *Cheyenne Sundown* whimsical. It was a love story, it was an adventure, it was a buddy movie, but it wasn't *whimsical.*

Maury thanked him and signed his old-fashioned autograph book, then asked which of *Dorian and Henry's* stars he was there to see.

The young man sighed mightily, in hurts-so-good pleasure. "I'm here to meet Alvee, of course. It's the dream of a lifetime!"

This was the reason that he'd recognized the director, had seen all of his films. It wasn't that Maury was a flexible genius or that *Kinship* was gritty or that *Cheyenne Sundown* was whimsical or that *Downpour* deserved anything other than its straight-to-video anonymity. Story, pacing, cinematography – none of that mattered. He liked Maurice Claremount's movies because of their star.

"He so loves meeting his fans," quoth the director, which thrilled Alvee's devotee to his very core.

Slumming uncharacteristically, the auteur now addressed the young woman, stating the obvious. "And you're here to see Armand?"

She nodded reverently, unable to speak. She had not a clue who this skinny old guy was, why he would be talking to her. Her entire being practically moaned, *OMG! Where's Armand?*

I remembered the first time that Ruthanne and I had met Franck. He could immediately tell that it was Ruthie that was his fan (and not me, not then), simply by her dazed, love-struck appearance. But the overcome young woman here today was blonde Armand's fan, not raven Alvee's.

Maury and I said our *Nice to meet yous,* and our *Good lucks,* and took a few steps away from the fortunate winners towards the door to the theatre.

I was absolutely, unequivocally, positively sure that Maurice Claremount, of the many, many responsibilities, could not possibly have had anything whatsoever to do with something as not-related to filmmaking as deciding the winners of a rabid-fan contest. Still, I thought it would've amused him to choose a besotted young man to pay homage to *not even remotely curious* Alvee, and an eager young woman for the commanding British sodomite, so I asked him suspiciously, "Did you have something to do with picking these particular fans?"

"I most assuredly did not," he said, with that embarrassed-for-me, *Really, Carol* face, the one he usually reserved for my stupidest questions.

"Choosing contest winners is a little bit below my pay grade, wouldn't you say? I'm sure someone in marketing chose them. Or maybe a machine chose them, by keeping track of how many superlatives and *I love yous* appeared in each entry. Aren't they cute?"

He stepped into the theater, and the two fans, about to live out the dream of a lifetime, were utterly forgotten by Maurice Claremount, as if they'd never been born.

In what seemed like another lifetime, in the bar of a Las Vegas hotel, as prelude to his faux proposition, Franck O'Day had told me, "I've never had to seduce anyone, Carol, never had to talk anyone into it, never even had to ask. They always ask me. I'm not saying that the entirety of womanhood has always thrown itself at my feet."

That's precisely what you're saying, I'd thought.

"There are girls too young and women too old, and happily married women, and girls that like girls. I'm not everyone's type. But if I am their type, and they're bold enough, they always wind up asking me, sooner or later."

Now, at the premiere for *Dorian and Henry,* I should've gone on into the theater with my director. But professionalism be damned, I had to see how this played out. Call it childish, but I wanted to witness my darling Alvee's reaction to a young woman who was not there to see him.

The stars entered the building and paused politely while the handler introduced them to the contest winners.

The girl's face was slack with wonder; she stared silently up at Armand. She was quite unable to reply when he asked her something. Whatever clever words she'd written to beat out all his other fans abandoned her. She would hate herself later, I reckoned, relive the moment over and over in her mind: *Why didn't I answer him? He spoke to me!*

She did get her precious selfie, however. With some kind of ingrained instinct, as if her hand moved of its own volition, she silently handed her phone to the tall Brit, so he could snap their picture.

She noticed irresistible Alvee Smith-Killem not at all.

I'd wanted to see Alvee's reaction to Armand's fan. I wasn't quite sure what I'd been expecting, but really, I should've known. Alvee didn't notice the young woman any more than she'd noticed him. He simply wasn't her *type.* There had to be a few, after all. From across the lobby, he grinned at me as if to say, *You can't win 'em all.*

Alvee's fan was the girl's opposite in nervousness. He chatted effusively, so much that Alvee couldn't get a word in edgeways. He just smiled as if the young man's words were the most interesting and unique he'd ever heard.

The girl had felt it completely within her fan-rights to touch Armand, however. When he'd put his arm around her for the picture, she'd leaned in close to him; she'd recovered her nerve enough to give him a big hug afterward.

After his selfie with Alvee, the young man had to settle for the more societally-acceptable handshake, even though I would've bet the farm that the kid would've sold his very soul to embrace my black-haired charmer. He did clasp Alvee's hand in both of his for the entirety of their brief conversation, however.

It struck me that, if Armand and Alvee had been on the prowl for action, like rock stars trolling for groupies, then this particular encounter with two of their very biggest fans would've been a monumental bust, laughable in its barking-up-the-wrong-tree ridiculousness.

Girls will be boys and boys will be girls, it's a mixed up, muddled up, shook up world.

Thus, the agony of art.

****

A few days after the premiere, when the reviews came out, *Dorian and Henry's* black-haired leading man was astonished that I disagreed with them, that I thought the film should be nominated for an Academy Award.

"Really? You think it deserves an *Oscar?* It's –"

"If you say, *it's a fag picture,* I'll drown you like an unwanted puppy," Maury warned.

Alvee held up his hands in a defensive, warding-off gesture, and the scar on his palm was clearly visible. I knew that when he was filming, the make-up team hid it with a little flesh-colored, Band-Aid looking thing.

"I wasn't gonna say that at all. I was gonna say, *it's been done.* Didn't you say that enough times?"

Maury reluctantly nodded. Nobody else on-set had dared to utter the damning phrase, but he was the director.

"I think it turned out to be a great film. But not quite Oscar caliber." Alvee batted his enormous baby blues. "Didn't I put my heart into it? Wasn't I believable?"

Maury narrowed his eyes, and half a leer curled his lip. "Did Armand believe you?"

Alvee was noncommittal. "What do you think?"

"I would wager that he most assuredly *wanted* to. Nothing would've thrilled him more than to discover that Dorian's heart beat within your exquisite body."

"And as always, you would've won."

Oscar Wilde's words returned to my mind: *For curiosity's sake he had tried the denial of self.* For curiosity's sake had Alvee played a gay man. Just to see if he could pull it off.

Maury grinned in wicked glee. "What did he say?"

Alvee smirked. *Adonis,* I thought, *Narcissus; Hyacinth and Dorian Gray himself, and Alvee.* All beautiful and all quite aware of it. *Convinced,* Ruthie's voice said in my mind.

"You keep asking me that, and I keep telling you. He didn't say anything. Not a single word, ever. But now that he's going home, I did receive a letter this morning, delivered by courier." Alvee patted the pocket of his shirt.

"How mawkishly Old World of him," Maury marveled. "Let me see it."

"Down, boy. It's none of your business. I'm not one to kiss and tell."

"You never kissed Armand." It was a statement, devoid of any doubt whatsoever. Maury had known Alvee for a very long time. "You wouldn't have kissed him, had he begged, had he crawled on his belly like a reptile."

Alvee shrugged.

"Let me see this missive."

"I will not. Your critique would be too scathing. But I'll summarize to satisfy Maki's curiosity." Alvee winked at Maury's partner, and with an evil smile, rattled off several lines in Japanese. Maki glanced at me and his mouth dropped open in perfectly embarrassed astonishment.

"He didn't even use her name?" Maury exclaimed.

"He did not." Alvee chuckled, squeezed my hand.

"He did not what? What about my name?"

Alvee affected a fair imitation of Armand's accent. *"I know you amuse yourself with that screenwriter, and I'm sure that she worships you as only a woman can . . . How tiresome that becomes,* he said, and did I not agree? Then he offered to show me what worship was really all about –"

"I thought he liked me," I said, before I'd quite realized that the words had come out of my mouth. "I liked him."

"He never liked you." Maury's wicked grin intensified. "Not on your life, my darling. You've quite ensorcelled Alvee with your *screenwriter's* charms, and trust me when I tell you that *Rubio* hates you quite completely for it.

"How tiresome indeed, is a woman in such a situation. How she does stand in the way! And what is a woman, after all, but a fat, smelly bag of useless emotions? A woman cannot possible grasp the timelessness, the art and ecstasy of the Hellenic ideal, the perfection of the love that dare not speak its name . . ."

When I blinked at him in wounded disbelief, Maury immediately said, "Come, Carol. Don't be so devastated. We're friends. Of course, I don't think of you that way. You're not fat at all."

He didn't wait for my feelings to recover. I could either choose to be offended by his tender jab, or I could get over it. Either way, Maury cared not.

He leered at Alvee. "Did Armand give you any description of this promised worship?"

Alvee giggled, again said something in Japanese. Maki's expression, usually so blankly dignified, burst into a smile nearly as wicked as Maury's. He was one of Armand's biggest fans, after all. Then Maki quickly composed himself and blinked innocently at me again.

I was about to become annoyed at not being allowed in on the dirty part of the joke, when Alvee said, "His letter got very romantic and cloak and dagger and European from there. He told me that he'd be leaving this afternoon, gave me the airline and the flight number and the terminal and the gate, and what time the plane boards.

"I'm to come away with him, you see. If I don't show up, he said, he'll know that it had been a mistake to finally confess his devotion. He'll know that all his outpourings of love have been in vain . . ." Alvee theatrically put his hand to his forehead, then concluded, "The limo's picking me up in twenty minutes."

Again I blinked in dumb disbelief, and his amusement positively sparkled at my speechlessness. "That's right, Carol. I'm leaving on a jet plane to merry olde England, your favorite locale, with Maury's favorite twink."

Alvee was merry indeed.

He squeezed my hand again. "I think you, of all people, know me better than that. I'm neither romantic nor cloak and dagger nor European. Armand's an actor, and a damn good one. I consider us friends. I'll say goodbye to him like a friend. Besides, if I don't show up and tell him how it is, he'll always harbor some hope . . ." Alvee winked at me. *You know how that hope lingers.*

Maury tilted his head sagely, and a slight, mysterious smile curved his lips. "Remember, it's only queer if you look 'em in the eye."

Alvee's expression was now become one of total innocence. "I have no idea what you're talking about."

I suddenly kenned that I might have an idea what Maury was talking about, because another memory assailed me, a quite raunchy one in fact, another chapter from those interviews with Francis Joseph O'Day. He'd again been relating the tale of his first days in Hollywood, of his first break in the business, a further insight into why Robert Ecksmith would later believe that he possessed a certain *affability.*

Franck's words: "My Uncle Jesse, by what luck I'll never know, got me a little casting couch meeting with Patrick Morrison." Morrison, he explained, was a powerful director at RKO Pictures.

"I was almost twenty-three, certainly no baby, but I was still surprised by his offer. He was actually very straightforward about it. 'Suck my dick,' he said, 'and I'll give you the lead.'"

I was amazed at the ease with which Franck told the story. He was talking to a complete stranger about being propositioned by a male director, but he was relating it with no compunctions whatsoever, without a trace of self-consciousness.

"I'd read the script for Morrison's picture. *It was not all that,* as the kids say. But this was RKO, so I didn't just laugh in his face. I told him that I didn't think I was quite up for the lead, and asked him what else was available.

"'Well,' he said, and smiled at me. 'If you let me suck *your* dick, there still might be a small part in it for you.'"

Without extrapolating further, Franck told me that he got a part in the movie.

"I even had a few lines, but they wound up, as such things often do, on the cutting room floor. But the best connection I would ever make came out of my . . . *brief association* with Patrick Morrison and RKO. It was Morrison, you see, who introduced me to Bobby Ecksmith.

"It was at the wrap party. As I walked up, Morrison leaned in and whispered something in Bobby's ear. Bobby smiled at me. He and Morrison both smiled at me, like I was on the menu. I smiled back. Adoration is adoration, as I say, no matter where it comes from, no matter if you don't return it in the least. It's all positive energy.

"After a moment of smiling at me, Bobby said, 'Patrick tells me you're quite the up-and-comer.'

"I kid you not, Carol, he actually said that to me, and with a moderately straight face. I looked mildly at Morrison, who perhaps expected me to be shocked or embarrassed or worried. I was none of these things. Even at twenty-three, I knew which secrets were inviolate, and which secrets were shared and with which people. Morrison could say whatever he wanted about me. I knew exactly how far it would go, and was not concerned at all. After all, it wasn't me that was the cocksucker."

It hadn't been any kind of display of gratitude on Franck's part that had landed him the role, now had it? The privilege that Francis Joseph O'Day had allowed Patrick Morrison, the once in a lifetime opportunity to touch his exquisite person, had worked. Shrewd young Franck had already been seeing that hungry look for some years; he recognized that allowing the director this small liberty was the thing to do at the time for a young actor wanting to get ahead in the business (pun definitely intended.) It had been a one off, had served to make him all the connections he would ever need. So what? He wasn't the cocksucker. Franck had felt no shame at the time, no shame at the telling, decades later.

Now, the man who had once been Bobby Ecksmith was intimating that Alvee was willing to allow Armand Hambrick similar liberties, for no other reason than that he had begged to do so.

"Ah, yes the VIP Lounge at LAX, secure from looky-loos and the paparazzi. The two of you should be able to find a private spot in there."

"It's not like that, and you know it." Alvee sighed.

I'd never seen him angry, unless he was acting, but I thought that Maury's insinuations annoyed him. Alvee and I were together, more surely and permanently than if we'd been wed, and the activity to which Maury alluded was not one in which a happily married man engaged. The very suggestion that Alvee would even consider it was an affront to what we shared.

Then he grinned suddenly. "Armand's not even from RKO."

It was a joke between the three of us, a reference not only to Patrick Morrison's pass at Franck O'Day, but to the same proposition once offered to *neophyte* Alvee Smith-Killem, as well. That one had come from *New York Times'* film critic Cary Stuward, at a party after the premiere of *Cheyenne Sundown.*

"I could be a good friend to you, Mr. Killem, if you'd be a good friend to me," the chubby writer had told Alvee, saying that he'd be more than willing to turn in a stellar review of his performance in the western, if only Alvee would be willing to perform certain sex acts upon his person.

Alvee read neither *The Times* nor *Variety,* and regardless, Cary Stuward was no Roger Ebert. It was not the 1950s, and Alvee made movies for fun these days; he was not hardly a hungry *up-and-comer.* He laughed in Stuward's face, and said (as he told us later), "You're not even from RKO!"

Now Alvee's blue eyes were all round and solemn with feigned concern. He was such a good actor. "Seriously, my love. You'd don't think that I'd really allow Armand to . . . to . . ."

I waited for him to say *touch me,* but he never quite got it out.

"Of course not." I knew which way Alvee *swung.* He wouldn't *allow Armand to . . . to . . .* not even for the novelty of a different kind of worshipful energy. I knew that Alvee was mine, and that our connection precluded such adventures, with men or women, even if Maury seemed to think otherwise.

I kissed my boyfriend. "I'll see you when you get back from the airport. Tell Armand that *the tiresome screenwriter* wishes him well."

****

Alvee's guffawing dismissal of Cary Stuward's intimate proposition had made him an enemy in the business. As the critic exited the premiere party for *Cheyenne Sundown* in a huff, Maury had also had the nerve to grin knowingly at him. So in his savaging of the film in *The New York Times* the next morning, Stuward had taken a few potshots at the director, also.

He'd deemed Alvee's jaw-dropping love scene with Camellia Swanson to be *gratuitous* and *underlit.* It had been neither – it was Maurice Claremount's gift to the world. His languid shots of Alvee's nude train-robber had made the *neophyte* and his sexiness household words. Forget reviews – hell, forget plot, setting, characterization – Alvee's perfection in that one scene would be all that anyone would ever remember about *Cheyenne Sundown*. Ryan who?

Other than Cary Stuward's pan, the movie met with fair to good reviews. And far more importantly, it topped the box office its first weekend out. The ticket-buying populace loved it.

Old sins (or a giggling refusal to commit them) cast long shadows in the movie biz, so it was not in the least bit surprising that Cary Stuward would also hate *Dorian and Henry*, concentrating his malice on the dark-haired lead. Golden Armand Hambrick was indeed golden, but *Alvee Smith-Killem, best known for playing criminals, was completely miscast as the titular character. He possesses neither the diction nor the range of emotion to bring Wilde's tortured anti-hero to life.*

Stuward, no doubt thinking himself quite impossibly clever, then paraphrased the immortal Oscar Wilde himself: *It is not good for one's morals to see bad acting, Mr. Claremount.*

None of the other reviews found fault with Alvee's performance in particular, yet, across the board, the critics had but a lukewarm response to *Dorian and Henry*. The film was not much more than okey-dokey to all, except for the columnist for *The Village Voice*, who'd enthusiastically proclaimed it *an outstanding allegory for the 1980s AIDS epidemic and its chilling aftermath.*

Maury smiled ruefully "Well. It certainly wasn't that."

Then he giggled at *The Voice's* wrong-headed interpretation, and his giggle grew into a good old-fashioned belly laugh. None of it, neither reviews nor commercial success, mattered in the least to Maurice Claremount. He made movies for fun. His beloved muse had wanted to play another bad guy, so the director had accommodated him.

Maury believed that our screenplay, his costumes, his direction and his stars made *Dorian and Henry* a superb retelling, one for the ages. As did I. So what if Alvee himself declared that *it had been done,* and the critics thought it was *meh,* and Oscar ignored it as if it was a drunken cousin at his daughter's wedding? It didn't top the box office, but it did a little bit better than break even. There were still DVD sales to come, and there was always the potential for it to become the next Netflix guilty pleasure.

And most importantly, Alvee had enjoyed making it, had enjoyed playing the heavy again. Nothing else mattered to Maury.

"However," the director said, "for your next picture, my darling, I think we should go with something a little bit lighter."

"Kyōgen?" Alvee smiled at Maki and he smiled back.

I reached for my phone, but Maury covered my hand. *"Kyōgen* is traditional Japanese comic theater."

I glanced at Alvee is surprise. "You mean, like with the make-up?"

"That's *Kabuki."* Maury favored me with his standard, *You* are *an ignorant little American girl, but you're trying* expression, then considered his flippant leading man. "What would be wrong with a comedy?"

Alvee snorted. "And now for something completely different. Maurice Claremount writes comedy."

"I didn't say I had to write it."

Maury wordlessly questioned me and I shook my head. I reckoned I could do adventure, romance, a little sci-fi, *gritty* drama, perhaps. But not comedy. It just wasn't my thing.

Maury shrugged. He took out his phone, scrolled, spoke. "Send me some comedies."

Maurice Claremount Directs Comedy

Despite his command to an overseas underling at Title XVII to *send him some comedies,* and despite the fact that scripts arrived every day, dozens, hundreds – it took almost two years for the filmmaking trio of Maurice Claremount, Alvee Smith-Killem and my humble self to choose one.

And even then, I wasn't completely onboard with what my director and leading man picked. The plot was linear, as Maury preferred, the stock, non-confusing three act structure, blah, blah, blah, but my small professionalism as a screenwriter was offended.

The plot involved two friends who fall for the same woman; hilarity ensues. It had been done, and repeatedly. For *decades.* I related a memory from childhood to Maury; I didn't know when exactly, or where I'd seen it, but there was an episode of *The Monkees* with just this plotline. All the boys in the band fall in love with Julie Newmar.

Maury told me not to bother him with obscure, long-forgotten Americana.

I said, okay, how's this for not forgotten: The movie he'd chosen for Alvee had the same plot as *Rushmore,* Jason Schwartzman's star-making debut. Everyone lives happily and appropriately ever after at the end of that one. And there had been that Tom Hardy/Chris Pine/Reese Witherspoon vehicle, *This Means War;* each character got the girl he deserved in that one, too.

I mentioned another one I'd seen, some years before. It was indeed obscure, straight to video, yes, but not American. An import from the Great White North, it starred doomed

Canadian Edison Forbes and a young Mitch Barlo, and was called *Two's A Crowd.* Both black-haired and blue-eyed, these actors even resembled Alvee a great deal.

The formidable Maurice Claremount sniffed in irritation that a nobody such as myself would dare to question his script selection for his muse's next picture. "There are only so many plotlines under the sun, Carol."

"Man against machine," Alvee said. "Man against society, against nature, against God, against self . . ." When I peered at him in surprise, he added, "But what do I know? I'm just a dumb actor."

Maury pontificated. "In rom-coms, or at least in this one, the conflict is man against man, with the lovely woman as the prize."

I pointed at the script on the table. "But neither gets the prize in the end."

"The Third Man gets her."

"It's been done," I insisted emphatically. It was basically the same plot, the same ending as *Two's A Crowd.*

Maury looked to his leading man for an opinion. Alvee shrugged. He was a bit of a *chancer* himself, an actor's actor. He would play any part. It would be good to see his name in lights again, even if it was for a soon-to-be-forgotten rom-com fluff piece. Alvee made movies for fun.

His phone beeped, and when he saw who was texting, he grinned. "Always on cue. Did you say *casting call,* Maury?"

"What are you talking about?"

Alvee typed on his phone, again smiled at the response he received. "Armand says hi."

In the two years since *Dorian and Henry* had faded into obscurity, I'd rarely given Armand Hambrick a thought. If he did cross my mind, I was invariably reminded of how he'd so mistakenly dreamt that his blonde beauty would be able to undermine my relationship with his costar. How he'd believed he'd be able to surpass my *tiresome woman's worship* of Alvee with his own.

On the heels of these recollections came smug satisfaction. The Brit may indeed be beautiful, talented, famous; but the one thing of which he dreamt was mine. Exclusively.

Since his return to his native land, Armand still corresponded with Alvee online, and he also frequently sent little taste-of-England care packages via old-fashioned post. All in a bid, I reckoned, to lure his favorite colonial across the pond for a visit. I knew it was laughably futile: one-time plane crash survivor Alvee Smith-Killem hated to fly. It would take more than the oft-cited wild horses, and most certainly more than the long-distance adoration of a foreign pouf, to get him on any airplane, and especially not on a trip that involved a ten or twelve hour flight. *As if.*

Maury would gleefully consume the UK foodstuffs Armand mailed: *Rowntrees Blackcurrant Fruit Pastilles, Fray Bentos Steak and Kidney Pies, Batchelors Chip Shop Mushy Peas, Branston Pickles.* He'd regale me with reminiscences of the *auld sod* with his mouth full. Alvee ignored the edibles, but always handled the little Union Jack buttons and Manchester United memorabilia and other trinkets that Armand sent. Like Franck O'Day and his green keys, Alvee absorbed Armand's loving energy from these items, then tossed them carelessly back into the box.

Alvee insisted that *Rubio* had never made a pass at him whilst they were making *Dorian and Henry.* When he'd showed up at LAX and informed Armand that his love was not returned, Alvee said that the Englishman had taken it well.

But time and distance had made Armand bold in his emails. Alvee occasionally featured us with a few of the blonde thespian's flowery tenders, all borrowed (and with not much originality, I thought) from the poets of old.

How had Armand referred to me? I was *tiresome?* I thought him tiresome indeed in comparing Alvee to a summer's day; and Christ, could anything be more tiresome than counting the ways he loved Alvee, even after death? The memory of Alvee's eyes, as blue as *the sea and wind when both contend which is the mightier* were *his spell against a cursed day.*

Maury's eyebrows rose at that one. *"That's an ill phrase, a vile phrase."* He winked at me. Armand's mixing of Shakespeare and Mario Benedetti, his banality in apparently Googling *popular poetry* to find praises for Alvee, tickled the hell out of the famous director.

He rose, and projecting masterfully, emoting as if he was an actor himself, he held forth: *"By that Heaven that bends above us – by that God we both adore – tell this soul with sorrow laden if, within the distant Aidenn, it shall clasp a sainted maiden whom the angels name Lenore – clasp a rare and radiant maiden whom the angels name Lenore!"*

I giggled in nasty arrogance. *"Quoth the Raven, 'Nevermore.'"*

Alvee considered us silently over his phone, then typed, scrolled, came up with a quotation of his own. Deadpan, as if he really believed it, he read, *"While the laughter of joy is in full harmony with our deeper life, the laughter of amusement should be kept apart from it. The danger is too great of thus learning to look at solemn things in a spirit of mockery, and to seek in them opportunities for exercising wit."*

Maury, of the classical education, needed no electronic helps to counter. *"Isn't it the sweetest mockery to mock our enemies,* Carol?"

"Armand's not her enemy," Alvee said.

"He's not even competition," Maury agreed. He nodded at Alvee's phone. "But not from lack of trying."

"You people are cruel." Alvee thenceforth stopped reading Armand's love letters to us.

I knew that the besotted Brit continued to send them, however, because I would sometimes catch a faint smile pass Alvee's lips when he was perusing his computer. There was a different quality to it than when he read his correspondence from the rank and file of his fandom.

Alvee read all his fan mail personally, both snail and email. But the email was of course the most convenient, and that love-energy was useful to him, after all, even when received electronically.

The computer wizards at Title XVII had made him a little app that allowed him to answer his fan's emails, too, with what seemed like a wonderfully personal touch. All he had to do was hit one key, and the fan received a quick video – how unscripted and homey they seemed, with the pool in the background! Alvee had been so moved by the fan's heartfelt . . . whatever, that he'd just gone right ahead and recorded a few words, just for that fan! Maury would snicker uncontrollably whenever Alvee would record new clips.

They were all variations on *Thanks so much for your kind words,* and *It's so nice to hear from you, please feel free to write again.* At the bottom of these bot-generated return emails, the fan was instructed to *Click here if you'd like to purchase* any or all of Alvee's four films on DVD.

Soon, I thought, the link would suggest, *Click here to purchase advance tickets to this tiresome, been-done rom-com I'm about to make . . .*

I felt bad about thinking that, so I again ruminated on Armand Hambrick's affection for my boyfriend. Since I was aware of his continuing florid emails to Alvee, the fact that the modern convenience of texting had also been added to their correspondence shouldn't have surprised me. But I have to admit it did. I knew about the emails, but I'd never known that Armand and Alvee texted like school chums until just that moment.

"Should I tell him you're about to cast the new project?" Alvee asked his director.

"For the love of God, don't do that!" Maury shook his head, and I was surprised at the firmness of his conviction. Alvee was surprised, also.

I figured that perhaps the director thought that casting Armand as Alvee's rival for the affections of a woman would confuse the ticket-buying populace, after their turn as lovers in *Dorian and Henry.* But that wasn't it at all.

"Have you *seen* Armand lately, my darling?" Maury asked. "I mean, I realize that you talk to him frequently, which I'm sure warms his very cockles, but have you *seen* any recent pictures of him?"

Alvee shook his head, and Maury sighed. "Alas, it is a cautionary tale. Behold, my children, the dictionary definition of *letting oneself go . . .*"

The picture that Maury showed us wasn't *that* bad. In the two years since I'd last seen Armand, he had grown a shade puffy; a trifle stout and jowly, in an aristocratically English kind of way. His locks were of course still blonde, but his hairline had receded quite a bit. Maki shook his head with infinite sadness at his favorite's transformation, as if Armand had died, instead of just beginning to show the lash of Father Time.

"Hell, Maury. He doesn't look that bad. He's, what . . .?" I had no idea how old Armand was. I'd figured he was probably about the same age as Alvee appeared to be. I considered a discreet Google to find out, but Maury was watching me.

"From this picture, how old would you guess he is?" Maury studied it again. "This is his head shot for whatever he's doing now. Some play."

"He's doing theatre again?" Alvee asked in surprise. "He didn't tell me that."

"Perhaps there isn't a lot of call for paunchy, bloated blondies in cinema at the moment."

"He's not paunchy, Maury." It felt odd to defend Armand, but really, he didn't look that bad.

"This is a *publicity shot,* Carol. Done by a *professional.* This isn't some lucky pap snap taken the morning after a particularly grueling night at the Hellfire Cave." Maury grinned. *"Fais ce que tu voudras,* and all."

Alvee rolled his eyes and translated for me: *"Do what thou wilt."*

"This is the best Armand looks nowadays," Maury said, considering the picture again. "I suspect even this may've been Photoshopped somewhat. It's shocking."

Alvee sighed. "How dramatic you are! It's not shocking. He just looks a little tired."

"And old. And fat."

Alvee commented no further. "Never regret growing old," he'd told me once. "It's a privilege denied to many."

But he wasn't one of them. According to his bio, Alvee Smith-Killem, of Bromley, Kentucky, was thirty-five, three years younger than me. With the right lighting, he could make twenty believable, but in the day-to-day world, he looked an utterly delectable thirty. Besides myself, Maury and Maki and Kimura, no one that still stalked the earth knew that he had once answered to the name of Franck O'Day, and that he'd been born in 1933, damn near a century ago.

"Seriously, Carol," Maury repeated, "from this picture, how old would you guess Armand is?"

I reckoned that I'd only seen *Rubio* in the daylight during the shoot for *Dorian and Henry,* when he was in make-up. The dim ambiance of LA's finer restaurants, where the four of us had often dined, was legendary. I'd always found Armand to be as youthful and pretty as Alvee, but perhaps he'd always just been fortunately well-lit. Maybe he was older.

"I dunno. Forty, maybe? Forty-two?"

"Armand is barely thirty-two."

If that was true, then his state *was* a little bit shocking. I tried to feel pity for the still comely Brit, aging so badly, but I figured that he'd probably brought it on himself. Who knows what kind of hijinks such a haughty, full-of-himself actor might've been getting up to over the last two years? London swings like a pendulum do. If Armand burnt the candle at both ends, it was bound to take its toll on his looks. It was his own fault.

And besides, he didn't like me, so my pity for him remained minimal.

I chortled at Maury. "If everyone has the face he deserves at fifty, I'd suggest that perhaps it's time Armand got on having one of those magical portraits painted."

"Before it's too late." Maury giggled appreciatively at my wit. "Like, stat."

Alvee, however, was not amused. I sensed that he'd grown bored with our mean deconstruction of his former costar's appearance and wanted to move on.

"So no part in this as yet untitled epic for Armand?"

Maury said something to Maki. He shook his head sadly. "Papa-san says, 'When the old rope walked into the bar, what did he say to the bartender?'"

"'I'm a frayed knot,'" I supplied, not daring to look at Alvee.

He sighed. "I guess I deserve that. This *is* supposed to be a comedy."

****

Instead of personally choosing Alvee's costar, this time Maury conferred with his staff across the pond at Title XVII; someone over there was supposedly adept at casting comedies. The choice of who would play The Girl was also left to underlings.

It occurred to me that my director's artistic genius wasn't totally onboard for this picture. It wasn't that he wasn't enthusiastic – Maurice Claremount made movies for fun, regardless of the genre – so he was always enthusiastic. I just got the impression that this was more of a business move than a creative one to him. Maury thought that the time was nigh for our favorite leading man to prove that he could play any part. It was time to preclude Alvee's being typecast as only a dramatic actor.

I sensed a different kind of calculation to having Alvee appear in this film, something I hadn't felt when Maury used his own material. He would direct his muse in this (barking dog), but still, not unlike myself, comedy just wasn't Maury's thing.

So it seemed a little odd to me that he would want to oversee the casting call for the role of Mark, the Third Man, the guy that gets The Girl in the end. Any way you sliced it, it was a minor role. The character also could've been labeled The Ex, and the part consisted of only two scenes: the break-up in the exposition and the make-up in the (it's been done) resolution.

It was odd that busy, busy Maurice Claremount would want to sit in on the cattle call for this bit part, when he'd allowed staff to cast the major roles. It was even stranger that he wanted me to also sit in. Who was I? Neither Maury nor I had had even the most perfunctory input in the screenplay for this one; someone else wrote it, and with the director's blessing, Title XVII had bought the rights, as is.

I didn't even particularly like it. OMG, it finally had a title – *She's A Peach* – and I had expressed my humble opinion that the name was particularly awful. So I couldn't understand why Maury wanted me along at all, and especially for this detail. But he was the director, so I did what I was told.

Title XVII rented a meeting room at the Hilton for the event, and on the limo ride over, Maury explained how it all worked.

"There'll be someone to check them off a list and then send them in to us. They give us their resume and their head shots. We can ask them a few questions about what they've done . . ." Maury waved his hand impatiently, and again I wondered why he was involving himself in this. "There'll be an X on the floor in front of the table. They read the scene . . . We jot down our impressions and thank them, and the next guy comes in."

"Just you and me?"

"Sometimes there's a cameraman, if we decide to tape the auditions. Sometimes one of the other actors will be there to read the scene with them, to see how they mesh. But it's a small part, so yeah, it's just you and me, this time. You can read The Girl's lines if you want."

I was horrified. "Oh, no, Maury, I couldn't . . . I'm not an actor . . ."

The impatient, sardonic, unimpressed auteur that he sometimes became frowned, and I thought that my cowardice disappointed him. The further thought struck me that perhaps

78

everything I did disappointed him: the way I dressed, the way I spoke, the way I wrote, the way I amused his leading man . . .

Such was the power, the effect of Maurice Claremount's frown upon me. It was because of him (more than Alvee, really) that I was living the dream of being a participant in Hollywood. Pleasing him meant a great deal to me.

We arrived at the hotel, found our area. One of the production company's hired local functionaries had already set everything up. Here was the hallway; there was a little table with the check-in clipboard, and a line of chairs for the hopefuls. Here was the room, with another table from which we would judge the auditions; another clipboard with a list of names was on it. There were three or four copies of the script, there was the X on the floor. What there weren't were any other people. No one to check the actors in, no actors to be checked in.

Maury's phone beeped. He answered it, asked the caller to hold on.

"I must take this, Carol. I might be a minute. If I'm not back by the time they start showing up – just point to the X and listen to them read. Write down what you think. I trust you."

I opened my mouth to object again – I couldn't audition actors, I wasn't qualified – but Maury was already back on the call, and already out the door. I listened to his familiar accent as it receded down the hallway.

I sat behind the table for several minutes, doodled on the clipboard, read the paper-clipped scene.

INT. BUSY MALL FOOD COURT - DAY

                MARK
       I got the job, Marci!

   (MARCI looks at him in disbelief. It was
   not the news she'd been expecting.)

               MARCI
   So that means . . . you're leaving?

```
                        MARK
        It's the opportunity of a lifetime. You
    know I'll always love ya, baby. I'll keep in
                        touch.


            (MARK kisses her quickly, gives her a
        little squeeze, waves. Then he's gone.)


                        MARCI
            But . . . I thought . . .
        (She puts her hand over her face)


                        VICTOR
        (striding heroically across the food court)
            Are you all right, Miss?
```

And so on. I thought Victor might've been Alvee's character, but maybe not. I'd only read the script once, and the thing was so formulaic, I wasn't sure if it was Alvee's character that made the first Play for The Girl or if it was the other guy.

In the scene before this one, Marci's sure that the surprise Mark has for her is a marriage proposal. But the audience already knows that he's gonna let her down, that he's asked her to meet him in a public place so she won't cause a scene.

After Mark takes off, the New Man (Victor) comforts her. Second Man arrives to have lunch at the mall with New Man (they're buddies). He's also taken with Marci, and she with him. Indecision on her part ensues, with the accompanying outrageously competitive attempts to win her, the requisite threats to the men's friendship.

In the end, Mark returns. He's settled in at the new job, but he realizes that he can never be completely happy without Marci. He proposes, the music swells, she dumps New Man and Second Man, as the hilarity of their pursuit has been annoying to her all along.

They *Ah, shucks* it back to being friends again, but then another pretty girl walks by and they both approach her.

Christ, that left the possibility of a sequel!

I just didn't like *She's A Peach.* It had been done.

I tossed the script back on the table, arose and peeped out of the room. The hall was still empty. I sat back down, and after several more minutes, a nice-looking guy knocked politely on the door frame.

"This is the audition for *She's A Peach?*" He gestured behind him. "There's no one . . . I signed the roster."

"Yes," I mumbled. "Please come in."

He handed me a manila envelope, took a script off the table and stood on the mark. He told me his name, recited several commercials in which he'd appeared, and a small non-speaking part as somebody's henchman on a long-running cop show. This was not his first audition.

As it was such a short scene, I did what Maury had suggested and read Marci's lines. The young man adequately communicated Mark's excitement at his new job prospect, appropriately missed Marci's chagrin at his departure.

Feeling as if I was in a movie myself (another one that had been done), I said, "We'll be in touch."

He thanked me for my time and exited, stage right.

Beside his name on the clipboard, I wrote *Adequate.*

The next one also knocked on the doorframe – no one ever did show up to man the table outside. After the second guy, I just told him to send the next one in on his way out.

They all seemed familiar with the drill, all seemed to be professionals. There were four more come to audition in quick succession, then there was a lull. I noted that there were fifteen names on the list, and I reckoned that Title XVII must not've advertised this one too much – I'd imagined that it was going to be an all-day affair, with candidates lined up out into the lobby, all eager for a chance to appear in the famous director's latest.

I really didn't know how a casting call worked, how it was advertised, but I thought that if Maury didn't return soon, he was gonna miss all the auditions, and then he'd have to rely on my . . .

Then it hit me.

Sometimes I feel like the goose of popular expression, as if I wake up in a new world every day, completely ignorant of events that have occurred in the past. Maybe if I just paid a little closer attention . . .

But now I had it.

Once upon a time, there had been a fan and a not-fan of an actor named Franck O'Day. The fan had tragically perished in a fire, and the not-fan had showed up on Franck's doorstep, after hearing his voice (returned from the dead) in a trailer for some Ryan Gosling western. She had there met irresistible Alvee Smith-Killem. She had been introduced to Maurice Claremount.

Sometime afterward, the director and the now-never-to-be-biographer had the following conversation.

"I understand you aspired to be a writer at one time, Carol."

"All my life," I told him truthfully.

"A noble ambition," he replied. "But setting nobility aside for a moment, have you ever tried your hand at writing a screenplay?"

Academy-award nominated director Robert Ecksmith was asking me if I'd ever written a screenplay. I thought of the stack holding down the corner of my desk at home. Crime stories and romances and science fiction and drama. Period pieces and heist stories and cautionary tales of love gone awry.

"Yes, sir, Mr. Claremount, sir. I've done quite a few screenplays. Nobody's ever read any of them, but I've done quite a few."

He grinned at me. "I'd like to see them."

"I don't think so, Maury. They're awful."

"Oh, you're too modest, Carol."

When Maury requested that I bring my stuff to him, I thought he was kidding, and I wondered if he realized that I would be heartbroken, crushed, if this was some kind of famous-Hollywood-director-makes-fun-of-aspiring-writer joke.

But he assured me that it was not.

I was still living in Riverside at the time, had not yet succumbed to Alvee's charms. I mailed Maury my screenplays, and when he chose one – it would have to be revised, of course, to be up to real filmmaking standards – I whined that I couldn't do it. I thanked him for choosing something I'd written, and while his confidence made me believe that it might be true that I could indeed tell a story, I was certainly no screenwriter.

I had trouble with the formatting. I was too descriptive. They ran too long. I whined so much, in fact, that Maury just went ahead and wrote the screenplay for *Kinship* himself. But it was still my story.

He insisted that I contribute to the screenplay for *Dorian and Henry,* however. Alvee and I had become a couple by then, and Maury said it was therefore about time I started earning my keep. About time I became a member of the team. Alvee would appreciate me all the more if I could demonstrate that I, too, was a trouper.

And sitting in the empty conference room of the Hilton, after having written *Adequate* next to six actors' names, I realized that Maury was doing the same thing again. He'd *ordered* me to become part of the team the first time; he'd *demanded* that I help write *Dorian and Henry.* He'd been a slave driver, and I had done my best, but in the end, my help had been minimal.

Now he'd *tricked* me into being a part of the team for *She's A Peach.* He'd disappeared because he wanted *me* to pick the actor to play the Third Man, all by myself. The method in his madness instantly became crystal clear: if I had a hand in the decision-making on this dog, maybe I'd stop bitching about how *it had been done.*

It was a small role, so whomever I chose – I couldn't mess up the film too much. But I would have a stake in it then. If any critics carelessly mentioned the performance of the actor who played Mark – well, hot damn. For better or worse, the review would be about the actor that *I'd cast.*

I hated Maury then, and loved him in equal measure. He'd shoved me out of my comfort zone – I was just barely a screenwriter, and now he was forcing me to pretend to be a casting director. But it showed that he had faith in me; and the thought of famous director Maurice Claremount having faith in a nobody, regular gal from Riverside, California – that was just about the greatest thought ever.

If *I* was to cast the Third Man, he should be Olivier, he should be Gable! He should be as cruel as a young Brando in his callous disregard for Marci's feelings, and the audience should hate him for it! This was a comedy? His delivery on the eventual apology should be as hilarious as Belushi's Jake Blues. *It wasn't my fault, I swear to God!*

A feeling of professionalism seized me, and I sat up straighter in my chair, neatly stacked the scripts in front of me. I reviewed the list of candidates again, tried to recall their auditions with more discernment. But none of them had been anything more than adequate.

The next actor knocked on the doorframe. "Is this the audition for –"

"Yes, yes." I waved him in, my hand arcing lazily through the air in fair imitation of Maury's indifference. Ego spoke in my head: *You should make a little sign and put it on the table: Auditions for She's A Peach. Carolyn Adyon, Casting Director. Please sign in and have a seat.*

The actor paused for a second; he seemed a little confused. He was about thirty, of average height and build, not gloriously tall (taller than me, anyway) like Alvee or some of the other candidates. He had big brown eyes that matched his chocolate-brown hair. He had gone for the grizzled look, but the trope was complimentary. He was not matinee-idol sexy, so instead, he chose to broadcast an air not unlike that goose I had thought of earlier: like he woke up in a new world every day, and anything that happened to him was gonna be a surprise. It was cute and endearing, and I thought it appropriate for the Third Man character. Mark was oblivious to the feelings of those around him, and it was only after the customary loneliness of this new job in a new city that he awakened to his own emotions and those of others.

I realized that I was reading all of that into the poor script to *She's A Peach,* but with one glance, I thought this guy could perhaps bring it out.

He stared at me in what seemed like frank amazement for another split-second, then recollected his purpose for being there. He handed me a folder containing his resume – paused to look at me again – then gestured at the neat stack of scripts. I nodded, and he took one, found the X on the floor and stood on it.

His said his name was Steve Shea. With an adorable, self-deprecating smile, he said that he'd done a great deal of local theater, had appeared as an extra in a popular beer commercial. I couldn't place him in it.

"So this is your first movie audition?"

Again that bashful smile. "I've done a lot of auditions. Movies, television . . ." He trailed off and stared at me again.

I felt warmed by his modest smile, again thought he would be great for the part. I nodded at the script in his hand, picked up my own.

He paged back through it, to see what had come before, to grasp Mark's *motivation,* I imagined. He read over the brief scene, then looked up at me again.

"I got the job, Marci!"

The expression on Steve Shea's pleasant face communicated Mark's joy and anticipation at achieving this goal, but there was also something extra there. He knew that Marci was gonna be disappointed with the news. He knew that she loved him, but it just couldn't be helped right now. He was sorry to hurt her, but . . . He just couldn't worry about a girl when he'd just scored the big promotion.

It was *amazing.* All that emotion, in just one glance! I mentally patted myself on the back – I'd known immediately that he'd be great for the part!

I looked down at the script, even though I knew the stupid line. I *felt* like Marci. Mark loved me, it showed on his face, but our love wasn't as important as his career. I felt selfish, but still . . . What about me?

"So that means . . . you're leaving?" I thought I emoted well. Steve's great acting was making me feel my own part better.

"It's the opportunity of a lifetime." Mark had made the decision to just ignore Marci's feelings. He made a joke out it. "You know I'll always love ya, baby." Steve's eyes communicated Mark's sudden need to flee. He felt a moment of regret at what he was doing, but . . . it couldn't be helped. "I'll keep in touch."

It wasn't necessary for me to read Marci's line, but I found that I wanted to *act,* I wanted to speak her sad confusion, because Steve had made me *feel* it.

"But . . . I thought . . ." I put my hand over my face in sorrow, as the stage direction indicated.

In the ensuing silence, I peeped through my fingers at Steve Shea.

He returned my gaze, then quickly looked down at the script again. "Should I read Victor's lines too?" He turned over a few pages of the script, perhaps searching for Mark's next scene. I knew he'd be looking for a minute. Mark didn't appear again until the last act. It was a very small part.

"No," I said apologetically. "Victor's already been cast."

"Oh, okay. Of course." He offered me a kind of quizzical look and didn't move from the X.

"Are you excited to audition for a Maurice Claremount project?" Maybe it wasn't the most professional thing to say, but what did I know? I liked him; he was a good actor.

His quizzical expression expanded. "Is that what this is?"

"You didn't know?"

"They don't say what . . . My agent just said to show up for the audition. It was listed as a comedy, of course. . . But I should've realized when I saw you . . ."

Of all the words in all the world that I could've expected to come out of this actor's face – his next were not them.

"You're Carolyn Adyon." Again, that plain, friendly smile. "I saw you on *Entertainment Tonight*. At the premiere for *Dorian and Henry*. With the director. Maurice . . ." He struggled to recall the renowned last name.

If I thought my astonishment couldn't have gotten any bigger – this guy knew my name! – I was mistaken. He was saying that he remembered me from a split-second interview from some two years previously, when I had appeared on the red carpet with *the director*. Whose name he *didn't* remember.

I was speechless. He went on. "I thought your screenplay was great. The movie wasn't really my kind of thing . . ."

You and most of the ticket-buying populace, I thought.

". . . but the adaptation was awesome. You wrote the story for *Kinship,* too?"

My eyes probably bugged. Why, this guy had . . . *followed my career!* I felt flooded with a pleasant warmth. I nodded, still dumbstruck.

"That one was a bit . . ."

"Outré," I supplied. "Yeah, I didn't . . . I didn't have a lot of input on the screenplay for *Kinship.*"

"But it was still your idea." Steve grinned. He remembered the brief blip of *From a story by Carolyn Adyon* in the opening credits.

I couldn't help but grin back at him. Critically acclaimed *Kinship had* been my idea, and I realized in that second that, besides Maury, not too many people had ever put it into words to me.

The silence threatened to lengthen; I retrieved my professionalism from beneath where my stroked ego was sitting on it, and said, "Well, thanks for the audition, Mr. Shea. We'll be in touch."

"Thank *you,* Miss Adyon." He stepped off his mark and set the script on the table. "It's been a pleasure to meet you." He wanted to shake my hand, but his own professionalism prevented it.

"We'll definitely be in touch," I said brightly. "Could you do me a favor and send the next person in?" Steve Shea returned my smile, nodded, and quickly left the room.

Of the remaining hopefuls, there were three no-shows, and the rest, like the first six, were also only adequate for the role.

Maury returned moments after the last one departed. I took it as a small sign of respect from my director: he might've tricked me into this casting gig, but he wasn't going to make me wait around after the task was completed. Maury might make actors, and screenwriters, and the occasional interviewer wait – he was arrogant, old-Hollywood to his core, after all. But he was prompt with his friends.

He sauntered into the room, blithe, innocent. "So sorry, Carol. I was detained. How did it go?"

"You are an unmitigated son of a bitch, Maurice Claremount."

"And you are far too hesitant in your ambitions, my darling. You insist on maintaining a fear and awe of this business . . ."

He gestured at the empty room. "Were they not just people? Only actors, and quite polite, hungry ones, at that? Casting this itty-bitty part . . . I imagine it was as boring as interviewing applicants for dogcatcher. But you know what we're looking for, do you not? Has not this epic *been done?* Did you find the perfect Third Man?"

I put a damper on my enthusiasm. No need to crow wildly about Steve Shea's performance. Maury would go with my choice; there was no call to express *awe* at one unknown's dead-on grasp of one *itty-bitty part.*

"I did," I said with studied unconcern. I gathered up the small stack of envelopes and folders, then proceeded to paw through them, as if I hadn't already singled one out. He'd had me at, "I got the job, Marci!"

(He had you at, "You're Carolyn Adyon," my ego said. But I ignored it. It wasn't that at all. All the other guys had been merely adequate, but *this guy* had *nailed* the part. He was a good actor. The fact that he'd recognized me, that he'd

followed my career . . . None of that had anything to do with my choice.)

"He was number six or seven, I think," I told Maury, as I handed over his resume.

The great auteur perused it with not a lot of interest. "Steve Shea. Never heard of him."

"You, nor anyone else." As if on cue, the actor appeared in the doorway. "Excuse me," he said, and stepped past Maury, summarily ignored him.

"I'm sorry to bother you, Miss Adyon. But after the audition –" that cute, *dumb-me* smile again "– I left my phone on the table when I had lunch. It was of course gone when I went back. I'm gonna go get a replacement, but you know how long that can take, so I wanted to give you another number where I can be reached, in case . . ."

"You've got the part, Mr. Shea," Maury told him.

Steve glanced at him, with no recognition whatsoever, then back at me. I felt a little embarrassed at his faux pas – he was ignoring the great Maurice Claremount, in favor of a nobody from Riverside, California. I quickly introduced them.

They shook hands and Steve said he was a big fan of the director's work. But then he again turned back to me for further instruction.

Maury was amused. He took a card from his pocket, touched Steve's arm so he would look at him. "First production meeting's at nine am, next Monday morning. We'll send a contract before then. Please be on time."

"I will, sir." Steve shook the director's hand once more, then mine. "Thanks, Miss Adyon."

I nodded, and he smiled at me for another heartbeat. "Well. I guess I'll see you guys next Monday, then." He left the room with hardly any awkwardness at all.

Maury sighed and flopped down into the chair beside me. He thumbed idly through Steve's folder, briefly studied his photograph. "Steven P. Shea. Consummate nobody." He skewered me with a filmmaker's appraisal. "What made you pick this experienced thespian, Carol?"

"He nailed the part," I replied, allowing a little enthusiasm out. "The rest of them were just . . ."

"Adequate." Maury nodded at the clipboard on the table. "Yet I see you've circled Mr. Shea's name several times." A languid, curious smile. "What struck you about him, more than the others?"

"He struck me as the better actor."

A little warning bell chimed in my head. Was this some new trick? Maury had given me this task, and I'd made my choice. Why was he now cross-examining me about it?

"And that's the only reason? His recitation of what – two lines?"

I nodded and endeavored to affect Alvee's standard, always-convincing expression of innocence.

Maury studied me for another second, then laughed. "You really must get out more, my darling. Being around me and your beloved all the time . . . You don't even realize . . ."

I blinked blankly at him, Alvee Smith-Killem-in-the-role-of-schoolboy-stylie. I even repeated his standard line. "I have no idea what you're talking about."

"I truly believe that you don't, so allow me to enlighten you. Alvee has initiated you into the secrets of the universal energy – you feel it from him, and to a lesser extent from me. You know we love you.

"But you don't realize – young Mr. Shea likes you, too. It's quite unmistakable. And his affection – like that which Alvee receives from his fans – any kind of admiration touches those of us attuned to it, Carol. Perhaps you've just never felt it from a stranger before, but you did feel it, didn't you?"

Had I felt it? That little rush of warmth when Steve Shea smiled at me, when he complimented my work?

I did indeed love Maury, but he was cagey. What was he trying to get me to admit? Admiral Ackbar spoke in my head: *It's a trap!*

"I have no idea what you're talking about, Maury. He was just the better performer."

Again, Maury laughed. "It's quite all right, Carol. What does Alvee always say? *Attention is attention. Love, adoration. It's all the same. It's all energy.* And he is living, breathing proof that it's quite unnecessary for it to be returned."

I remained silent, and Maury studied Steve's headshot again. "As you were quite unaware of Mr. Shea's admiration, I'm sure your choice was indeed a professional one. I have no doubt that he was the best performer out of this meager showing."

Maury grinned wickedly. "Young Master Shea likes you, and as only genuine affection completes the mystery, perhaps our darling Alvee should buff up his game. Perhaps this young hopeful will give him the oft-mentioned run for his money."

I barked surprised laughter. "That'll never happen, Maury. No one, except for maybe you, loves Alvee more than I do. Steve Shea . . . He's just a good actor."

"Admiration, to those of us who know how to assimilate it, is like a drug, my darling. Like I said, it doesn't have to be returned to be useful."

It's Been Done, Being Done Again: First Meeting for *She's A Peach*

Title XVII Productions, through innumerable contracts and negotiations that I could not understand (and certainly did not want to), had rented a soundstage on the backlot of storied Warner Bros. Studios. In a moderately-sized conference room adjacent, the first meeting for *She's A Peach* would soon begin.

Alvee could've played the fashionably late mega-star if he so chose, but he did not, this time. It had been over two years since the premier and subsequent fade of *Dorian and Henry,* and he was excited to start a new project.

After all the behind-the-scenes-functionaries, he was actually the first talent to show up. He hailed and shook hands with the members of the crew with whom he'd worked before, then took a seat near the head of the table. Ever at ease, he put his feet up on another chair and began idly perusing the script. I sat quietly beside him.

Steve Shea was the next to arrive. He glanced cautiously into the room, then smiled when he saw me. He came in and effusively thanked me again for giving him the part.

"I don't mind telling you, it's my first real break, Miss Adyon," he said, with his nice smile.

Alvee glanced up from the script with a perfectly blank, nonplussed expression on his famous face, as if I was conversing with Cecil B. DeMille, returned from the dead. There was no one in Hollywood that I knew that he didn't also know, especially not a pleasant-looking actor that was so enthusiastically shaking my hand and talking about breaks.

It was not that Alvee was in any way jealous. The concept of jealousy was as foreign to him as the idea of Franck O'Day ever having to make the first move in that *paso doble* that makes the world go 'round. Alvee was just patently and completely surprised.

I took in his astonishment and giggled. "Stop calling me *Miss Adyon*, Steve," I said blithely. "You make me feel like an old maid. Carolyn also makes me feel old. Just call me –"

"How about Sissy?" Alvee said with a lisp. "If you're our little sister, will it make you feel younger?"

He could be so cute. I said to Steve, "Allow me to introduce the star of our little endeavor." Did I sound like Maury? I certainly hoped so. "Steve Shea, this is Alvee Smith-Killem."

"Do I hyphenate that?" Steve asked, offering his hand. "Use both?"

Alvee featured the newcomer with his inimitable killer smile, and without rising from his chair, shook his hand. "Just call me Alvee."

He looked to me for further explanation, and it was wonderful to be the center of his and Steve's attention at the same time.

"Steve's playing the Third Man," I said. Since this was evidently news to the picture's lead, I added, "I cast him."

More amazement, but Alvee recovered beautifully. "Nice to have you on board, Steve."

How Alvee had failed to hear about my pushed foray into the casting arena, I didn't know. He hadn't mentioned it, so I hadn't mentioned it. I figured that Maury would've told him.

Steve sat down across from us. The two actors chatted, and it pleased me to see that Alvee liked him immediately, as I had. I imagined that he was warmed by Steve's genuine friendliness, just as I was.

Maury came in next. As Alvee was laid-back, with his feet up, so it struck me that our director was unusually casual in his entrance. This was a comedy, after all.

With Maury was Mina Reed, the film's female lead. She was pixie-adorable, with short, reddish hair and laughing hazel eyes. I'd seen both of her movies, other comedic fluff in the same vein as *She's a Peach*. I have to admit, I was a little nervous to meet her, as she was just as cute as the oft-mentioned button, and I was rather a fan.

At the premiere for *Cheyenne Sundown,* I'd been similarly awed with Camellia Swanson, Alvee's costar. She arrived late, and I never did get to meet her, but I saw her sitting several rows ahead of us. She was beautiful, in a fragile, antique-doll kind of way. When Maury whispered in my ear that Camellia was a *gold star* (I had to Google it), I wasn't sure exactly how I felt about that. Remembering the realism of her scenes with Alvee, I thought she was certainly a spectacular actress.

For the entire epoch of geologic time that was *Kinship's* endless shoot, Melissa Holloway and Alyson Rushtin, the actresses who had respectively played Alvee's cheating lover and hapless daughter, had looked at me as if they smelled something bad. Melissa's dislike came from the fact that Alvee ignored her *come-hither, American boy* invitations in favor of some hanger-on that wasn't even really the screenwriter; and I think Alyson just didn't like Americans in general.

But I soon found Mina Reed to be as down to earth as were the girl-next-door characters she'd portrayed. After the director introduced us, she sat beside me and told me she loved my nail polish, told me that she thought *Dorian and Henry* (which, like Steve, she was sure I'd written) was *cute.*

Well, I thought, mimicking Maury in my mind, *it certainly wasn't that.* But it was all right for her to think so. She was just as lovely and unpretentious as she wanted to be.

After another few minutes of walking around, chatting with his crew, uncharacteristically informal Maurice Claremount took his seat at the head of the table. Crew members that had worked with him on more serious projects fell silent, waiting in *fear and awe* for His Directorship to begin his oratory.

Maury glanced around the table. He sighed, then zeroed in on Sylvia, the script girl. "Would you ask Mr. McCown if he would be so kind as to grace us with his presence? I believe he's out in the hall."

Sylvia hopped up to do as she'd been commanded. Maury's phone beeped, and he stepped away from the table to take what was undoubtedly another important call. All of Maury's calls were undoubtedly important.

"Wow," Steve said to Alvee and Mina and me. "Mike McCown. Wow."

Alvee was delighted with the Third Man's completely fabricated reverence. "Who?"

"Michael McCown!" Mina gushed. She didn't get the joke. "We have the same agent. I almost had the lead in *Unparalleled,* but it went to Hayden Panettiere."

Mina stared at the door in anticipation, willing this guy to appear. Finally, she leapt right up and walked out into the hall.

Alvee smiled questioningly at Steve. *"Unparalleled? That's a movie?"*

"Really? Someone as famous as you? You didn't see *Unparalleled?"*

Alvee shook his head, and Steve said *Wow* again, as if Alvee hadn't seen *Star Wars.*

"Mike infiltrates some Russian, not-quite-the-Bolshoi dance troupe where Hayden is the head cheerleader, or dancer, or whatever. He's a former parkour star, whose career was cut tragically short by an accident caused by a nefarious rival. Hayden's just cute." Steve winked at me.

"Since recovering from his injury, Mike's become FBI, now undercover. Or maybe he was FBI all along. Maybe he was *born* FBI. I don't remember.

"Anyway, there's a villain in the troupe. Could it be the same guy that tripped him and made him go splat in New York City? Damn right it could!

"Mike does karate, he dances, he leaps hither and yon. The troupe is revitalized by his modern moves, executed between dark shoot-outs and circus-style acrobatics. There's not a whole lot of dialogue, however.

"Mike dispatches the bad guy, gets the girl, and makes America safe once again for interpretive dance. Think *Step Up* meets *The Transporter.*"

Alvee grinned. "Gee. I don't know how I missed that one."

I could tell that he dug his new friend's derision for this *celebrity.* Maury had often said, "Doctors will seldom talk about other doctors; and even lawyers – they'll seldom dis one another. They all have that professional brotherhood, you see. But actors? They'll savage each other faster than you can say, 'Let me see your SAG card.'"

Alvee looked at me. I shrugged. I hadn't seen *Unparalleled* either. He said to Steve, "So he's like, an *action* star?"

"One of the best, so they say."

"And now he wants to do a comedy?"

"Maybe he's a *chancer,*" I suggested.

Michael McCown ambled into the room, his arm around Mina's waist. I recognized him immediately; I'd seen his face plastered up on billboards all over LA. I don't know if the ads had been for *Unparalleled* – action movies aren't really my thing – but they'd been hard to miss. In them, he glowered smokily at the viewer, with piercing dark eyes and a luscious little half-grin. *Get to know Michael McCown,* the tagline said, *in . . .* But somehow, the light had always changed and I'd driven on, so I'd never quite gotten the title of the flick.

In person, he was tall, slender, lithe, dressed in some kind of pricey black leather jacket, the inevitable wife-beater, dark jeans, black shades, red Chucks. His attire reminded me of Alvee's, the first time I'd met him: gloriously, carelessly *young.*

Michael McCown's hair was a lighter shade of brown than Steve's, sandy almost, an impeccable blend of highlights and undertones, as if he was a surfer or life guard, or some other beach-local dream come true. I suspected that the amalgam might come out of a bottle or perhaps several bottles: *his hair, as the old song said, was perfect.*

He was adorable: that superbly built, athletic, irresistible boy-next-door, like Dawson Leery or Dylan McKay, the kind that really only exists in the movies. He was probably all of twenty-three.

Mina, giddy at his attention, brought him up to the table. "Michael McCown, I'd like you to meet –"

"I know who he is, hon." With studied nonchalance, the actor removed his shades and tossed them onto the table. Mina was now forgotten, and he just flat out ignored Steve and me. As we were not recognizable faces, we were non-persons to him. "Nice to meet you, Alvee. I'm Michael McCown."

This offhand, false-modest understatement was a classic, frequently used by those most narcissistic of *Homo sapiens,* the ones we call *famous:* actors and athletes; the occasional race-car driver; hip politicians. At our first meeting with Franck O'Day, he'd done precisely the same thing. As if my wide-eyed friend Ruthanne, come some seventy miles to see him, might've had some doubt as to who he was.

After Alvee, Michael McCown featured himself the most famous name in the room – yet (again, as if anyone could possibly not know who he was), he'd offered this simple introduction.

"Hiya, Mikey," Alvee said. He couldn't look at me or Steve, lest he bust out in laughter. I felt as though I could read his mind: *Who does this refugee from Enter The Dragon think he is?*

"It's Michael," he corrected firmly.

His phone call concluded, the director returned to the table. From the frown he aimed at the action star, I kenned immediately that Michael McCown's having to be fetched had brought Maury's austerity back from its vacation. He had no time whatsoever for actors trying to make an entrance.

I remembered how he'd crucified Alyson Rushtin for being tardy at the first production meeting for *Kinship.* She'd flounced in after the rest of the cast had already been introduced.

"Ah, Miss Rushtin, how nice of you to join us," Maury began, amicably enough. "Take a good look at Miss Rushtin, everybody."

Which is just what she wants you all to do, I'd thought.

"Because if she ever interrupts one of my meetings again, it will be the last time you see her." Maury was not kidding, not in the least. He glared mildly at the young actress. "In the future, Miss Rushtin, if you find yourself running late, please wait outside until the meeting has concluded. If you miss anything important . . . Well, maybe you should make the extra effort to get here on time."

Miss Rushtin sat down, suitably chastised.

I waited with a kind of mean-spirited anticipation for Maury to lower the boom this time. Mikey McCown might think he could get away with ignoring me, and even Steve, but . . .

Maury glanced imperiously at his people, and the table fell silent.

"Mr. . . *McClown,* is it?"

Steve shot me an *Oh, shit!* grin of pure glee.

"It's McCown, Mr. Claremount," Mike said softly.

"Right. Of course. I'm sorry I haven't had the chance to speak to you before this, but that's why they call it the *first meeting.* We're all here to get to know each other. You've appeared in several action films, am I correct?" Maury pantomimed getting winged by a bullet. Someone at the other end of the table snickered. Mike nodded.

"And in such films, I imagine that timing is everything. If you or a stuntman is a little off in his timing, why, I imagine you could accidentally get kicked in your pretty face?"

Mikey grinned self-consciously, searched around the table for a friend. Only Alvee grinned back at him. No one else would even meet his eye. "Yeah. I guess you could say that, Mr. Claremount."

"So it is with my production meetings. They can become rather boisterous. Latecomers, well . . . Your face is your paycheck, Mr. McCown. I wouldn't want you to get kicked in it. In the future, please be on time."

Before Mikey could reply, Maury started the meeting. The action star was left to meekly take a seat.

I'd Like to Thank the Academy . . . Not

The table read went well.

Alvee, of course, was the best actor present. He was brilliant in dramas, and while they hadn't been comedies, he'd had a few light moments in *Cheyenne Sundown*, and, under a different name, in a different era, in *High Times in Manhattan*. While a thoroughly comedic turn was certainly new to him, owing to his unnaturally long life and unshakeable confidence, it wasn't anything he couldn't do. My fascinating leading man had once been someone else, but even then, he'd been a great actor. Alvee Smith-Killen could be anyone he wanted to be.

Steve again nailed his small first scene, reading more into the few lines than had been written there. He made Mark more than just a one-dimensional placeholder, the guy that would (oh, *so predictably,* I thought) return in the last reel to complete the silliness of the whole plot. Steve gave Mark nuance; he was a human being, he had feelings; he wasn't dumping Marci because he didn't care for her. The situation just couldn't be helped.

Mina brought a shade of on-the-rebound cruelty to her character. Mark had hurt her, so she was going to make these new, unsought suitors jump through as many hoops as she could, just for amusement. She pretended to be receptive to both, but there was just something in her eye and smile that let us know that she wasn't ready for a new love, wasn't ready to expose herself to the risk of another heartbreak.

The most surprising performance came from Michael McCown, however, if I must say so myself. Gone was the smugness, the conceit, the jaded, *Do you really think I need* you *to tell me how sexy I am?*

He *became* the artless all-American boy, ignorant of his own delectable cuteness. In the first scenes, he's unaware that Victor is also out for Marci; Michael was positively *bouncy* in his unsuspecting declarations to his friend of how he was gonna win her.

Alvee could do innocent, but it was not called for in this part. Victor was by no means as deceitful as the baddies he'd done in his previous flicks – this was a comedy after all – but Alvee's was still the older and wiser character this time. And while Alvee appeared to be an undeniably irresistible thirty, Michael McCown was twenty-three and played his role as if he was a hometown twenty.

Even though it was just the first table read, it could not be denied that Mike's portrayal of innocence and naïveté upstaged Alvee's worldlier Victor. One glance at the film's helmsman and I could tell that even he was impressed. Alvee was, without a doubt, the star of *She's a Peach;* but Mikey's character was definitely more appealing.

Not one of these subtle distinctions of characterization was inherent in the lousy script, of course. I marveled, not for the first time, that black upon white, especially when presented in 12 point, 10 pitch Courier typeface, could sometimes only be brought to any semblance of life when spoken aloud by talented actors.

Based on the table read, Maury's choice of this cast would go a long way toward making a silk purse out of a sow's ear. They were going to make it the best film it could be. Regardless, I was still glad I hadn't had anything to do with either the story or the screenplay for *She's a Peach.*

When the first meeting concluded and faded into the history books, its storied director also did a fade. He wouldn't lower himself to associate with his actors; perhaps not at any time during the shoot, but certainly not here, at the outset. This was a comedy after all, and he couldn't have them mistaking him for their buddy, their *compagnon d'armes,* in the midst of all the hilarity.

****

In just that spirit of companions-in-arms, however, Alvee asked his new cast mates if they'd like to join us for a late lunch there on the back lot.

Michael McCown looked disinterestedly over his sunglasses at hopeful Mina; she returned his casual glance eagerly. I then recognized a familiar *What* is *that smell?* expression when Mike considered Steve and myself. When he'd again donned his cool-guy shades, the action star had also regained his arrogance.

"I think I'll skip the *cafeteria,* Alvee, if you don't mind. But you call me later. Let me give you my number."

What kind of an incredible bit of unasked for awesomeness was this? Thespian of (not) Shakespearian-caliber Michael McCown was offering Alvee his *personal cellphone number?* My darling tried to assume Steve's earlier air of (fake) reverence, but failed. He wasn't that good at comedy yet.

He took his phone out of his pocket. "What is it?"

Mikey considered the rest of us as if he might've suddenly felt some kind of mild abdominal pain. "Why don't we just . . . Let me type it in there for you." *A guy can never be too careful of his privacy these days,* went unsaid.

He's right, I thought. *If he would've said his number aloud, why, I would've been powerless not to instantaneously memorize it, then go right on ahead and tweet it immediately to the Michael McCown Fan Club.*

Alvee blinked his baby blues at us *(there* was that innocence) and handed his phone to Mike. He typed, pushed the button, and his own phone rang in his pocket. It was a slick trick – now Mikey's had his famous costar's number, too.

Alvee didn't sweat it. He was used to Hollywood vanity.

Once upon a time, under a different name and in a different era, Alvee had shared bed and board (in the house where he now lived again) with beautiful actress Jessika

Yerdlay. Franck O'Day had said of her, "She listened to her own press too much. She believed that she was so talented and sought-after that she could get away with presenting that bitchy, stand-offish attitude to the world. In her defense, I must say that damn near everyone let her get away with it. But I was not impressed – Jessika Yerdlay thought she was a whole lot more wonderful than I thought she was."

Although Franck had said that his impression of her never really changed, from the stories her daughter told, Jessika had certainly loved him. Despite his brief marriage to another, through tragedy and then better times; and even after Franck abandoned her and she splashed her condemnation of him all over the front page of *The Los Angeles Times* – still, deep down, Jessika never stopped loving him. When his plane had disappeared in Japan, she'd shut herself up in her mansion to grieve. Jessika went to her grave still loving Franck, believing that he had preceded her to that great Orpheum in the sky.

But he was still here, and because he had known far grander egos than Michael McCown's, Alvee handled the kid's hubris with surprising grace. He was certainly not impressed, as was star-struck Mina (who I thought should've known better.) Nor was he in the least bit offended, as were Steve and I.

"We'll talk soon." Without a backward glance at the rest of us, Mike swaggered out of the room.

Steve opened his mouth to spew fresh insults, but Alvee cut him off with a smile. "He's just a kid. He listens to his own press too much."

Steve inclined his head to indicate Mina, looking wistfully after the action star. "Apparently he's not the only one."

"He's *unparalleled,*" I said and we shared a giggle at Michael McCown's hyper-inflated sense of self-importance.

Our mockery passed Mina by. "Where do we eat? I've never been here before."

During lunch, Mina seemed to forget all about Michael McCown. Her remaining famous costar was my boyfriend, so she treated him with the playful respect she might give to an admired older brother, and turned her attention pointedly toward young Master Shea. She seemed to warm up to him quite a bit, giggling prettily at his self-effacing witticisms and lavishing him with happy smiles.

As lunch ended, she received a text, and told us that she had to hurry to another appointment. She gave me a friendly hug, and a sisterly one to Alvee. She squeezed Steve's hand and gave him a little kiss on the cheek, told us that she would see us on the morrow. Then the female lead for *She's A Peach* was gone.

Steve sighed. "Are you a gambling man, Alvee?"

"It depends on the bet."

"What would you wager that Mina's sudden appointment is with Mr. McClown?"

"Ah, Steve, she wouldn't do that," I blurted out. "I think she really likes you."

He smiled politely at me, because he was polite, and he wanted to communicate that he was sure that whatever I thought was all okey-dokey, artichokey. But it was Alvee's opinion that he wanted. I don't think Steve believed Alvee necessarily knew any more about *women* than he did – they appeared to be about the same age, did they not? – but perhaps the accomplished star knew a little bit more about *actresses*.

"I'd give it even money. They have the same agent and all."

"There are tears for her love; joy for her fortune; honor for her valor; and death for her ambition." Steve winked at me. "But it's all good. I'm not complaining. Everything's coming up roses and daffodils. A triangle is one of my favorite shapes, as a matter of fact." Then he sang, *"I do know one thing, though. Bitches, they come, they go . . ."*

I finished the line for him. *"Saturday through Sunday, Monday. Monday through Sunday, yo."* We high-fived.

Alvee's black eyebrows went up in startled pleasure. "That's one way of putting it."

While he knew his Sinatra and his Liberace ("Now *he* was a peach," according to Maury), and he'd taught me the difference between Buffalo Springfield and Dusty Springfield, Alvee had lived in the wilds of Japan for almost forty years. And while it was also true that he'd been back in the States since 2006, it could still be said that he'd not entirely familiarized himself with all the myriad trends that had occurred in the world of music since 1968. In other words, Alvee had never heard any Eminem, and our rendition of the misogynist lyrics shocked him, in that way you're shocked by a dirty joke that you also find hilarious.

He laughed and slapped Steve on the back.

I found it wonderful that the two of them seemed well on their way to becoming friends, because, in my estimation, friends were something of a novelty for Alvee. Besides me, he only had one.

Hollywood can be a rough town, where trust and honesty are often no more than commodities, as Maury (and Franck) had often told me, but in all incarnations, the two of them were troupers. They shared an enjoyment and an identically realistic perception of this business we call show; so for more than half a century, they'd had each other for friendship, and had not needed anyone else.

Maury loved Alvee; Alvee was his muse. And Franck O'Day had once said of Robert Ecksmith: "Bobby was the only person in the business that I ever knew that didn't want something from me."

But in an unexpected way, since Alvee and I had fallen in love and everything *that* entailed, since I'd come to live and work with Maury in the big old house in Beverly Hills, I liked to think that I'd become another kinda-show-business friend to the director. From his bottomless store of knowledge and experience, talent and vision, he was showing a beginner the ropes, and enjoying it very much.

I thought that it was the same for Alvee with Steve Shea. He recognized that Steve had talent; it was only natural for one great actor to befriend another.

****

Alvee claimed to know how to drive, but also insisted that driving involved entirely too much stress. So, as always, he'd summoned a limo, and the black car idled silently by the gate, waiting for us.

Maury thrived on stress, so he put it much more concisely: *Rank has its privileges.* Neither famed director nor renowned heartthrob (of either era) could possibly lower themselves to operate a motor vehicle.

No Porsches or Jags or Mercedes; neither of them even owned an automobile. The immense, three-car garage at Jessika's mansion played host only to Kimura's modest Honda and the (only slightly more pricey) Toyota on which I'd splurged after getting paid for being the author (if not the *screenwriter)* of *Kinship.*

Because cabs were also too plebian, Alvee and Maury took limos wherever they went. They could certainly afford it.

"Can we drop you anywhere, Steve?"

"Sure. I'm at the Alto Nido."

"You're not!" Alvee was amazed.

"I am, actually, but not for long. The ambiance is great, right? But the square footage, for the price, is very small. Since I got this part –" he smiled gratefully at me "– I've decided to move to a bigger place – upgrading *to the vicuna,* so to speak."

Alvee instructed the driver, and I tried to remember where I'd heard that word before. I couldn't exactly form a picture in my mind, and for the twenty minute ride, I still wasn't quite sure what a vicuna was – some kind of clothing, made from some kind of animal fur, surely, but was it a rabbit or a sheep or what?

When we pulled up in front of the tan-brick, vaguely-Spanish-looking building, the film buff in me spoke. I still didn't know what kind of animal had been mentioned, but I remembered the line.

"As long as the lady is paying for it, why not take the vicuna?"

The building had been in black and white in the movie, of course, but the sign was pretty much as it had been in 1950.

Steve Shea lived in the same apartments as had Joe Gillis, William Holden's down-on-his-luck screenwriter in *Sunset Boulevard*. Such things are only possible in the City of Angels.

Of course Alvee would recognize the name of the place. Billy Wilder's *satire noir* of a star desperate not to be forgotten was one of his very favorites. I'd watched it with him several times, but I must here note that ya can't really call it Netflix and chill with my leading man: Alvee Smith-Killem's house boasts its own screening room in the basement. It seats about twenty people, but not unlike Norma and Joe viewing her old silents on a reel to reel, the two of us have always screened *Sunset Boulevard* alone. Maury claims that the movie depresses him.

As Steve opened the limo door, Alvee said, "You should come up to the house for brunch on Saturday."

"I'd love to, but that's moving day. You're welcome to help pack the U-Haul, though."

Steve grinned at the idea of *someone as famous* as Alvee Smith-Killem hefting couches and stuffing boxes into a rented moving van. *TMZ* would lose their collective hillbilly mind. The crowd of paps would stop traffic.

Steve was undoubtedly aware that world-renowned Alvee Smith-Killem seldom ventured out in public unless he sought some premeditated publicity, as when he'd hit the restaurants and nightspots with Armand Hambrick, to stir up a little interest in *Dorian and Henry*. Those appearances had been a necessary part of the biz, like attending premieres and the talk-show circuit. Otherwise, Alvee never went out into the world.

Alvee loved his fans – their adulation kept him young. And he actually liked the paps, because he made sure that when they were snapping his pic, it was at those times he deemed appropriate. What Steve couldn't possibly know was that Alvee's reticence to mingle with the unwashed masses was a result of his old-Hollywood sensibilities, more than a dislike of being plagued with those photographers. Alvee was from a time when famous entertainers were a type of American royalty; you wouldn't expect to see the Prince of Wales wandering around on the streets of LA, walking his dogs and going to Starbucks in his sweats, as actors did today.

Part of the draw of being famous was just the kind of seclusion that was necessary for Alvee to maintain his privacy. Why should he go out? Where did he need to go? He had his own pool, his own theater. The universe was at his fingertips via the internet. Kimura was the best chef in town. Alvee had his old friend and Maki and me for company. He thoroughly enjoyed the kind of isolation that came with being a movie star.

All that being said, he surprised me. He accepted Steve's invitation to get his hands dirty. "What time do you want me to be here?"

Steve was just as surprised as I was, and no doubt still thinking about the paps, he said, "I'll tell you what. You can help *unload.* The new place is a little more secluded."

"Text me the address." Alvee blinked blankly at me. "Could you turn your head, Carol, while I give Steve my number?"

That was uproariously funny to Steve Shea, and once cellphone numbers were exchanged (I gave him mine, too), our new friend once again expressed his heartfelt gratitude. "This has been the best day of my life."

"It was all on the casting director," Alvee said magnanimously. "And we don't have any scenes together, so I'm not worried about you upstaging me."

"I leave that to Mr. McClown." Steve blinked in embarrassment at his own words. Mike McCown upstaging Alvee might actually occur. He had certainly done so at the table read.

Steve quickly changed the subject back to the move. "Just do me a favor, will you? Have the limo drop you off at the end of the block? I don't want the whole town knowing Alvee Smith-Killem knows where I live."

"We'll do the bait and switch," Alvee replied, delighted. "We'll send the limo off, and then come out in Carol's car."

"Nobody ever follows me," I told Steve Shea.

Will the Real Slim Shady Please Stand Up?

The first week's shooting breezed by.

Mina fawned on Michael McCown between takes, but she went out to dinner with Steve after the shoot wrapped for the day. The action star preferred to appear solo after hours, or with some of the other macho types that had appeared in his movies: the young posse on the make. Like Alvee, the press and fans liked Michael McCown better single.

Steve Shea's self-effacing personality was genuine – he felt like the luckiest guy in the world to be making this movie with this director and this cast – but I also discovered that he was a shrewd Hollywood cognoscenti, for all that. Dining almost nightly with Mina Reed was nothing if not better-than-money-could-buy publicity for the unknown actor. Soon their names were linked as romantic partners. Steve might've wished it were true, and maybe it was, a little bit. But in the cold light of seeing his name in print, he could not possibly care less if Mina snuck off to see Mike McCown after their candlelit tête-à-têtes concluded, and the photographers went home.

"Yond Cassius has a lean and hungry look," Maury remarked to me one afternoon. "You could learn quite a bit about ambition from our clever Mr. Shea, Carol."

Mina was on hand to help with the *upgrade to vicuna;* like Alvee and me, she'd managed to elude the photographers. After we moved all of Steve's stuff into the nice little bungalow he'd rented, Alvee and I left, so the two of them could enjoy his new digs alone, maybe get to know each other a little better.

On the way home, I reiterated that I thought the actress genuinely liked Steve.

Alvee shrugged, sighed. "Maybe. Maybe not. Mikey has another engagement this evening."

"How do you know?"

Alvee offered me his best smile. "He's having dinner with us."

"Seriously?" I was flabbergasted. "Why would you invite that puffed-up *child —*"

"Because he's just that, Carol. A child. A kid. I've gotten to know him a little this week. He's really not that bad. All that action star ego is just a facade. Deep down, he's really just as thrilled to be working with us as Steve is."

Us? Oh, Alvee, aren't you the diplomat?

There was no *us* for whom the *kid* possessed even the merest modicum of respect. I was an utter nobody; I wasn't even a lowly screenwriter on this dog. Steve was an unknown, and Mina had breathlessly listened to Mikey's press and bought it wholesale, so what respect could he possibly have for her? Maury had taken him down a notch upon his arrival, and I'd watched the action star mock the storied director to members of the crew when he thought he wasn't being observed.

Alvee was willing to entertain Mike in his home because the kid's pride amused him, and because Mikey was thrilled to be working with *him.* There was no *us.*

"Does Maury know about this?"

Alvee shrugged again, became a trifle patronizing, I thought. "As I don't have to remind you, Maury's a professional, Carol. He understands the benefits of contacts in this business. He wouldn't condescend to dine with a mere actor, anyway."

Unless it's you. His eternal muse.

"He'll say a few words and then have some pressing engagement elsewhere."

"I don't know if I want to —"

"Of course, you can join him." Alvee smiled and squeezed my hand. "The kid's an idiot, Carol. He thinks we're buddies. It's hilarious."

"Whatever amuses you." *Hardy, har, har.*

Alvee and I gave Michael McCown the tour, and he was suitably impressed with the luxury of the old mansion. Dinner was to be served on the terrace, as always, and when we went outside, I noticed that the expensive antique china service was set for only two. I was being relieved of any further hostess duties. That was fine with me.

As Alvee had predicted, Maury put in a perfunctory appearance, welcomed the young actor to our home, then made some excuse about script changes, and the two of us walked back into the house.

But the moment we were just inside the still open French doors, out of sight, out of mind, Maury paused and I almost ran into his back.

I'd often thought that the dead and forgotten architect who'd designed the grand palace must've thoroughly understood that its owner might like to overhear whatever was being said while he or she was not present. With a clever, almost magical trick of acoustics, conversation at the table on the terrace was audible from just inside the house. The setting was thereby the equivalent of a hot mike to an unwary speaker.

Mr. McClown didn't realize that his director and I could hear him. Surely he wouldn't've had the insensitivity to say what followed, otherwise. Surely.

"Hot damn, Alvee! That ass! But I gotta ask you – can she write?" Mike guffawed. "Who cares, right?"

Alvee grinned in *Did you really just say that?* astonishment.

"And what's it like, living in the same house with the old homo? Do you catch him listening at the keyhole when you're going at it with Karen?"

"Carol."

Alvee glanced for a split second across the veranda, through the doorway; he knew Mike had an audience, even if

Mike did not. He wanted us to see how much he was enjoying the incredibly bad taste of the kid's remarks.

"Do you ever have to fight him off? I know how pushy they can be. The make-up guy on *Unparalleled* actually had the nerve to slide his hand up my thigh once. He'll never work in this town again, that's for sure."

"Say his name," Maury whispered. "I'll hire him for the whole shoot."

As if Alvee had telepathically heard him, he asked Mike the question.

"How the hell do I know? Like I know the names of all the fags running around on-set. You can't swing a dead cat without knocking out five or six of them in this town."

"How droll," Maury murmured.

"Christ! My last director! You know, it's only pussies that file sexual harassment suits, but I'll tell ya, I could've made a fortune." Mike rolled his eyes and Alvee stole another glance at us.

He thought it was all hilarious. Just like he'd told me, Michael McCown, big-time action star, was a big-mouthed idiot. He was one of those people that just naturally assumes that everyone he perceives to be like him thinks the same way he does, ready to make fun of *the other*. It was not the way to be in a business where everyone wore masks, I thought. He was cute, but he wasn't *that* cute.

Earlier in the week, Steve had mentioned that Mr. McClown believed himself to be so famous that he was above giving interviews. The image he set forth was that of the mystery man, sly and sexy, just as unknowable as the undercover operatives and CIA spooks he portrayed. He flat out refused to talk to the press.

I realized that it wasn't mystery that he wanted to project, however. That wasn't the case at all. His agent had no doubt clamped the gag order upon his talent because he could probably never guess what outrageously insulting thing was gonna come out of this ignorant kid's mouth next. When it came to the internet backlash from a celebrity's insensitive remarks, it could be said that there really was such a thing as bad publicity.

"But tell me more about Karen. I'll bet she . . ." Mike leaned in a little closer to Alvee to impart his filthy speculation, and at the same time, Maury took my elbow and led me the rest of the way into the house.

"Aw, shucks, boss. I wanted to hear Alvee describe my talents."

Maury ignored my attempt at humor. "It's a pity he's so adorable."

"Pretty is as pretty does," I opined.

"Not in this town."

"What the pity is, is that he's already signed the contract, and you've already done a week's shooting."

Maury shook his head, waved his hand in familiar dismissal. He wasn't angry, wasn't considering taking steps to ensure that the action star *never worked in this town again,* like I would've been, if I had Maury's connections. Despite his tiresome homophobia, his redneck misogyny, Michael McCown was a bankable star. Maury had been hearing the kid's not at all unique brand of ugliness since before Mikey's grandfather had climbed out from under whatever rock had hatched him. The director was used to it.

"I was going to say, it's a pity he's so adorable because . . ." Maury trailed off.

It was not like him to *trail off.* "What?"

He considered me carefully for a minute, like he might hold forth at length on the ignorance of young actors these days. But in the end, he only said, "Let's just hope that he holds onto his money. Looks are everything in this business, and a little boyish talent and looks are all he's got."

"I dunno, Maury. I think he's got a few years left." It was hard to compliment the little bastard, but it was the truth.

Maury pursed his lips, shook his head. "You never know. Remember Armand?"

"Armand was Cary Grant compared to this twerp." I also shook my head. "I can't understand why Alvee would invite him to dinner."

Now Maury smiled like a shark, showing all his no-longer crooked teeth. "Alvee's decided to try on the role of mentor, Carol. He senses that this boy looks up to him, and he digs that. The kid's admiration is not unlike the purple prose he still receives from sadly dissolute Armand."

"It most assuredly *is* unlike it," I said, thinking how much more I preferred the *commanding British sodomite* now that Alvee had a new kind of admirer. At least Armand had been polite.

The Moving Finger Writes; and, Having Writ, Moves On . . .

There's that scene in *Sunset Boulevard* where Betty Schaefer says, "I just think pictures should say a little something."

Desperate screenwriter Joe Gillis replies, "You'd have turned down *Gone With the Wind.*"

"No, that was me," sighs the producer. "I said, 'Who wants to see a Civil War picture?'"

Now *She's A Peach* was neither *Gone With the Wind* nor *Sunset Boulevard.* Not in this lifetime. But it turned out to be the one thing that I hadn't expected it to be: a huge hit.

The prospect of seeing Alvee Smith-Killem and Michael McCown in their first comedic roles had (inexplicably) appealed to the ticket-buying populace, and they'd packed the theaters. Their collective funny bones tickled, they'd told their friends and neighbors. Maurice Claremount's off the rack, *been done* rom-com soared to the pinnacle of the box office, foreign and domestic, leaving *Cheyenne Sundown,* his previous money-making success, in the red Wyoming dust.

The comedic timing of the newcomers to the genre amused the critics, as did the chemistry between all the actors: Alvee and Michael as the feuding buddies; Mina and each of her suitors. No one said, *Casting Director Carolyn Adyon's choice of Steve Shea to play the Third Man was awesome,* but *Variety* did say it was the last time anyone would refer to him as an unknown.

Even Cary Stuward's catty first line – *The joke's on Alvee Smith-Killem in She's A Peach, the freshest comedy to hit your local multiplex in many a moon* – wasn't really an insult. The chubby critic from *The New York Times adored* the picture.

I read the review aloud to the film's director. *"Michael McCown demonstrates that beneath the cool detachment and alluring physique of an action star can beat the heart of the naïve boy-next-door. Mina Reed got up and ran with the meager script – in a surprising triumph for the ladies, she's not taken in by the charms of the newest peacock on the block (nor his adorable chum) after so recently being dumped by her thoughtless boyfriend.*

"Christ, he's a terrible writer!"

Maury just giggled fitfully and gestured for me to read on.

"After his dismal performance in the equally as dismal and thankfully forgotten Dorian and Henry, Alvee Smith-Killem has found his niche, brilliantly conveying the dumb surprise of the Don Juan turned down."

That's because he's a brilliant actor, Cary, I thought. He'd never been turned down in his preternaturally long life. He'd never even had to ask, yet his comedic portrayal of rejection had wowed the vindictive, long-memoried critic. My Alvee can play anything.

"Neophyte Steve Shea steals the entire flick in just two brief scenes. At the outset, he has a tough decision – girl or career? He makes his choice manfully, reluctantly, and I positively cheered when he realizes his error and corrects it, communicating his contrition with soulful brown eyes and just the perfect measure of sorrow in his voice. His apology is truly the highlight of the film.

"She's A Peach is an entertaining retelling of a familiar story, with the clever twist of the girl holding out and getting the boy she wants for a change. It's a welcome bit of empowerment. Trust your friend Cary, gentlemen. The cutie from Starbucks that gives you her best smile in the morning? Take her to see She's A Peach. It's the perfect first date movie."

Maurice Claremount continued to giggle. He laughed, he slapped his knee, he nudged Maki, but couldn't translate the reason for his mirth, because he couldn't stop giggling. This time around, he'd starred his muse in a comedy, because he'd felt it time to demonstrate Alvee's acting chops, time to show the world that the black-haired, blue-eyed pretty face could indeed be anything Maury imagined for him: butcher, baker, candlestick maker; superbly lit, naked cowboy or vengeful drug-dealer; debauched homosexual or hilariously rejected Don Juan.

Maury laughed because *She's A Peach* was a hit, and he hadn't expected that, any more than I had. The film would soon be forgotten, but its reverberations would not: the director had given Mina Reed a vehicle to show a little depth to her acting. He'd shown that there was a funny streak to Michael McCown, that there was more to him as a performer than just getting the girl and kicking ass (without much dialogue). He'd *discovered* Steve Shea, launched his career. Based on the reviews, the sky was now the limit for the guy who had become my friend. Maury had made them and himself richer, *sought-after,* in a very tough business.

But none of these truths mattered to the director, and that's the other reason why he laughed. He made movies for fun and the chiefest joy in that, well . . . He'd loved one particular actor for more than a half a century. Alvee liked to see his name in lights. He knew how desirable he was, and the adulation he received from his fans kept him young. Maury laughed because his picture was a hit and the only thing he cared about was that this fact pleased Alvee.

****

For the entire time that the picture was in theaters, Mike McCown kept in touch with Alvee, made frequent visits for dinner. They went to Catalina together, appeared courtside at a Lakers' game. They hung out at the pool.

Alvee told us that, despite the kid's successes so far, he was a babe in the woods as far as the business was concerned. Alvee didn't have an agent as such; since bursting from obscurity with *Cheyenne Sundown,* he didn't need one. Any offers from hopeful directors and studios were referred to Title XVII Productions. There had been quite a few, but so far, none had appealed to him. Like DeNiro and Scorsese, Johnny Depp and Tim Burton, Alvee preferred to work with Maurice Claremount and his production company.

But Mikey had an agent in whom he placed all his trust, and thereby was the kid woefully represented, in Alvee's opinion. Alvee himself wasn't much for perusing his own contracts; Franck O'Day had once told me, "Legal matters have always bored me, absolutely. That's what we pay lawyers for, to understand and handle all those really important things that bore us utterly." It was what he had Maurice Claremount's crack legal team at Title XVII for.

But even a cursory examination of Michael McCown's agreement with his agent had led Alvee to believe that his mentee was not only being robbed blind; Alvee also thought the kid wasn't being offered the right parts because his agent was incompetent.

"There's gotta be a way to get him out of it," Alvee commented to Maury. "I was thinking that maybe there might be someone you could recommend . . ."

Maurice Claremount loved Alvee, deeply, truly, madly; for his looks, for his talent, for his lifelong dedication to their friendship. But other actors . . . Even the ones that he felt had talent, the ones he felt were going places; Maury sometimes subjected them to his wicked sense of humor, too. But that was all in good fun. The heat, the kitchen, and all. If they were gonna make it in this business, they had to be able to take a joke.

The actors Maury didn't like, however, whether for personal or professional reasons – he *despised them.* Robert Ecksmith had once said of that aforementioned 1960s actress: if she was the last woman on Earth and he had to film a message for visitors from the future, he still wouldn't cast her. He'd drunkenly, publicly, toasted Franck at his wedding to another: "Congratulations on your lovely bride, my friend, and kudos to your escape from the sharp and desperate talons of Jessika Yerdlay!"

And by all accounts, despite her off-screen personality, the late Miss Yerdlay had been a great actress. Bobby hadn't liked her simply because of the way she'd treated Franck.

Now I watched Maury raise one blonde eyebrow. He most assuredly didn't like Michael McCown. "If his teeth were on fire, I wouldn't cross the street to –"

"Never mind, then." Alvee smiled faintly. "I just thought I'd ask." He wouldn't bring it up again.

In the next two years, I saw another larger than life advertisement for one more Michael McCown action flick, but soon forgot all about him, because another familiar face smiled down at me from billboards along the Sunset Strip: Steve Shea.

He did another comedy, for Sony. He starred and it was another hit. Then he took the lead in a drama, and it also topped the box office. Alvee and Maury were happy for him, but I was happiest of all. Steve was a nice guy, and a great actor. No one thought he deserved success more than me.

Steve didn't visit – he was far too busy getting famous – but he called and texted me regularly. Michael McCown kept in touch with Alvee; he frequently told us, "Mikey says hi!" just to see the expression of dislike cross our faces, I think. But the trips to Catalina, the visits to the house and cheering on the Lakers, slowly ceased.

When he had not been around for several months, nor had Alvee mentioned him, Maury asked, "Whatever happened to your protégé?"

Alvee looked at him blankly. "My –?"

"The action star. The one that thought you were his big brother."

Alvee shrugged, then grinned at me. *"Bitches, they come, they go.* He still writes, though."

Texts, Alvee. Or emails. Nobody writes *anymore.*

"I guess he's been busy."

"Oh?" Maury said with completely fake interest. "He's making another picture? Funny, I haven't heard about it."

Alvee studied his phone. "It's somewhere overseas, I guess."

Maury glanced at his leading man, found him pointedly not looking back. "*Overseas?* Scratch one career."

I murmured, "Couldn't happen to a nicer guy."

Alvee considered our smug admiration of the universal law of *what goes around comes around,* then changed the subject. "Steve's doing television."

Maury nodded. "Writer, producer, star. A man after my own heart. I'm quite proud of him."

Steve's gig on the small screen was news to me. Sometimes it seemed that my famous housemates *treated* me as if I was that goose. No one ever told me anything. Michael McCown's career tailspin, Steve's triumvirate of success in television – writer, producer, and star! I was always the last to know. I needed to start paying closer attention.

While Maury and Alvee chatted, I surreptitiously called up Steve's *IMDb* page. Under *Filmography,* it listed *She's A Peach,* and his hit comedy, and his hit drama. There was the new one: *Letters to the Editor (TV Series).* I clicked on the *in production* link, and was taken to a page that invited me to *Become an IMDbPro Member Today,* to sign up for a free trial. The thought crossed my mind that perhaps I might be a little bit more hep to what was going on with my friends in the biz, if I did just that. But Wikipedia was free, and if *Letters to the Editor* was in production, there should already be a page for it.

The synopsis was brief. Steve Shea starred as Geordie Crowson, editor/chief reporter of a small Midwestern newspaper, struggling to stay afloat in the digital age. Each week's episode would revolve around the news story that the paper was covering, whether humorous or dramatic, romantic or criminal. It was slated to premiere in a few weeks.

Humorous or dramatic, romantic or criminal. I thought that my second-favorite actor's range could cover all that. Like Maury, I was so proud of him!

****

The screening room in Alvee's basement was actually more and less than that: there was a curtain, like in an old-timey theatre, and it, as well as the walls and the seats, were all done in a midnight-blue crushed velvet. A dark, impossibly polished hardwood floor was beneath our feet. It was an old-Hollywood tribute to the place where its product met its consumers.

But when the curtain was rolled back, via remote control, it revealed not a silver screen at all, but a state-of-the-art Panasonic television, just as huge and thin as it wanted to be. The wall at the back of the room no longer contained any little windows behind which the once-necessary projectionist would've sat. In addition to controlling the curtain, the remote also dimmed the recessed lights in the ceiling, called up cable and broadcast programs, retrieved any of the encyclopedic number of movies Alvee had stored on a computer kept (somewhere) strictly for that purpose. He might not be up on the last half-century of modern music, but when it came to our viewing pleasure, he had a home theater system done new-Hollywood-style.

Almost as if he wasn't a director of blockbusters, and as if Alvee Smith-Killem wasn't a star of mega-wattage, Maury and my leading man settled in with a bowl of popcorn every Friday night and watched *Letters to the Editor* in this awesome room with me.

The show was pretty good, light, mostly, with just enough drama to make it interesting. Mid-season, for example, just when we were getting to know all the characters, Steve killed one of them off in a spectacular car explosion, as part of the expose-of-a-local-Mafioso storyline. That certainly re-captured waning attentions.

Maury didn't comment on the plots or the acting, but said the production values were quite good, and the music was outstanding. Alvee, on the other hand, praised Steve's writing, how he portrayed Geordie Crowson, the harried reporter, as a good guy gone just a little bit bad, a once upstanding citizen who had gone a little to seed, a little to drink, a little to falling into bed with the wrong kind of women.

I thought *Letters to the Editor* was fantastic, overall.

After the Season One finale, Alvee commented to his director, "Since you haven't come up with another movie, maybe I should consider doing some television."

"Perhaps you should," Maury replied evenly.

It had been almost four years, and no scripts sent from Title XVII had caught the director's eye, no plots for new Alvee Smith-Killem-starring vehicles had occurred to him. Alvee was beginning to feel that itch again. It didn't quite need to be scratched yet, but the idea was again presenting itself: Alvee wanted to get back to work.

And This Week, Guest-Starring Dorian Gray

When the whim of doing television occurred to my leading man, he knew the guy to call. Writer/producer/star/good friend Steve Shea was overjoyed, and immediately wrote him a character and five-episode story arc.

In episode eight of Season Two of *Letters to the Editor,* Alvee's introduced as Geordie Crowson's nemesis-from-way-back, Bellamy Fritz. The first show is entirely exposition, about how Geordie and Bell had been best pals in journalism school. Then both are hired at a big New York daily, and the intense competition turns them into one-upping frenemies. Next, Geordie gets the girl that Bellamy wants, and that strips bare whatever tatters remained of their friendship.

The girl, Loren, is troubled. But not unlike the character he portrayed in *She's A Peach,* Steve's Geordie is too ambitious to notice that his girlfriend drinks a little too much, that she is becoming fonder and fonder of prescription drugs. Geordie finally sees, but she refuses to get help, so he leaves her. He has his career as an up-and-coming newsman to consider, after all. He can't be burdened with the albatross of a druggie girlfriend.

The exposition comes to an end when Loren, despondent over their break-up, washes down a handful of pills with a swig of vodka. As she starts to get sleepy, she also starts to have second thoughts. She can't get Geordie to pick up, so she calls Bellamy, the man she knows never stopped loving her. He rushes across town, stymied repeatedly by the traffic that defines New York City. But he's too late.

Fade. To. Black.

In the next episode – now we know why Geordie Crowson is a little bit of a wreck. He has a lot of guilt over Loren's death, because he wasn't around to save her. Maybe she would've been better off with Bell from the out-set, because he hadn't really cared for her all that much in the first place. He's truly sorry that he's really just not that sorry. Was her suicide, in fact, his fault? Yeah, well, maybe . . . But maybe not. Round and round it goes in his thoughts. He left New York, took this slower-paced job in the Midwest, to get away from the memories.

Next we learn that in the intervening years since Loren's death, Bellamy has abandoned the dying biz of news-in-print. He became a founding partner in some kind of every-device-app, internet sensation. It's practically indispensable. While Geordie and staff are struggling to keep their concern afloat, Bellamy is as successful and impossibly rich as Mark Zuckerberg.

Now he's arrived in Geordie's little town, all limos and expensive suits, hell-bent on ruining his former friend's life, for kicks, for no other reason than that he can. Over the remaining four episodes, Bell's revenge takes many forms: he tries to buy the paper (he fails). He tries to frame Geordie for embezzlement, and thereby get him fired *and* arrested. Bell fails at that, too.

In his last effort, Alvee's slick and good-looking, wealthy and confident Bellamy succeeds, however. In a scenario as old as time, he aims to seduce and then carry off Geordie's girlfriend. Sweet and a little dumb, Debbie succumbs to the big city charmer, and the Season Two finale shows her and Bell cozied up in another limo. They board his private jet and wing off to the lights of New York City.

Executive Producer, Steve Shea

It was a helluva finale! I was so proud of him!

The questions swirled, but the fans would have to wait until Season Three: How will Geordie cope with the loss of pretty Debbie, a girl he thought he really did love? Because

Bellamy only wanted her as a means to hurt his enemy, will he soon tire of her? Will she come crawling back?

And most importantly, would gorgeous Alvee Smith-Killem be reprising his role when the show returned in the fall?

I was not privy to the story arc of the third season of *Letters to the Editor,* so I couldn't answer the first questions. But the answer to the last one was a definite no.

Letters to the Editor was shot in the Big Apple. Steve put Alvee up in his own apartment for the entirety of his guest-starring stint. Like one big vacation, they toured the town's world-famous sites and had a good ol' time palling around. But other than his friend's company, my decades-long California-boy hated New York. He hated the weather, the restaurants, the inescapable congestion; he hated the accents of the people on the crew.

Broadway entertained Alvee a great deal, however.

From his *IMDb* bio: *Alvee Joseph Smith decided he wanted to be an actor at a young age. He was born* [on May 1, 1988, three years and two months after me] *in the little town of Bromley, Kentucky, but spent his teens and twenties kicking around London and its environs, sampling the theater scene. He says the Killem part of his stage name comes from something his first director there told him: "If you ever get to Hollywood, kid, you're gonna kill 'em." The rest of the cast referred to him as Killem after that. The name stuck, so he hyphenated it onto his name for his first movie role, Downpour. "It's so much more memorable than just Smith," he said.*

Of course, that was all bullshit. Franck O'Day's birthdate was April 29th or 30th, 1933. He'd been born on a farm in Ohio, so far back in the dim reaches of time that they hadn't even keep an accurate record.

As was once related on the long-defunct *TwoGreenKeys.com: Franck's father, Thomas, was killed at the Battle of Normandy, June 6, 1944. The following year, Franck moved with his mother, Louise, to Los Angeles, to live with her brother. In 1946, she remarried. Her husband,*

Howard Smith, did not adopt the then thirteen-year-old Francis, so he retained his father's last name.

His stepfather's brother (Uncle Jesse of the hungry looks), got young Franck bit parts around town for ten years. Then he introduced him to RKO power player Patrick Morrison, and the rest is forgotten Hollywood history.

My point is, Alvee never did any theater in his life. So watching the best and brightest tread the boards on Broadway was a novelty to him. It was still acting, but unlike any he'd ever participated in personally. Attending the theater made him forget a good portion of his homesickness.

But Steve Shea had done a lot of theater in Cali before he hit the big time, and he was a television star now, not to mention writer and producer of his own show. He didn't particularly like to be reminded of whence he'd come, not that many years before. So Broadway wasn't his thing. Maury made a few phone calls, and had a Title XVII minion, in the Big Apple on business, accompany Alvee to the theater.

Yet still he missed California's eternal sunshine; he missed his house and pool. He missed his director and his monk-friend. He missed me.

Alvee called on the last day of shooting. *"Start spreadin' the news*, baby. *I'm leavin' today."*

Doing television had been different and fun, he said, and he'd surely be down to do it again. But only if it was filmed at home.

****

The first season of *Letters to the Editor* was a minor hit. Ratings fell off somewhat for the first seven episodes of the second season, however, but came roaring back in number eight, with the debut of Alvee's lusciously vicious bad guy, Bellamy Fritz. After that, the show's ratings ascended again, all the way through to the season finale. Steve's show was golden; Nielsen sung its praises.

Unfortunately, the viewers were mightily disappointed when Bellamy Fritz didn't return for Season Three. Ratings positively plummeted. A change to Thursday nights helped not at all, and *Letters to the Editor* staggered to ignominious cancellation at the end of its third year.

"It died quietly, just like the printed word it portrayed," Maury proclaimed sadly, in his customary theatrical style. "A pity. But on a lighter note, perhaps Steve'll now abandon the dreary East Coast and come back to Hollywood. Where the action is."

The Two-Minute Drill

Alvee Smith-Killem was restless. His foray into the world of the small screen (already a year passed) had somewhat soothed his itch to once again appear before the cameras, but now his desire to work again consumed him.

He said to his director, "Maybe if you would come up with a new project, you could come up with a part for Steve, too."

It was my cue to reveal the idea that had been gestating in my mind.

"You should be able to pitch your idea for a new movie in two minutes, Carol," Maury had instructed me. "Any longer than that, and my eyes start to glaze over. The visions of dollar signs dancing in my producer's head begin to stumble. By three minutes, the length of your average pop song, you've lost us."

Maury called this synopsis the *Two-Minute Drill*. Thinking that it might be a standard filmmaking rule, I'd Googled it once. The internet said the term applied to *a type of hurry-up offense instituted after a two-minute warning in American football.* Not a single mention of nervous screenwriters trying to summarize their ideas to bored directors.

Since he was absolutely ignorant of football, American or otherwise, I was sure Maury had not borrowed the expression from the world of contact sports. Even though the words were the same, I was sure that Maury's *Two Minute Drill* was another strict regime of his very own devising.

I don't like the *Two Minute Drill*. It clashes with my storyteller's sensibilities. I like to *weave* my tale, to describe locations, ambiance, emotions. I like to relate dialogue. He's the far better screenwriter, anyway. He's the goddamned director. He can summarize. He can show instead of tell, once he puts it on film.

Maury, Alvee, and I were sitting at the terrace table. Maki had slept in that morning. Kimura had just cleared away the brunch things. Alvee still frowned, so I spoke up.

"I've been thinking about a plot for a new project." I didn't say *screenplay,* because then my director would expect me to *summarize* it, to condense it down to his impossible two minutes.

"Indeed?" he said with an encouraging smile.

"It would start something like this . . ."

I took a deep breath, then noticed Kimura standing in the doorway across the terrace, trying respectfully to catch my eye.

I nodded to him and he silently came forward, bowed slightly. "A man just called at the gate for you, Miss Carol. I told him you were not at home."

Such was par for the course for persons without appointments, but . . . Usually as calm as a breezeless summer day, this unexpected visitor seemed to have ruffled Kimura.

"He was a policeman."

Maury's eyebrows rose and he asked something of Kimura in Japanese. While I still haven't picked up very much of the language in all this time, the name *Franck O'Day* was recognizable in his reply.

Maury translated. "The message is: He's from Las Vegas, and he says he has some new information about the fire. And he mentioned Franck."

I watched Alvee's blue eyes widen.

"He requests that you give him a call at your earliest convenience," Kimura said, and handed me a business card. I thanked him and he bowed again, and quickly, gratefully, disappeared back into the house, sparing a split-second to exchange a glance with Alvee.

I reckoned that these few sentences were probably the most dialogue I'd ever heard in English from Kimura, but I didn't have time to ruminate on that because Maury spoke.

"I know this is a very tender subject, Carolyn. You lost your best friend in that fire, and that's why I've never brought it up with you." He cast a sidelong glance at our uncharacteristically silent leading man. "But since the gendarmerie are paying us a visit, and after all this time, maybe you should tell me –"

"I missed the fire, Maury. Franck sent me back to the hotel to get the guestbook."

Now I considered Alvee, who once upon a time, before the mystical inundations of the universal energies, the ensuing fire, the restoration of youth, and the assumption of a new identity, had been the person that had sent me back to the Wynn. He remained expressionless.

"So why does a cop want to talk to you about it now?" Maury studied Alvee as if he expected him to explain the mystery. Alvee shrugged.

"If we're suddenly to be interrogated by the authorities regarding anything to do with poor, burnt-up Franck, perhaps we should develop a more in-depth backstory for our unbruised youth," the auteur then suggested.

****

His mother paused with a handful of popcorn halfway to her mouth. "Christ, Jeff! It's Franck O'Day!"

"Who?" he replied irritably, not looking up from his phone. He knew he shouldn't react like that. Lots of people called him *Jeff,* until he corrected them, told them that he preferred *Jeffrey.* If they persisted with the abbreviated version, he didn't correct them again.

It really didn't bother him that much. His mom had called him *Jeff* all his life. It was only the fact that Libby had also called him *Jeff* that made it seem so irritating now.

His mother pointed at the TV. "Right there!"

Jeffrey looked up reluctantly. He'd been reviewing notes he'd taken earlier in the day regarding a liquor store hold-up down by Fremont Street; he'd been paying as little attention as possible to whatever his mom was watching on television.

Stella Naylor hated commercials, so she muted them. Sometimes she was a little slow on the uptake turning the sound back on when her program resumed, so Jeffrey was always missing what was going on. He suspected that Stella actually liked things better without the sound.

But it was nice to have someplace else to go besides back to his lonely apartment. Mom didn't mention Libby at all, as if she'd simply ceased to exist when she'd left him. So Jeffrey figured that the least he could do was pay attention when Stella was excited about something.

She fumbled for the remote, hit the sound.

"– for chatting with us, Alvee." A correspondent with a microphone turned away from a good-looking, dark-haired man dressed in an expensive black suit. Jeffrey was astonished to recognize the woman standing beside him.

The reporter said, "Alvee Smith-Killem's latest opens nationwide tomorrow. Back to you, Kevin."

Stella clicked the sound off again. "Well, I'll be goddamned. He hasn't aged a day."

Where have I seen that woman before? Jeffrey was asking himself. *Some case . . .* He realized that his mother was waiting for him to pick up his side of the conversation.

"What did you say, Mom?"

"I said, I'll be goddamned. I just saw Franck O'Day on *Entertainment Tonight.* He's making movies again, and he hasn't aged a day."

At the mention of the old movie star's name, just like fingers snapping in his mind, Jeffrey remembered where he'd met the woman he'd just seen on TV. He'd spoken to her after the VFW fire. The woman – Cathy? Karen? Her name had been among those listed on the rental agreement for the hall. She had been the only one left to interview because she hadn't been there when the place burned down.

Jeffrey concentrated, attempting to recall the details of the case. She'd returned to the hotel for . . . something. He'd talked to her the next morning, and she'd shown him the flyer for the event that had been underway when the fire started. He'd only

131

recognized the actor's name, and the name of the movie, because his mom was a big fan of the guy.

"Franck O'Day's dead, Mom. He died in that VFW Hall fire."

Stella shook her head firmly. "I remember you telling me that then, Jeff. And I remember telling *you* – that guy at the VFW hall was some kind of an imposter. Franck O'Day disappeared in the 60s. They never found a body. If he'd suddenly decided to come out of hiding, after all those years, why would he be having a – what was it they were having? At the VFW?"

"They were showing that movie you like."

"High Times in Manhattan," Stella supplied. "It was the only thing he was ever in. But he was great in it." Stella clucked sadly over Franck O'Day's stunted career. "But now he's making movies again. That's great!"

Jeffrey was thinking about the woman he'd just seen on TV. Her exact words escaped him, so he called up a mental picture of the flyer she'd shown him. It had said something about answering questions and signing autographs. It was supposed to be the actual guy, not some kind of tribute.

"Franck O'Day was there, Mom. After the fire, the witness said –"

"I don't care what she said. It wasn't him. He disappeared when I was in high school." Stella gave him that *I don't care if you think I'm crazy* look. "Did they identify his body after the fire?"

"That I don't know."

Jeffrey assumed that there had been no unidentified remains; he would've heard about it, otherwise. If the old actor was there, his body had been catalogued with the rest.

It had been a tragedy, sure, but a non-mysterious, run of the mill one. The fire hadn't been set. LVFD had decided right away that seventy-five people had died because of faulty wiring. The arson boys' investigation concluded that there'd been some kind of short, an overload; it'd started above a perhaps too-modern projector hanging from the anciently-wired, not fire-proof ceiling. Sad, but not criminal. As far as LVPD was concerned, case closed.

Stella said, "Don't you think that if they'd found Franck O'Day's body in a fire after he was supposed to've already been dead for forty years – don't you think that would've made the news?"

"I dunno, Mom. Nobody's ever heard of –"

"He was big, Jeff. When he disappeared, it was in all the papers. But he didn't die in a plane crash, and he didn't die in a fire, because I just saw him on the TV."

"That guy couldn't be more than thirty-five or so, Mom. It couldn't be him. And they said a different name. Alvin –"

"Alvee. Alvee Smith-Killem. Isn't that the most ridiculous name you've ever heard? I've seen a few commercials for his movies . . . None of them was very interesting, so I didn't pay a lot of attention. But even then, I thought he looked like Franck. But seeing him right there on *Entertainment Tonight* . . . I don't care what he's calling himself. That was Franck O'Day, Jeff."

"If you say so, Mom."

Jeffrey knew better than to argue with his mother when her mind was made up, especially about something so insignificant. Stella had her share of crazy theories: there were aliens on the dark side of the moon; JFK was set up by Johnson; Bush knew about 9/11 beforehand. What difference did it make if she believed that some young actor was Franck O'Day returned from the dead? Jeffrey knew that it was an impossibility.

But it was definitely the same woman, though, the one who'd claimed that Mom's favorite old actor had been present at the VFW hall, from whence no one had come out alive.

Funny that Mom would connect this young guy with that old guy, and there's the same woman . . .

A tiny chime pinged in Jeffrey's mind; it was precisely the same sound as after the line in the old Pink Floyd song: *Okay, okay, okay, just a little pinprick . . .* He'd always heard that soft little chime, all his career, whenever something struck him as just a little bit odd, or funny, or off in some way. Whenever something seemed strangely . . . coincidental.

And then his cop's curiosity would tilt its head like that famous dog: *his master's voice. When?* That voice might ask, or any of the other interrogatives, and the rest of Jeffrey's clicking mind would rally to answer. Once some detail spoke to his curiosity, there was no unseeing the oddness, the offness.

Jeffrey didn't really believe in coincidences, you see.

Now it was *How?* How was this woman now appearing on television, on *Entertainment Tonight,* beside a famous actor (that resembled Franck O'Day)? That woman, the woman that had missed the fire because she'd been on some convenient errand – she'd been some kind of secretary, Jeffrey recalled. Now she was on TV.

Her friend had been a secretary, too, the one that'd burned. It had all been a small, economical event, held at a tiny, firetrap of a venue. Maybe the guy hadn't really been Franck O'Day at all, as the flyer had claimed. Maybe he *had* been an imposter.

Maybe the imposter, then, had been this actor he'd seen on TV, now. But just like the fortunate woman, he wasn't dead.

Not only weren't they dead, they were wealthy, famous. At least he was. Now that he thought about it, hadn't this Alvee Smith-Killem been in some TV show? And Jeffrey had also seen his face on posters at the Cineplex a few times, when he and Libby used to go out. Like Stella, he'd heard the guy's name, but hadn't seen any of his flicks.

Jeffrey Googled *Franck O'Day,* tapped *Images.* There weren't very many. A few grainy newspaper black and whites of him and a good-looking blonde. The same head shot of him in a tux, repeated in black and white and in color. A picture of him with long hair and mutton chops, wearing aviator shades, with some blonde guy. No other pics.

Next Jeffrey Googled *Alvee Smith-Killem,* again hit *Images.* His mom, and the robbery report, and even brooding about Libby and her departure, were forgotten. The role of the guy in charge of Jeffrey's thoughts would be played by his curiosity this evening.

There were many more pictures of this young actor. Hundreds more. In character from his films, that TV show; giving interviews, on the red carpet at premieres. In this last type, the woman from the fire was always on his arm, or standing a little off to the side.

Jeffrey saw how Stella could easily mistake Alvee Smith-Killem for Franck O'Day. The resemblance was very striking, but it couldn't be the same guy. Just like the old daguerreotype from the Civil War was not evidence of an ageless Nicholas Cage, nor was Keanu Reeves immortal just because he resembled the guy in some 18th century French portrait. Sly Stallone was not Pope Gregory IX, still alive and making bad movies. The internet was awash with consideration of those kinds of ridiculous time-wasters.

Some people just resembled others. That was about the only kind of coincidence Jeffrey and his curiosity were willing to admit, however. This guy wasn't Franck O'Day. He just looked like him.

Wasn't it funny how the same woman – what was her name? He'd have to look it up. Wasn't it odd that the same woman, the one that had miraculously been elsewhere when all those people died, at some kind of event featuring Franck O'Day – wasn't it coincidental that she'd show up all rich and famous on the arm of some guy that, hey, what d'ya know, just happens to look a whole helluva lot like Franck O'Day?

Maybe this guy *had* played the imposter all those years ago, but if it'd been him, why wasn't he dead? Nobody had ever come forward saying that they'd escaped the fire. Actors love publicity – if it had been this guy, he would've stepped up, just to get his silly name and his picture in the paper. *Alvee Smith-Killem, Franck O'Day Impersonator, Escapes Fire That Claimed Fans.*

But no survivors had ever come forward. Jeffrey wondered: had it been some kind of con? Some kind of insurance scam? The details of the case were just not coming back to him. It had been a simple electrical fire that had consumed an old building, and something criminal about the whole deal seemed highly unlikely, and yet . . .

If this woman had lost her best friend at a Franck O'Day event (not to mention Franck himself) . . . Jeffrey remembered her tears, her grief, her plaintive questions: "No one got out? No one at all?"

How unlikely was it that she'd end up rich and famous with some guy that looked just like . . . It was just *off* somehow.

"Your sister called. Asked how you're doing, since . . ."

Stella's remark broke her son's concentration. "And what did you tell her?"

"I told her you're doing great." Maternal concern creased her already wrinkled brow. "You do look a little tired though, honey. You should take a vacation. Get out of town. Some new scenery'll give you the chance to forget about . . ."

She who shall not be named. Jeffrey appreciated his mother's loyalty. Break-ups are seldom exclusively one-sided, and being a cop, maybe he hadn't been home as much as he should've been. But none of that mattered to Stella. Her boy was the victim here.

Jeffrey smiled then, probably his first genuine smile since he'd found the note and the bare closets and the drained bank account – all that Libby had left behind when she took off to Reno with that blackjack dealer.

"You're right, as always, Mom. I do need a vacation, and I know exactly who I'll visit."

Stella was wary of her son's sudden good mood. She'd told him not to marry that trampy waitress, and while Libby certainly deserved whatever she got – Jeff had a gun, and his mother didn't want to see him in prison.

"Who?"

"Julie."

Stella relaxed. Julie was her daughter, Jeff's sister. She lived in Los Angeles.

Jeffrey figured that after a quick perusal of the case file to recall her name, it wouldn't be hard to find the woman who'd escaped the fire. Or this young actor that bore such a resemblance to Franck O'Day. All Jeffrey would need to find *him* would be a *Map to the Stars' Homes*, available on any street corner in the City of Angels. Alvee Smith-Killem had just appeared on *Entertainment Tonight,* after all. His new movie was opening nationwide. He shouldn't be hard to find.

****

Detective Jeffrey Naylor of the Las Vegas Police Department should've felt a little silly when he pushed the button on the intercom before the gate of Alvee Smith-Killem's Beverly Hills' estate.

It wasn't like he was there on official police business. The fire at VFW Post 864 had occurred way back in 2013, and it'd been deemed electrical in origin by the professionals at the LVFD. The place had been adequately insured. The woman who'd escaped – her name was Carolyn Adyon – had not filed any claims, nor had anyone from the estate of Franck O'Day. His were not among the remains identified, nor was his name mentioned anywhere in the insurance company documents, either as living or deceased, past the fact that the unfortunate victims had gathered there at the VFW Hall to see an old movie in which he'd starred.

But Jeffrey didn't feel silly as he reached for the red button on the intercom, because even though no insurance claims had been paid out to this Adyon chick, he'd discovered that the plot of the Franck O'Day angle had definitely thickened.

There was a young woman that worked at the DA's office, who'd always been a little sweet on Jeffrey. Her name was Courtney and she was, bless her heart, a good fifteen years younger than him. In a different world, maybe . . .

Even when he'd still been married to Libby, Courtney had always been friendly. And after his divorce, whenever he'd had an errand to her office, she'd been positively maternal to the now sad and saturnine cop, he who'd once been so talky and upbeat. But Jeffrey wasn't ready for a new girl yet, and Courtney was entirely too young for him, anyway . . .

None of this stopped him from asking her to do a little research for him, however, and that was why Jeffrey didn't hesitate to push that button. Between the details of the case file on the fire and what Courtney had uncovered, the whole deal had just become curiouser and curiouser.

Jeffrey had explained to Courtney that the whole thing was off the record, just his inquisitiveness messing with him about the coincidences. He'd quipped that the after-hours' Sonny Crockett part of his brain was working overtime. Courtney had smiled blankly, blinked politely. The *Miami Vice* reference had passed her right on by. *Yeah, she's way too young . . .*

He took her out to dinner at a nice restaurant – he figured it was the least he could do. She presented him with several documents, no doubt printed up at the expense of the good people of Clark County, whilst Courtney had been at work.

The first unexpected bombshell: sex-abuse allegations had been leveled against Franck O'Day by one of his costars, Jessika Yerdlay, way back in the 60s.

Courtney paged through the copies of articles from *Variety* and *The Los Angeles Times*. Like a good researcher, she gave Jeffrey the gist: "Franck and Jessika stared in some movie together –"

"High Times in Manhattan." Stella's favorite.

Courtney nodded, smiled. Her eyes twinkled; her affection for the detective was on display. *If only you were ten years older,* Jeffrey thought, *and if I wasn't such a mess . . .*

"The two of them had been an item for a while, then Franck married someone else. Jessika's brother killed her –"

"Killed Jessika?"

"No. Jessika's brother killed Franck's wife. Murder-suicide." Courtney passed the article to him.

Jeffrey skimmed it, and his only response was, "Wow."

"After this tragedy, Franck eventually went back to Jessika." Courtney paused to watch Jeffrey's eyebrows rise at that tidbit. "They announced their engagement, but then Franck took off with his director to Japan. Apparently, Jessika waited for him to return, and when he didn't . . ." Courtney passed across another printout.

"Jessika accused Franck of having molested her daughter, Dolores Adamson, when she was fourteen. The LA County DA didn't file anything formal, but Franck issued a statement through his studio that he would be returning to the States to face the music, anyway."

Jeffrey read from the article. *"I look forward to my day in court to answer Miss Yerdlay's sad charges. I have no doubt of my certain exoneration."*

"But he never made it."

"His plane went down in Japan."

Again Courtney smiled. "They found what may or may not have been the wreckage in 1982. No bodies.

"Fast forward to 2013. Tragic fire at VFW Post 864, during a Franck O'Day Fan Club screening of *High Times in Manhattan.* The Coroner's Office identified all the remains, none of which belonged to Franck O'Day. Yet there was one set . . ." Courtney now slid a copy of an autopsy report across the candle-lit table.

The restaurant was dim and the print was small, but Jeffrey could still make out the name. "Dolores Adamson? The girl he was supposed to have molested? She died in the fire?"

"According to the dental records."

Jeffrey had read over the case file before his dinner date with Courtney. None of the names mentioned in Carolyn Adyon's statement had stood out to him then, but now . . .

He'd asked, "Why weren't you there? Why did you go back to the hotel alone?"

"Franck asked me to go back. He'd forgotten the guestbook. It was a present from his friend, Lori."

Jeffrey had asked for clarification and Adyon had given the woman's full name. Dolores Adamson.

"It gets better," Courtney said, like the very best girl Friday. She slid another page across the table. In flowery script, it read *Last Will and Testament of Dolores Adamson.* Again Courtney summarized. "A few months before her death,

Dolores executed this. It leaves everything – and she had a lot of everything, Jeffrey. She had been her mother's sole heir, and because he'd never had a chance to change his own will after he left the States – she was also Franck O'Day's sole heir. She got an enormous chunk of change, seven or eight years after he went missing.

"In her will, the never-married Miss Adamson left everything to Alvee Smith-Killem. He and Carolyn Adyon live in the grand old house Dolores inherited from her mother, to this day."

"I'll be goddamned," Jeffrey murmured, unconsciously mimicking his mother. "There's the angle right there. Alvee Smith-Killem and this Adyon woman – it wasn't for any kind of insurance money. They brought Dolores Adamson to our little town and set her and seventy-four other people on fire for this million dollar estate."

"Several million."

****

So Jeffrey Naylor didn't feel silly at all pushing the intercom button.

He was turned away, of course. He didn't have an appointment. Jeffrey had gone on to have a nice dinner with her sister and her husband. Carolyn Adyon had called in the middle of it.

She was curious as to why a policeman had come all the way from Las Vegas to stir up all these sad memories, all these years later. She'd made him an appointment for the next day.

Alvee Smith-Killem's house was incredible, fantastic, like something out of a dream of film industry opulence. Jeffrey didn't get to see much of it, though. A silent Asian servant admitted him, led him across the gleaming parquet floor of the foyer, beneath the twin grand staircases, then out through French doors to the Italian marble-tiled veranda.

Jeffrey recognized Carolyn Adyon immediately. It hadn't occurred to him when he'd seen her on television – memory is a funny thing – but the thought struck him now that she hadn't

140

aged a day since he'd interviewed her after the fire, way back in 2013. If anything, she looked better. But on the other hand, she'd been grief-stricken then, agonized at the loss of her best friend. Or had she?

Now she was rich, a Hollywood screenwriter, he had learned. Now she was regal, consort to a world-renowned actor, mistress of this magnificent estate.

The man sitting at the table with her was probably in his mid-forties, well-dressed. Everything about his bearing screamed lawyer. *How did you come by all this luxury, Miss Adyon, hmm? Why do you need an attorney present to discuss an old, tragic event with me?*

The presence of an attorney didn't necessarily broadcast guilt to Jeffrey, not when he was dealing with moneyed . . . *yeah, let's just call her a suspect.* Persons such as Carolyn Adyon had multiple interests to protect, after all, and once upon a time, when it had been necessary for her to work for a living, she'd been employed by an attorney. She'd been a five-digit a year legal secretary then, and see how far she'd come. The goddamned pool cost at least six digits. Had she and her actor boyfriend accomplished all this through mass murder?

Jeffrey shook hands with Alvee Smith-Killem's woman. She introduced the distinguished gentleman as Jackson Mauer, of the firm of Woods, Kaffee, and Finch.

"This is just an informal meeting, Miss Adyon," Jeffrey said, feeling like a character in a police procedural. "You don't need an attorney present."

She laughed and replied, "A good friend of mind says one can always benefit from the presence of an attorney, Detective. But Mr. Mauer isn't *my* attorney. You said that you had questions about some kind of *connection* between the late Franck O'Day and Alvee. He's unavailable today, so Mr. Mauer is here in his stead. To answer your questions."

"So you're Mr. Killem's lawyer?"

"I'm an estate attorney, Detective. I represent Mr. Smith-Killem's estate, as well as those of other entertainers. What is it, exactly, that interests you?"

141

Jeffrey didn't like lawyers in general, and especially not this one in particular, already. He was a foreigner, some kind of Englishman or Australian or something, judging by his accent. That accent made the cop feel as though he was being talked down to, and that summoned up the Colombo in Jeffrey. He *had* these people, in black and white, just the arena in which this smarmy mouthpiece dealt, and Jeffrey was certain he wasn't going to be able to talk their way out of it, regardless of how much money they had.

"Here's what interests me, *exactly,* Jack. I'd like to know how it happened that Dolores Adamson, heir to Jessika Yerdlay's millions . . ." Jeffrey gestured at their surroundings. "Heir to the estate of the late Franck O'Day, suddenly changed her will and left it all to a nobody named Alvee Smith-Killem, and then just as suddenly wound up dead in a suspicious fire in Las Vegas."

Mauer opened a folder before him on the table. "The fire wasn't deemed suspicious."

Funny how an *estate lawyer* would have a copy of the police report, and so quickly. Jeffrey had let them know he was in town to see them only yesterday. The things money could expedite . . .

The lawyer said, "But it isn't necessary for us to get into the details of the fire department's findings. Allow me to restate your accusations."

"I'm not accusing anybody, Jack. I'm not even here officially." *Not yet, anyway.* "I saw Miss Adyon on *Entertainment Tonight.* I remembered that I'd interviewed her after the fire. Taking a little walk down Memory Lane, I reviewed the old case file, and discovered a few . . . curious inconsistencies, shall we say?" *That surely sounds like something out of CSI.* "I'm in town visiting my sister, so I just thought I'd drop by and satisfy my mind. Such a thing will bother me forever if I don't have it answered."

Jeffrey told the lawyer the truth because the truth, he'd once been told, was just liable to set a body free. It wasn't the Las Vegas cop that had anything to hide.

"Allow me to explain all, therefore, and ease your mind. You seem to see some unlawful, possibly criminal reason behind Miss Adamson's bequeathal of her estate to Mr. Smith-Killem?"

"I couldn't find any connection between them, other than her will. I couldn't find much about him at all, actually. He came out with his first movie, not long after the fire. It was foreign-made – how had Miss Adamson come to leave her estate to a foreigner? How did she even know –"

"This stranger? A valid question for an intrepid policeman."

If Jeffrey had any doubt as to the lawyer's attitude of superiority, his patronizing smile confirmed it.

"I have documentation to dispel all your concerns, Detective. Miss Adamson and Mr. Smith-Killem were by no means strangers, and he certainly isn't a foreigner. In very broad, by-marriage terms, you could called them relatives, almost."

He paused to let that revelation sink in. Jeffrey waited.

"I must apologize in advance for the Byzantine twists and turns of the history I'm about to relate to you. It's all documented, as I say, but it'll be vastly easier to understand if I just tell it to you.

"First, the players. You've no doubt heard of Franck O'Day."

"I heard that he didn't die in the fire, as Miss Adyon told me."

"That is correct. But she didn't purposefully deceive you, Detective. I'll get to that part momentarily.

"As I'm sure you're aware, Franck was once involved with an actress named Jessika Yerdlay. He was acquainted with her daughter, Dolores Adamson."

Jeffrey decided not to mention what the papers had said about Franck's *acquaintance* with his paramour's teenaged daughter. If it became necessary to bring it up, he could do so *momentarily.*

"As I'm sure you're also aware, the relationship between Jessika and Franck didn't endure, and he married someone else."

"She was murdered."

"Yes. It was a senseless tragedy. And in the wake of that tragedy, other events occurred, of which I am quite sure you are *not aware*. No one knew of them, except the parties involved, and then not even all of them knew. Yet I am prepared to reveal what occurred to you now, to assuage your curiosity. When I'm finished, you'll be able to continue your vacation, and worry no more about the lives of anyone who lives here." The lawyer, too, gestured around him.

"Franck's wife was murdered in 1965. In his sorrow, he returned home to Ohio to grieve, where he'd spent his childhood. There he met a woman named Alva Smith. Alva comforted the sad actor, and through her affection, his sorrow passed; he soon returned to California. But Mr. O'Day left part of himself behind in the Midwest. In 1966, a son was born to Alva Smith. She called him Joseph.

"Children born out of wedlock were still quite frowned upon at the time, so after Joseph's birth, Alva relocated to Bromley, Kentucky. She manufactured a story of a husband, killed in the war . . . Perhaps she dreamt of someday journeying across the country and presenting Franck O'Day with the son he didn't know he had . . . We can never know. But any dreams of that sort were cut short when the actor's plane went down overseas in 1968.

"Time passed, as it inexorably will." The lawyer featured Jeffrey with an emotionless smile. "Joseph Smith grew up. As I say, we don't know if he knew who his father really was. But someone knew, because someone revealed the truth to Joseph's own son, Alvee."

"That he was Franck O'Day's grandson."

"Yes. Alvee embarked on his own theatrical career. He traveled to the UK, made a little name for himself in theater over there, starred in one film. He got to thinking about his heritage, and through the connections that all show-business people acquire, he got in touch with Dolores Adamson. You see how I say they were almost related – had Franck ever wed her mother, as he'd once intended, Dolores would've then been his stepdaughter. Much older sister, if only by marriage, to his son, Joseph. Dolores would've then been Alvee's aunt."

The lawyer waved his hand dismissively. "Of course, Franck never did marry Jessika, so none of these connections have any legal bearing. But because he perished in Japan before he had a chance to change his will, all of his holdings still eventually went to Dolores. Perhaps Franck wouldn't have changed it, regardless. Even though things had not worked out with her mother, Franck had always been fond of his almost-stepdaughter."

Quite fond, according to her mother, Jeffrey thought.

"And of course, Franck knew nothing of the son he had fathered in Ohio. So maybe he would've left his will unchanged.

"Dolores was a fair woman. Once she met Alvee, the fact that he was indeed kin to her almost-stepfather was undeniable. I'm sure you've noticed the resemblance. She didn't have any heirs, either, so it was only natural for her to leave her estate – essentially *Franck O'Day's estate* – to his only living blood relative."

Mauer paused, then continued abruptly. "As I say, I have documentation for all this, Detective. Birth certificates and the like. Franck is of course not listed as Joseph's father, but I have copies of affectionate notes to Alva, in Franck's hand, that he wrote whilst he was in Ohio with her –"

"Why did you tell me that Franck O'Day was in Vegas with you, Miss Adyon? That he died in the fire?"

The screenwriter didn't hesitate, didn't glance at the lawyer for assurance. Whatever she was going to tell Jeffrey – maybe it was the truth, maybe it wasn't. Either way, it had been rehearsed.

"My friend Ruthanne was a big fan of Franck O'Day. She belonged to his fan club. She told me that, on its website, they maintained that Franck hadn't died in the plane crash. I'd always wanted to be a writer, so when she suggested I do a bio on him, we got in touch with the webmaster of his fan site. Come to find out, it was his stepdaughter, Lori Adamson. She invited us to LA. We met Franck."

"Except it wasn't really him."

Carol nodded, a trifle too eagerly, Jeffrey thought. "No. The guy we met certainly *looked* like him, although I did think he seemed a little young . . ."

"They can do wonders with make-up these days."

Still she didn't hesitate. "Lori came up with the idea for the comeback show in Vegas. It wasn't until after the fire . . . I really believed it was Franck, and that he'd died, Detective.

"A few years later, I saw an ad for *Cheyenne Sundown* on television. I thought I heard Franck's voice. But it was impossible. Franck was dead. But, just like you say . . . I couldn't get it out of my head. So I drove down here.

"I met Alvee, and he told me the whole story. He was Franck's grandson, and he and Lori had come up with the idea for the thing in Vegas, as a kind of tribute. At the end of the show, they were going to reveal to the fans that he wasn't really Franck at all.

"Alvee escaped the fire, went back to England. When he received word that Lori had left everything to him . . . he came back to the States, made *Cheyenne Sundown*. I met him – re-met him, actually, because I'd once believed he was Franck – and we . . . Well, we've been together ever since."

Another pause. It all seemed too pat, too compact and perfect to Jeffrey Naylor. They still could've offed Dolores Adamson for the money. Kin did that to kin every day, without all the *Byzantine twists and turns of the history* that they'd just related to him. Jeffrey was still suspicious, but the story wasn't without merit, if it checked out . . .

****

I trailed off, leaving the LVPD detective to reflect on what he'd been told. It still needed a clean ending, and I had one more twist for that. But I'd told enough for the time being. I

146

waited eagerly for a reaction from my director and leading man.

After what seemed like an eternity of silence, Maury said slowly, "You got a major detail wrong, Carol. And unfortunately, it sinks your entire premise. Lori didn't leave her estate to Alvee. That would've taken some rather *involved* legal wrangling of the after-the-fact sort. The word *illegal* springs to mind. You're correct about part of it, however. When Jessika died and Franck came back here to live with Lori, she did indeed execute a new will.

"But as you know, Lori, may her *perturbed spirit* rest in peace, never met anyone named Alvee, did she? So she couldn't have left him any *bequeathals.*

"All of Jessika's assets, as well as those she'd inherited from Franck – Lori willed them to the estate of Robert Ecksmith in merry old England. There was nothing whatsoever suspect about that. As you say, Lori had never married, had no children. She and Bobby had been friends when she was a girl. Even though he was dead . . . Franck had told her that Bobby's executors still managed his production company, that they still cranked out a few films every year. She was a child of Hollywood; she wanted to keep her money in the movie business.

"And when she passed, her assets indeed went to Bobby's estate, and not a legal eyebrow was raised about it. Sometime later, a portion of that estate was ceded to Maurice Claremount – for walking around money, if you will – and a portion of that was ceded to our Alvee. So as far as this story goes –"

"Why would you want to do a movie about my life?" Alvee cried angrily.

I jumped; he'd never before shown anger toward me, not once in our entire relationship. As a matter of fact, I'd never heard him utter a single discouraging word, as the song says, above mild annoyance, and then it had never been aimed at me. But now he was furious.

"The names could be changed to protect the –"

"None of this is even remotely funny, Carol." He glowered, blue eyes aflame.

I couldn't tell that him a cop really had interviewed me after the fire, had mentioned that his mom had been a fan of the now-definitely-deceased Franck O'Day. I couldn't tell Alvee that I'd thought up the whole *curious inconsistencies* angle after remembering the paranoid journal I'd written, still gathering dust in a safe deposit box. I couldn't tell him that if Maury had liked it, had wanted to do it – hell, I could hammer out the screenplay in a couple of days. I already had the notes for it. I'd even pictured stout and condescending Armand Hambrick as the smarmy British lawyer; Steve Shea as the cop.

But it had been a thoughtless gambit on my part, a dangerous game, not even remotely funny. The dead were buried, all of them. No use kicking over rocks and disturbing the ghosts, even if it would've made a great flick.

Still, I persisted another moment. They still hadn't heard my twist ending.

"How 'bout this?

"The cop goes back to Las Vegas. He's still unsure about the whole thing, but all of the paperwork checks out. Apparently, Alvee Smith-Killem really *is* Franck O'Day's grandson.

"Still, the detective doesn't like coincidences, especially ones that dovetail so precisely. The actor's name is still floating around in his head.

"He's always been a brainy type, for a cop, and he's got this little game on his phone. Anagrams. You put in a word, and it comes up with all the possible phrase combinations.

"For grins, he types in *Alvee Smith-Killem.* He gets a bunch of gobbledygook. It's a lot of letters, after all. He smiles to himself: one of the combinations is *Hammiest Level Ilk.*"

"Did you actually *research* this?" Alvee asked. He was still up to his eyebrows in disbelieving anger.

I waved away the interruption. "Next, the cop enters Franck's name, then combines the two names. Still nothing but garbage, thousands and thousands of combinations. Then, he sees a phrase, there, almost to the bottom. It contains the name of some historical figure –"

"Someone *Byzantine,* perhaps," Maury suggested blankly.

I wasn't going to let him interrupt me either. The big finish was in sight.

"Again, just for grins, Jeffrey Googles the historical name. And what do you know? The painting or mosaic or whatever, looks just like Alvee! He does more research, makes more anagrams. He finds depictions of a Renaissance playwright, an old tintype of a turn-of-the century preacher. Every one of them is Alvee! The cop realizes that not only is Alvee indeed Franck O'Day, just like Stella said, he's been around for centuries! He's actually an immortal –"

"Vampire demon alien." Maury tittered viciously at me. It stung like a slap. He winked at Alvee. *"There can be only one."*

I knew the director's next words were going to be *Really, Carol,* following by the guillotine of the coup de grâce, and I was not disappointed. "It's been done. You should've stopped while you were ahead."

"It's . . . terrible!" Alvee declared. "All of it! Why would you ever want to . . . Christ! What's wrong with you?"

I didn't know what I'd been expecting, but undisguised derision from Maury and towering fury from Alvee certainly hadn't been it. I leapt to defend myself. "I was just trying to come up with some new ideas."

This mollified him not in the least, so I tried a different tack. "It's a joke, Alvee. I was just kidding . . ."

It was all still not even remotely funny, but Maury came to my rescue. "You don't actually have to worry about any new material right now, Carol. I've got a little something up my sleeve. But I did like your characterization on the cop. Abandoned by his wife; bitter. That's all been done, too, of course, but I liked it."

He eyed Alvee. "Maybe we should run with the whole Franck's grandson thing. That was certainly *imaginative* on Carol's part. The boys in legal could come up with the requisite *documentation.* They manufactured Alvee Smith and his life story once; surely they could retool it and make all this work.

"Imagine the publicity! We could call a press conference, resurrect the whole sad story of the whole sad crew – dead Franck and Bobby, Dolores and Jessika; her brother; poor, murdered Bridget – and then plop you right down there in the middle as Franck's one-generation removed bastard. We could remake *High Times in Manhattan,* and star you in it as a – what did you call it, Carol? As a tribute!"

Alvee gritted his perfect teeth. "You've got to be kidding."

"Of course I am, my darling." He patted Alvee on the shoulder and his seething anger seemed to dissipate somewhat. "I have a surprise for both of you. You said that if I came up with a part for Steve Shea, he might come back from New York? I'll do you one better. Not unlike our frightfully long-memoried biographer here . . ." Maury shook his head, rolled his eyes. "Alvee's right, Carolyn. What were you thinking?"

I glanced down at the table in shame.

Satisfied with my contrition, he continued. "Steve's got his own idea to pitch. We're meeting with him tomorrow, as a matter of fact."

When Alvee remained silent – he was calmer, but he was still pissed – Maury said to me, "You're welcome to sit in on that, of course. I know he'll be thrilled to see you. Whatever this treatment he's got – maybe you can help with the dialogue. I thought his material for *Editor* was usually dead-on, in the mainstream, commercial sense. Timely, ripped from the headlines, and all that television claptrap. But he's taking a stab at *cinema,* this time, and arty he's not. His dialogue is atrocious."

The Way We Were

Steve Shea hugged me, held me at arm's length. I was warmed by his smile as I'd always been. He once again reminded me that all he had become, all his success, had been as a result of my giving him his first big break in *She's A Peach.*

"You might forget that, but I never will. I consider you my best friend."

I was speechless, but not at his gratitude, not as his declaration of fellowship. I'd always considered us friends, too. It was his appearance that shocked me, that left me dumbstruck.

When *Letters to the Editor's* ratings started to nosedive, I imagined that Steve had just let it *go gentle into that good night;* he did not *rage against the dying of the light. Editor* hadn't been *All The President's Men* after all, and three seasons was pretty damn good for a first effort. He'd had to just let it die, so maybe that was the reason that he was worn, tired, a little baggy around the eyes. Maybe that was why he'd put on a little weight, and why it didn't look good on him.

Steve had been out of the spotlight for some time, and perhaps he'd been tending other irons in other fires whilst *Editor* soldiered on to its inevitable conclusion. He'd allowed his actor's sharpness to dull, maybe even to rust somewhat.

"The audience is fickle," Maury said in greeting. It was the sum total of his commentary on Steve's series. In his estimation, there was no use in attempting to dissect the dead horse to try to figure out what had killed it.

"The audience loves Alvee Smith-Killem," Steve countered, slapping his friend on the back. "The ratings were good before, great when he was there . . . Then when he left, he took my show with him."

There was a split-second of bottomless disbelief in Steve's eyes as he stated this truth: his show had bombed after Alvee quit it. I caught the shade of self-doubt; maybe *Letters to the Editor* had never been that good. Maybe it wouldn't't've even made it three seasons, if Alvee's famous face hadn't saved it halfway through the second one.

But there was also a certain stubbornness in Steve's expression: his show *had* been good; different, fresh. Why had it only grabbed spectacular ratings when Alvee guest-starred? Steve could never know why – the audience is fickle – and I thought that the incomprehensibility of it ate at him.

Then he shook his head and offered us that ol' nice-guy, friendly smile.

"Let me tell you about my idea."

Steve's smile was still friendly – we were his friends, were we not, me especially? But I noticed a steelier quality now, engendered no doubt by the fact that he'd always known just how things work in Hollywood. He'd had a string of successful movies, then had helmed his own television series. That had been a partial success, but it, too, had faded, as every little bit of entertainment eventually does.

Steve was back in *What have you done lately?* Cali-for-ni-a, and he knew that professionals such as Maury and Alvee wouldn't be down to collaborate on a new project with him based solely on friendship. There would have to be some profit apparent in it for them; it would have to be a story interesting to the ticket-buying populace.

"There's this politician. He's old school, maybe a little shady around the back rooms, but he's done great and kind things for his constituency. He's not truly a dishonest guy. Then there's his campaign manager. It's his son or his son-in-law – for whatever reason, the politician can't just fire him.

"The campaign manager gets caught with his pants down – or maybe it's drugs or money laundering, or even something more serious. That needs to be developed, depending on how funny or how dramatic we want to make it.

"There's this other guy – I was gonna make him a reporter, but I don't want it to be too much like *Editor.* Maybe he's a friend or a relative – connected somehow to the politician or the campaign manager – or maybe the campaign manager's wife. Anyway, he finds out about the campaign manager's wrongdoing.

"The hook is that he has to decide if exposing the wrongdoing – if whatever this guy did – is serious enough to also bring down the basically honest politician. Whatever he decides – of course the world is left a better place."

I was impressed. Steve certainly had the *Two Minute Drill* nailed.

"You already have the script?" Maury asked.

Steve shook his head, smiled at me. "I thought Carol might want to take a crack at it. I'm kind of off screenwriting right now. I'm on vacation."

"How's your money holding out?" Alvee ignored my shocked look at his shocking question. "I mean – are you back at the Alto Nido again? How much money you've got determines how off of screenwriting you are. It limits the length of your vacation." Now he looked blankly at me. "Don't you think?"

Steve was successful: he'd written, produced, starred in his own TV show. But that was last year. Alvee knew that to people who'd lived only one lifetime, even in show business, money was always a concern. But I didn't think he'd had to spell it out just like that.

To stem the silence, Maury said, "Which is your part?"

Unmistakably, Steve looked down at his unkempt paunchiness, then over at Alvee, as fresh and fine as a summer day, as always. Doubt crossed his features again.

"Ah, I dunno, Maury. I figured Alvee for the crusader, and I've got a guy in mind for the campaign manager. He did a comedy, once."

When Maury looked dubiously at him, Steve's normal edge reasserted itself as much as was possible. "I guess I could do the politician. I imagined him as a little older, but . . . I guess I could do it. I guess I could help Carol write it, too." He winked at me.

"Nothing's more fluid than an unwritten script. It's time for your comeback, regardless. Forget about all this television . . . nothingness." That auteur's careless wave of dismissal. "We'll do it mostly funny. Alvee can supply the gravity with the authority figure. Who did you have in mind for the campaign manager?"

"For comic relief, I suggest . . . Michael McCown."

Maury grinned acidly. "Is he still alive?"

Steve's friendly smile also curdled into the picture of schadenfreude. "Barely. I hear he's been considering doing porn."

"What?" Alvee exclaimed. "He hasn't said anything about –"

"I'm just kidding," Steve admitted.

We all looked curiously at Alvee. None of us would've imagined that he was still in contact with forgotten Michael McCown.

Steve said, "I don't actually know what he's doing. Something overseas, last I heard."

"I haven't heard anything. *Mikey, we hardly knew ye.* That's why I asked if he'd died." This snarkyness delivered, Maury fell silent. He waited.

He didn't have to ask why Steve would want to cast someone he'd never liked in his new movie. It was inherent in those three words: *in his movie.* What better way to pay tribute at the familiar Hollywood altar of *What goes around comes around?* How magnanimous would it be for the former unknown to offer the lapsed action star a role?

Mike was still young, still bankable, Steve figured, if he was given another break, a good part. But as their positions in the biz had reversed, nice-guy Steve wasn't above shoving a little humiliation, humble-pie-stylie, down the throat of the no-longer-big-name that had once ignored him. A lesson in *Be nice to who you meet on the way up, 'cause you're gonna see 'em again on the way down.*

"I like how you think," was the director's only comment.

Another awkward silence; then Alvee asked, "You said there's a girl in this? The campaign manager's wife? Who do you think for that? Do you still talk to –"

"No. Yeah. Sometimes." Steve shook his head. "Mina married a producer."

I'd wondered why she'd faded from the scene. She'd only made one picture since *She's A Peach*. It had done well, I recalled.

"They're splitting up." Maury knew everything. "Perhaps she's looking to get back on the horse again, too."

"A reunion," Alvee said uncertainly.

"Indeed!" Maury was enthusiastic. He made movies for fun. "What kind of time frame do you television types need to turn out a script?"

He looked expectantly at Steve, then at me. Now I was suddenly a *television type?* How ridiculous was that?

"I was living in an apartment house above Franklin and Ivar. Things were tough at the moment. I hadn't worked in a studio for a long time. So I sat there, grinding out original stories, two a week."

"A month should do it then?" Maury asked, ignoring Steve's quotation. He'd never cared for *Sunset Boulevard*.

Steve smiled at me. It was great to have a friend, another Hollywood colleague with whom to work – one with whom I shared neither a bed and a raft of supernatural secrets, nor a childish awe at his filmmaking genius. I was so glad he was there; I was already excited about the movie we would write.

Steve had seemed a little down, and he certainly looked *quite a bit* down. But one conversation with Maurice Claremount had pepped him right back up.

Maury knew how to talk to actors. He'd convinced Steve that he'd be right for the part he'd thought up, talked him into casting an old flame for the female lead. He had my dubious services to help write the screenplay.

I believed that with a little bit of sleep, a shave, and maybe a few healthy meals, Steve Shea would be ready for his next close-up. He was home, after all, back with his friends. It was gonna be like old times.

She Don't Lie

We'd been working on the script for a few days and had a lot of nothing. Steve was back to not feeling being in front of the camera; he was having a hard time seeing himself as the politician, especially as he was not that much older than Mike McCown.

And what was Mike's character's crime? How was it funny or serious?

We had our laptops set out on the dining room table, across from each other, like duelists. Maury stopped in to check on our progress.

"Cast it, my children," he said, like an evil head master, "and the characterization will come to you, followed by the plot. Think of actors in other roles, and how they could similarly do these parts. Our darling Alvee can borrow some of his rich man's airs from *Editor;* throw in a portion of his charm from *She's A Peach;* perhaps a measure of his anger from *Kinship* . . . See what I mean?"

Steve frowned. "Or maybe we could just use some chemical inspiration."

Before I was quite aware of what he was doing, my friend began cutting up a generous pile of cocaine on a small mirror that he'd removed from his pocket.

I was not so green as to have never seen the stuff before. I'd been to enough Hollywood parties, and yep, it's true what they've always said: Tinseltown runs on any and all the drugs you can imagine. And I'd even tried it once, but not here in Hollywood. My lost friend Ruthanne had obtained some for a little celebration when we'd been hired on as legal secretaries.

I hadn't been impressed with the drug's effects; I hadn't felt much different from my normal, charming self.

I volunteered this information to Steve and Maury, proclaimed that in my one experience, cocaine was overrated. Neither looked at me; Steve was preparing and Maury was watching him. At last the director murmured, "Then whatever you had must not've been any good."

This was a distinct possibility, and I had no response. It wasn't that I was shocked that Steve was preparing drugs, right there upon Jessika Yerdlay's antique dining room table in front of God and everybody. I wasn't even shocked that illustrious director Maurice Claremount was following this unexpected development with interest. I was just surprised, that's all.

"We are such stuff as dreams are made on," Maury said, when Steve handed him a rolled-up twenty. *"And our little life is rounded with a sleep."* He grinned wickedly at me, and snorted up one of the thicker railers presented. "Or not."

He offered me the bill and before that look of disappointment could cross his face, I took it from him. I immediately caved to peer pressure, if I was so bold as to consider myself Maurice Claremount's peer. The so-far-unproductive screenwriting attempt was suddenly a party. Why the hell not?

"Have you ever thought about doing Shakespeare, Maury? On the screen?" Steve asked, swiping at his nose.

The director sighed. "There's no money in it." Then he smiled again. "Although Alvee aspires to play Richard III."

"He's too pretty for that."

Steve's brown eyes were expressionless, yet I marveled at his tone. He sounded like the ugly, smart girl who worked hard and was resentful of the easy breaks awarded to the attractive, dumb girls. I saw a flash of stubbornness – none of that should matter: beauty lasts for a season, but smart lasts a lifetime – then his eyes dulled over again. Alvee Smith-Killem remained pretty and lucky, and what had Steve's smarts and hard-working, writer-producer-star savvy gotten him lately? A cancelled television series, that's what.

"My thoughts, exactly," Maury agreed, again taking the proffered twenty.

I heard a footstep in the hall, was thankful that it was Kimura's day off. *"Something wicked this way comes,"* I warned.

Maury looked up and smiled mildly at his muse. *"Open, locks, whoever knocks!"*

Alvee observed the mirror and the powder. He didn't ask, *What is't you do?* as it certainly wasn't *a deed without a name.*

After a second, he smiled. "Ah! I see we're screenwriting!"

Maury giggled. Alvee declined a toot; he wasn't a screenwriter. He invited us to take a swim with him – if we weren't too *busy* – and when Steve declined, he departed.

"Try casting it, my darlings," Maury again advised, then went to join Alvee poolside.

"There's nothing as fluid as an unwritten script. *The last one I wrote was about Okies in the Dust Bowl. You'd never know because when it reached the screen, the whole thing played on a torpedo boat."* Steve grinned at me, a little drug-shine in his eye. "Who do we know that's available? *Cast it, my darling."*

So cast it we did. And change it. The kinda-good-guy American politician morphed into some kind of foreign diplomat – more mysterious, more ominous, that way. The only foreign talent I knew personally was Armand Hambrick.

"Who?"

"He played Henry Wotton. In *Dorian and Henry."*

"The Brit. Okay." So now the shady character was an English diplomat, and Michael McCown, his attaché, his –

"Son? Younger brother?"

"Son," I said, thinking that if Armand's dissipation had continued at its rapid pace, he probably looked old enough to play slick Mikey's daddy these days. "I doubt if Mike can do an accent, so . . . he was raised in the States. Because of that, he's a little distant from Dad."

"The conflict – something to do with . . ." Steve snapped his fingers. "A high-priced call-girl. She's playing both of them – but still, Dad's a good guy. He's a widower. He finds out about her and his son, catches them together. She gets hurt somehow – maybe she just falls down the steps or something, but it looks suspicious . . . Dad and son call an ambulance and do a fade . . .

"Alvee . . . Alvee's her brother! He comes to see her – she's in a coma – and he starts poking around, gets the diplomat's cell number from the ambulance company . . .

"A crime has been committed – this guy hurt his sister! He goes to the cops, but the diplomat's got immunity, so the cops won't even investigate. Just because he called the ambulance, doesn't mean he hurt her . . . She's just some whore, anyway.

"But Alvee's gonna make this foreigner pay. He visits the diplomat's office – of course, the guy's not there, he's at the UN or something. The son, the attaché, meets with him instead. He lets it slip somehow – 'How is she?' – so Alvee knows he's connected with it, too."

"That sounds good." Now it was the diplomat's crime and not the son's. It was different. Still a little more television than movie, but not bad.

"Now all we gotta do is write it." Steve sighed. "I need a drink. What about you?"

I glanced across the dining room at the grandfather clock. When I'd visited this house as an aspiring biographer, I'd been impressed with the gleaming, intricately carved wood, the precision of its old workings. I'd figured that it must've cost much more than a few months' salary, then. Now it was just a timepiece, passé, another part of the palace in which I lived. Something Kimura or one of the maids dusted.

The black hands declared that it was 12:03. A little early for a drink, but the sun was at least three minutes over the yard arm, was it not? The moment had already become a party, and now we'd hit on a fresh plot. Why not celebrate some more, even if the cursors still blinked on blank screens?

I nodded, and Steve crossed the room. My one-time secretary's mind was in a cataloguing mood today – perhaps it was from the coke. I'd remembered the worth of Jessika's tall clock, and as I watched Steve study the inviting array of liquors, I reckoned the cost of the decanters. I again admired the mellow glow of the inlaid ornamentation on the credenza, the rosewood and mahogany and walnut. Worth about half of what I'd paid for my car, it was one of my favorite pieces.

My fictional lawyer, Jackson Mauer, suddenly spoke in my mind: *Of course, none of this opulence belongs to you, Carolyn. From a legal standpoint, you remain just a guest here. If you had to go, you'd go with the shirt on your back, and maybe some residuals from having your name on a couple of Maury's movies. Since I'm just a character you made up in your head, I wouldn't be able to represent you in court if you decided to file a palimony suit.*

Why was I thinking about palimony? Like anything could ever come between Alvee and me. *As if.* It had to be the drug. It was true that my lover had been uncharacteristically cold to me since Steve and I had started working on this project. Well, maybe not exactly cold, but certainly cool, quiet, introspective. Maybe he was anticipating playing the part we were (mostly not as yet) writing for him. But it was more likely that he was still pissed about my outrageous suggestion of tossing his singular life onto the big screen, adapting it into something as public as an only slightly fictionalized true Hollywood story. And one that proposed a murderous, self-serving angle, at that.

Seriously, what had I been thinking? It was no wonder that my high-quality-this-time, coked-up mind was calling forth fictional lawyers and having them talk about palimony.

Whilst Steve clucked appreciatively over the liquor selection, Dolores Adamson again swam into my drug-busy thoughts. The part in my infuriating screenplay about Jessika's accusations that the absent Franck had molested Lori as a child – that had really happened. The outraged starlet had called a press conference on the steps of LA's City Hall and made her horrible proclamation to the world.

LM Foster

But it was all bullshit. Lori had indeed loved her mother's stunning boyfriend when she was a teenager, but it had all been in her imagination. She'd recorded her yearnings in those staples of a lonely young girl's life: two red-bound, gold-embossed diaries.

Franck had already deserted Jessika by the time she discovered Lori's virginal ramblings; he'd already absconded to Japan with Bobby. The confrontation between mother and daughter was brutal – *he's got the bluest eyes* was the most innocent of the girl's scribblings of adoration for her mother's boyfriend.

After reading these fantasies, Jessika viciousness erupted: *"Do you know why he left? He left because of you! He left because you're a dirty, stinking whore! He went all the way to the other side of the world to get away from you! How disgusted he must've been!*

"I'm gonna tell the whole world what a stinking tramp you are. And when Franck comes back, I'm gonna send you away. I'll see to it that you never set eyes on him again!"

Jessika screamed all these recriminations while kicking and punching her teenaged daughter, while pushing her and slamming her to the ground. She'd left Lori bleeding on the floor of her bedroom.

And it was all for nothing. Franck knew that Lori was fond of him, but perhaps he didn't know the extent of her infatuation; unlike her nosy mother, he'd never read the girl's diaries. He never even knew of their existence. I only knew because she'd given them to me, as background for Franck's biography, as explanation for why her mother had accused him of molestation. In addition to her lengthy and repetitive worship of Franck, Lori had also recorded her mother's insane rage in the second volume.

But Franck had never touched underage Lori. She'd only longed for him to do so, with the purple prose of adolescence. With all her heart.

What occurred years later was much more outré than anything my tame writer's imagination could've dreamt up. It

162

was more akin to the *subtle, yet controversial eroticism* of a film by Robert Ecksmith. To say that I was shocked when I learned of it would be quite the understatement.

In the *Byzantine* meanderings that only prove that truth is oft-times much stranger than fiction, in the fullness of time (as the poets say), Franck and Lori *did* become lovers. When she turned twenty-five and came into the money that she'd inherited from him, Franck summoned her (in secret) to Japan.

Only eighteen years separated Lori and Franck in age, and while such a span was a mightily insurmountable gap when she was fourteen and he thirty-two, now that she was twenty-five . . . Hell, he'd been fifty-two when Ruthanne was *born,* eighty when she'd met him, and that hadn't stopped my friend from falling into bed with him. When one was in love with Franck O'Day, age was just a number, something to be summarily ignored. His charm made one forget completely about the regular customs associated with Father Time.

And Lori had loved Franck more completely in her imagination than Ruthie had, for some eleven lonely years, since she was a mere teenager. Franck was just an attractive actor on the screen to Ruthanne, but Lori had once lived in the same house with him, conversed with him, *watched him,* wrote her secret sonnets to his blue-eyed beauty. She had weathered the tragedy of the plane crash that claimed his life, the event that had devastated her mother.

But not unlike Ruthanne, Lori had never really believed he was dead. What would she have had to live for, if Franck was dead?

Then Franck revealed the wonderful truth to her and her alone – he was alive, and living in Japan. Through the firm of Marish, King, and Ayers, he sent her a round-trip plane ticket.

A child no more, Lori had never been a shrinking violet. (I knew this from reading her diaries). When she beheld Franck again after so many years, the object of so many fevered fantasies . . . At her insistent instigation, one thing just led to another.

By the time Ruthanne and I met Lori, however, neither one of us would've ever guessed that there had once been something between the former matinee idol and his almost-stepdaughter. Never in a million years would the thought have even crossed our minds. As Maury would later tell me, Franck had *put their sordid little congress to the sword* years before Ruthanne and I met them. To us, they seemed to be nothing more than normal, bickering housemates.

That they had actually once been lovers was part of the bombshell that I'd uncovered, only a few hours before the fan club meeting at the VFW Hall. The saga of Lori's unrequited adolescent yearnings (as related in her diaries), plus a few *curious inconsistencies* in an internet search, had led me to the truth of who they really were to each other.

Furious that this incredible . . . *thing* had been kept from not only myself but Ruthanne as well, I confronted Franck about it. He was not ashamed; he was not even overly concerned. My outrage amused him. What had once transpired between him and Lori was of no consequence; it had been over for years. He blithely bid me go up to Lori's room and ask her all about it, if I so desired.

Before I had a chance to reply, Franck removed his cell phone from the breast pocket of his immaculately tailored suit. He pushed a button, waited. Then he said, "Carol would like to have a word with you. She knows, Lori. She wants to hear everything. It's time for your close-up, dear. Your long-awaited moment in the spotlight. Be sure to make it good." Franck listened, then disconnected. "She'll meet you upstairs in ten minutes."

Dolores Adamson told me the entire story in excruciating detail.

Her bitterness was a palpable thing; seeing it in her eyes, hearing in coruscate through her soft, wavery words, shocked me. Her narrative made it painfully clear that she'd never gotten over the fact that Franck had ended the affair, even though years had passed. She was consumed with resentment that he no longer returned her love, if he ever had. She was jealous of my friend's fresh, young presence in his life.

Lori's tale was compelling, if for no other reason than that it was so entirely unexpected. Who woulda thunk it? Jessika Yerdlay's irrational, baseless accusations about Franck and her daughter had come to pass in the end. But it was also uncomfortable to listen to Lori's confession – like the wicked queen's poisoned apple, her tale was laced with hateful acrimony. Some of the things she said about Franck were obviously just the venom of an old woman, jilted, cast aside. I yearned to escape from her sad gray eyes, and at last I was free.

Still reeling from this undreamt-of true Hollywood story, I again found Franck in the hotel's bar. It was then that he delivered his devastatingly effective warning that Ruthie should most assuredly not hear about it from me first. He then promised that he would tell his young girlfriend everything, immediately after the show. But Ruthanne didn't live long enough to learn the truth of Franck's former relationship with his almost-stepdaughter, because she and Lori were both lost in the fire.

I'm not sure if Ruthie would've believed it, anyway. Or, she would've dismissed it as merely an episode from the past, certainly of no consequence to the love she and Franck shared then. He might've been eighty, but he looked forty, and Lori – when we all traveled to Las Vegas for our meeting with destiny, Lori was in her sixties, and she looked every second of it.

Ruthanne believed that Franck loved her; she'd told me breathlessly that he made her feel as if she was the only woman in the world. She would've figured (as Lori herself had told me) that Franck couldn't possibly have any interest in a shriveled up, little old lady anymore, regardless of the passion – on her part, at least – that had once existed between them. Ruthie was young and beautiful; she wouldn't have been jealous in the least of one of Franck's old flames, even if they did live in the same house together.

"How does bourbon sound?" Steve asked me.

"Great."

My mind snapped back to the present. I was sure that Alvee was just about over being mad at me. No need to dwell on others that had once loved him, no matter how completely it had been. Ruthie was gone, Lori was gone. He had perhaps loved my best friend during their short time together, and he had been fond of Lori, at least fond enough to grant her the opportunity to love him, something that she'd dreamt of since she was a teenager. If he'd never felt the same passion toward Lori, if he'd not quite returned Ruthie's abject adoration . . . What difference did any of it make to me?

Why was I even thinking about it? His past entanglements were in the past. I doubted if they ever crossed his mind, so why should I waste my time thinking about them? Alvee was mine, even if he was put out with me at the moment. What we had together was incandescent, transcendental; we were halves to a whole. We shared *that damn near superhuman melding of love and respect and understanding between two people,* and because we did, we kept each other young. Everyone had tiffs; this was our first. Everything would soon be as it had been.

Steve and I drank and snorted coke and had an uproariously good time for the rest of the afternoon. And as we were *screenwriters* (Steve more than me, perhaps), we had the outline for the damn thing done when Alvee came in an announced that it was almost time for the fire show.

He was famous, and didn't feel like going out for dinner this evening, suffering the paparazzi, especially not with two drunken, coked-to-the-gills writers in tow. Since it was Kimura's night off, Alvee had summoned his preferred troupe of Polynesian musicians and cooks and hula dancers. The script for this yet-untitled Oscar-contender was well on its way; Alvee's chef was living his own life. Why not have a luau? It was one of his favorite things.

****

After another fortnight of drink and drugs, of many hours and hard work, Steve and I had the screenplay polished and ready to present to the director.

We called it *Diplomatic Opportunity.*

In our tale, it turns out that the call-girl *did* just fall down the stairs. It was an accident, there was nothing intentional to it on the diplomat's part, even though he was mighty angry and jealous to discover that his beloved rented woman was also seeing his son. The son, it turns out, doesn't care that she's been doing Daddy; he truly loves her. He can't stay away, and when he sneaks back to the hospital to see how she's doing after she comes out of the coma, her brother catches him.

There is a tense scene where the brother threatens to expose the son and his father to the scandal involved in the both of them seeing a woman of his sister's profession. He's convinced that they've hurt her, and he figures maybe it will make her quit her dangerous lifestyle – maybe if Mom and Dad, back in Kansas, see her on the news, her name dragged through the mud . . . It's cruel, but he doesn't want her to suffer any more "accidents."

But the son says he's willing to withstand the media firestorm. He says he'll stand beside her, no matter what her brother tries to tell the press, because he's just realized he loves her. He knows that his father would never intentionally hurt the girl, and she knows it, too. It really was just an accident, a turned heel on a dark staircase.

The call-girl sees that being loved is more important than money, better than having powerful men such as the diplomat and his son requesting (and paying handsomely for) her services.

When the older man at last shows up to see how she's recovering, she has a heartfelt chat with him. She tells him that he was always her favorite, but it's his son that she truly loves. After this conversation, she even starts to believe it herself.

The diplomat graciously accepts reality, and the call-girl and her loving man decide to move back to Kansas and start a wholesome life together. Dad'll miss them both, but he knows it's for the best.

He realizes just how close his appetites brought him to career-ending scandal. He offers the call-girl's brother a job as his new attaché: "I could use an honest man like you, looking out for my interests. Saving me from myself."

His sister returned home, he takes the job. Although there is pathos – both the diplomat and her brother are going to miss the girl – everyone has come out of the whole movie a better person. As the diplomat and the brother walk out of the hospital together, perhaps Coldplay's old song, *Viva La Vida* could play as the credits rolled, if they didn't want an arm and a leg to use it. *I used to r-u-u-u-le the world . . .*

Fade. To. Black.

I chewed my nails fitfully whilst Maury and Alvee read the script. Even though it wasn't quite noon yet, I asked Kimura to make me a drink. I sat by the pool and watched Steve walk ceaselessly around it, nursing his own drink. He already had a head start on me.

Finally, from the table on the terrace, Maury caught my eye. He nodded once, imperiously, the signal for the hired scribblers to come up and face the music of his opinion.

Would it be the jingling of delight, or a dirge of distaste? Or worse, would it be laughter, mocking, followed by the three most despised words in the English language?

Steve flopped down into a chair; he refused to stand beside the table as if he was being schooled. I, on the other hand, was too anxious to sit. This was the first screenplay on which I'd worked without Maury's guiding hand; his opinion of it meant far more to me than it did to Steve. The actor's vacation from the craft had been brief; he hadn't been rusty at all. He was confident in what we'd written.

Alvee was Steve's friend, and he respected him as a more successful actor, but he'd only ever starred, never written and produced, too. Alvee was more famous, true, but his fame was only the result of being in the business longer; it was only the whim of the fickle, ticket-buying populace. Like Maury, Steve wore more than one hat; one actor's opinion of our script mattered little to him.

But Alvee was the man I loved, and my first effort with him in mind as star had infuriated him. He did not, I'd discovered to my complete surprise, have any desire to portray himself, neither *the promise of his greener days,* nor *these he mastered now.* He wanted the unique secret of his life to stay exactly that, and had been appalled that I'd cobbled together a fairly accurate depiction of it (with some artistic license, of course). He'd been aghast that I'd been prepared to show it to the world. No. No *true Hollywood stories* for Alvee. For the love of God, no.

He preferred to headline in a good fiction, with the lights, camera, and action directed by his brilliant old friend. But what did he think of the story that his new friend and his woman and a sinful amount of cocaine had dreamt up? He was still reading the last couple of pages, and didn't look at me.

Maury silently waited for Alvee to finish. When I didn't sit, he commanded me to do so, and his tone made me jump. At last Alvee tossed the script onto the table, and glanced at his director.

The irresistible lips that could smile with so much import were straight, expressionless; his silky voice, silent. Alvee raised his black eyebrows, only a fraction, and the gesture said nothing whatsoever to Steve, nor to me. And I thought I knew him so well.

But Maury had known Alvee almost longer than Steve and I had been alive, combined. He communicated his opinion of *Diplomatic Opportunity* to his director (in its entirety) with one simple glance. Maury understood perfectly, whilst neither Steve nor I had a clue as to whether Alvee liked it or loathed it.

Another heartbeat of silence passed, then Maury said, "It's good. I particularly liked Vaughn's attitude about his sister's lifestyle. He doesn't judge her. She's grown, and if she doesn't care about society's pronouncements on what she does to earn a living, why should he? He only gets angry about it when Sandra suffers the injury – he's convinced one of her clients caused it. It shows him as a multi-faceted individual, that he can then embrace hypocrisy and threaten to expose her to parental shame. He doesn't care, but Mom and Dad will. That's how real people behave, taking whatever stance will serve them best in a particular situation. It's good."

But it wasn't *great* or *spectacular* or *fantastic*. Steve and I turned to Alvee, as if we were watching a tennis match. He didn't look at us, replied instead to Maury. "You're the director."

Then Alvee smiled at Steve and he smiled back. Both of them were *chancers*. Steve would do comedy or drama or television, and while Alvee might aspire to portray a Shakespearean villain – *to seem a saint, when most he played the devil* – he was perfectly willing to act in anything that Maury deemed satisfactory, even it was something made up by his amateur-screenwriter girlfriend and his buddy, who just might've spent too much time getting friendly with drink and drugs on the East Coast. It was all the same to Alvee.

But . . .

While Steve was content with the director's avowal that our screenplay was *good,* as well as with Alvee's going along with whatever Maury chose for him, *I* wanted more from my men, my *colleagues*. I wanted Maury to say *Diplomatic Opportunity* was stellar; I wanted to hear Alvee say that he *couldn't wait* to play the part I'd written especially for him.

But in the end, I accepted my esteemed director's praise, faint though I found it to be, as well as Alvee's deferral to Maury's judgment. Maurice Claremount was going to again make a movie out a story I'd helped to write, and my blue-eyed beloved was going to star in it. What more could a nobody from Riverside ask for than that?

"So, of whom, besides Alvee, shall the critics rave?" Maury inquired with bright gusto. When his screenwriters hesitated, he glanced expectantly from one to the other. "You have Michael McCown for bumbling ineptitude and later, for soulful expressions of love. You have Alvee for gravitas –"

"It's really Alvee's picture," I piped up. "His character expresses the most range."

Maury exchanged a glance with his leading man, then offered me that embarrassed-at-my-latest-faux-pas shake of the head. "Really, Carol?"

"It's always my picture."

"Ain't that the truth," Steve agreed, not at all surprised at Alvee's ego.

Maury smiled. Sometimes, I thought it was Alvee's ego that the filmmaker liked best about his muse. It was as big as all outdoors, and certainly not unwarranted. A million women in a million theaters had once fallen in love with Franck O'Day, and their granddaughters (and some of their grandsons) had done the same with Alvee Smith-Killem. The energy from their heartfelt cards and letters and emails, and that reflected back to him from the crowds crammed behind the velvet rope at premieres – it helped to keep him young.

His director had once said of him, "Alvee's not for sale – although he can be rented for between ninety and a hundred and twenty minutes at a time in large, dark rooms where lots of people sit in rows."

Alvee was Adonis, as I'd often thought before, gathering love from all those worshippers in the dark. My own ego smirked. *But it's me alone that's his Aphrodite. Only I get to have him.*

Maury was saying, "Since you've cast the lead, and the comic relief . . . Do you think Mina's *range* will cover a call-girl, Carol?"

"I think she'll do it if Steve asks her."

Steve shrugged. "Maybe."

Love Means Never Having to Say You're Sorry

During our coke-fueled, mostly drunken days working on the *good* script for *Diplomatic Opportunity,* Steve had regaled me with the story of the ups and downs of his association with Mina Reed.

At first, when *She's A Peach* had been in production, he claimed that he'd been immune to her, laissez faire in his attitude about their potential as a couple. Mina was ambitious, and thinking that a little play with the action star might further her career, she had not hesitated to come whenever Michael McCown called. Steve had not slighted her for that; he was ambitious himself. His own nights on the town with her had gotten his name where it needed to be, had they not?

I remembered also seeing Mina's name linked with Mike's *after She's A Peach,* however. I wasn't going to bring it up, but Steve did.

"Then there was the follow-up to *Unparalleled. Michael McCown is Unequalled!* Did you see it?"

"I saw the billboards."

"Yeah, it was big among action fans, I guess. Again, not too much dialogue. Since he was hot and making money, Mina was there with him. But she still called me, still talked to me, when he wasn't around."

A flash of bitterness, a slammed drink and a quick refill.

"But I didn't see her. She was all caught up in Mikey's fame – she told me she was going to star with him in his next one. *Unrivalled* or *Unexpected,* or something equally as banal."

I searched my somewhat fractured, under-the-influence memory. No more sexy billboards featuring Mr. McClown's sultry sneer came to mind.

"Was there another one?"

Now Steve grinned gleefully over the rim of his glass, shook his head. "Mikey got all uppity after *Unequalled.* Thought he could handle his own career, make his own decisions. So he fired his agent."

"It was probably on Alvee's advice."

Steve squinted, shook his head again. "His agent was Ronny Prince. *The King of Hollywood.*"

"I thought Maury was the King of Hollywood."

Steve giggled at my little poke at our director. Maury had had a couple of big-money, commercial successes with *Cheyenne Sundown* and *She's a Peach,* but the ticket-buying populace had mostly shunned *Kinship* and *Dorian and Henry.* He just didn't make enough movies; two hits and two critically-acclaimed-but-otherwise-flops did not a king make.

"In a different fiefdom, perhaps," Steve allowed. "But Ronny Prince, he's a king, definitely. He represented Mina – maybe he still does. And Mikey. Made 'em both famous. Did you see *A Random House Is Not a Home?* Mitch Barlo was nominated for an Oscar for that. Ronny Prince is his agent, too.

"But Mikey got it into his empty little head that he could do better. And what has he done since? Nothing. It was the dumbest move ever. My own agent – he laughed and laughed when he heard." Steve shook his head again. "I don't think Alvee would've advised Mikey to quit Ronny Prince."

I couldn't tell Steve that Alvee didn't know too much about the representation side of the business. In his career, he'd had only a single *theatrical agent:* his Uncle Jesse, and the one *audition* that his by-marriage kin had scored for him – with Patrick Morrison – had resulted in a walk-on part, and an introduction and lifelong connection to Robert Ecksmith.

Bobby had directed Franck O'Day in only one forgotten, universally panned dog, but the Englishman's friendship had been invaluable to the young actor's early career, nonetheless:

it had been none other than Bobby who had convinced Donald Sunnerfeld to star Franck in *High Times in Manhattan.* Academy award-nominated Bobby and critically-acclaimed Donald were peers; like at the grown-up's table at Thanksgiving, Franck never would've got anywhere near Donald Sunnerfeld if Bobby hadn't talked his colleague into offering him a seat.

After the role of Perry Calibri, the luminous Mr. O'Day's name had become a household word, without his ever knowing the influential services of a Ronny Prince.

Next had come Sunnerfeld's never completed *Two Green Keys,* and the plane crash, and decades of anonymity for Bobby and Franck in Japan. Then Maury and Alvee had emerged, started making movies together, hits and misses – Alvee had never needed an agent. So it was not outside the realm of possibility that he'd inadvertently given Michael McCown bad advice.

My fellow screenwriter continued with his *Two Minute Drill* of *The Steve and Mina Show.*

"So Mikey's out of the picture, overseas. Mina did *Up And At 'Em* – it was billed as *A Wall Street Farce.* They did some location shoots in New York. It was during the first season of *Editor.*" Steve smiled in fond remembrance. "She stayed at my apartment with me. It was great."

His smile fled. "When it was time for her to go back to California, I discovered that I didn't want her to go. New York's different, Carol. Show business – it's just a small part of the bigger and much more varied business that is New York. You can forget who you are, what you do, sometimes. At night, when we both finished shooting . . . We were just people, together. If we didn't hit the nightspots, which we didn't – nobody followed us with cameras. We were just *us.*

"I told her that I was in love with her, while we were in New York. But she had to go back to finish the movie, and I was in the middle of the first season of *Editor.* We lost touch for a week or so, missed calls, hours between texts. Work was paramount.

174

"Next thing I know, she tells me she's getting married. It all happened so quickly. There wasn't even a big ceremony. If there had been – I don't know if I would've flown all the way across the country for it, to get my nose rubbed in the fact she was now with somebody else. Maybe she wouldn't have invited me, anyway.

"I asked her – what we'd had in New York – hadn't that meant anything to her? She played it off with the standard cliché. She'd always love me, but . . . right. It was a whirlwind thing, she said, this producer had just swept her off her feet. That was also a cliché, if I'd ever heard one. She didn't love him either."

Steve frowned. "I sincerely believe it's just business, Carol. This producer – it was her ambition and his money that swept her off her feet." He again swallowed the rest of his drink in one gulp, a theatrical representation of jilted pain. But still, I felt for him.

"We talk on the phone, text. She sends me cute little memes a couple times a week. She says she's not happy with him. She says she misses me. But she hasn't been able to see me since I've been back."

"Maury said she's divorcing him. Have you told her about the part?"

"We haven't written the part yet."

****

But we'd written it now, and *Diplomatic Opportunity* had received the green light from its director (who would also produce – Maury had faith in the picture, and Steve's finances alone (as Alvee had guessed) couldn't quite mount such a large production at the moment. And hell, if it bombed, it wasn't like it was going to put a dent in Title XVII's bottom line). Its lead had also expressed approval (enough).

So now Maury was asking if the originator of the idea wanted to cast Mina Reed in the role of Sandra, our clumsy-on-stairs call-girl. I was sure Steve still loved her, and some romantic part of me thought that now was the time that she

175

could love him back. The whole thing was like a rom-com, its own self. All he had to do was make the call.

"So, we'll pencil Mina in for Sandra. If she's available." Maury penciled nothing. He wasn't even holding a pencil. The next steps involved phone calls, and then contracts, and the director had people at Title XVII to accomplish all those clerical details.

Now Maury pursed his lips, sighed; a ghost of disappointment fogged his enthusiasm. Steve didn't notice, but I would've felt shame had the expression been directed at me.

"Since you've changed your American politician into a foreign diplomat, I'm assuming that means you want to add directing to your resume?"

Steve choked on his drink. "You're the director, Maury. I'm just –"

"Just an actor. Or so I thought."

"I'm a screenwriter right now." Stone-faced, Steve shook his head. "Maybe I'll be an actor next time."

Maury glanced coolly at me, as if it was my fault that Steve didn't feel ready to get in front of a camera again. "Who for this role, then?"

I sat up a little straighter. The casting choice for the diplomat had been mine, after all. "We were thinking that Armand Hambrick would be perfect." When Maury blinked in simple disbelief, I added, "He's got the right amount of Old World decadence. Just enough aristocratic foreignness to make the audience suspect him."

Maury turned to the star. "Like to see Armand again, would you, my darling?"

Alvee rolled his eyes, but only ever so slightly. He didn't communicate contempt so much as extravagant and thorough unconcern. Alvee could not possibly care less if we cast pudgy and ever-so-slightly balding Armand Hambrick opposite him again. *Rubio*, of the flowery love letters: definitely still British, undoubtedly still a sodomite, but not quite so commanding anymore.

Alvee's shrug was positively cinematic: *I care not,* but he said, "Carol's right. Armand's good for the part."

"Indeed?" Maury narrowed his eyes. "Would you like to call him with the offer? I know the two of you still correspond."

"You call him." A whiff of annoyance. "You're the director."

The Cattle Arrive

The first get-together for *Diplomatic Opportunity* was informal, a reunion. Virtual ink was still drying on electronically-signed contracts; the initial production meeting, again on the backlot of Warner Bros., was still a week or so away.

Mina lived in town. She'd accepted Steve's offer of the role of Sandra, and they'd had dinner together the night before. They arrived for the meeting together, and I caught shy smiles, and unnecessary touching of hands and shoulders. From the cute-tentative nature of this, I could tell that they hadn't renewed their former bond on an intimate level after dinner; yet it was just as clear that they were both thinking about it.

Since I was the equivalent of the most satisfied of happily married women, watching for the possible springs of a new-old romance between them delighted me. I'd liked Mina immensely during the shoot for *She's A Peach,* and Steve – well, Steve was my best friend, my pal, my drug-and-drinking buddy, my fellow screenwriter. I wished to see them as a couple, as happily in love as Alvee and me.

Steve looked brighter and more bushy-tailed than I'd seen him since his return to the Golden State. Mina was as cute as ever, but the years had thinned her, given her a more womanly austerity. Gone was the utterly girlish gigglyness that had been her prior persona.

In a private moment before the meeting began, she told me about her husband. They were indeed divorcing, and when I said that I was sorry to hear that, she shook her head resolutely.

"Don't be. He's not who I thought he was. I'm just a commodity to him. He has a stack of scripts – all of the characters are horrible, Carol. A murderess, a junkie, some kind of evil witch. He says I need to do dramas, but they're all just bad, mean women – none of them are redeemed at the end, like Sandra is. I didn't want to play any of them.

"So we fought. I saw that he didn't want me as a wife; he didn't want me at all, if I wouldn't do what he told me. So I called my agent, and he got me in touch with a good lawyer."

The indispensable Ronny Prince. Her agent, but not Mikey's anymore.

Mina smiled. "Don't be sorry about it. It was just a wrong turn in my career. I think I'm getting back on the right road now." She smiled fondly at Steve, across the room, then grinned conspiratorially at me. "But tell me, my friend. How *is* Alvee?"

The tone of her question was not unexpected, because Alvee's charm was irresistible. "Everyone finds him attractive, to one degree or another," Maury had once told me, stating the obvious. "He's stunning. Even militant lesbians from Mars would at least have him as their house boy."

From the moment he'd stepped on-set for the shoot of *Kinship*, his costar, Melissa Holloway, had openly displayed her desire for him, right in front of me. She thought of me as nothing more than the lead's *on-set squeeze;* perhaps Alvee would be down for a little action more befitting his station, if she would just let him know that she was available. What possible difference could it make if she let him know while I was standing right there? Who was I? A nobody, that's who.

It was the same attitude expressed by some of his fans, too. The anonymous interface of email made them bold. *If you're ever in Albuquerque . . .*

There was a tatted-up tough girl that lived in a corner of my mind, and she would speak right up at this appalling disrespect. *He's got a girlfriend, bitch. Didn't you see me with him at the last premiere? Don't you watch Entertainment Tonight?*

179

But Mina appreciated Alvee for his talent. She was a good actress, so if she felt anything more than fellow-trouper camaraderie for him, she kept it hidden. She expressed no yearning for my man, past this winking request to hear how he'd been. I'm sure that she found Alvee attractive, as did everybody, but she never flirted with him, not in the least. She was my friend, and while she might indeed be ambitious, she was no homewrecker.

****

Through his inestimable contacts in the business, Maury had located Michael McCown in Australia, of all godforsaken places. He was no longer unrepresented, however.

"His agent is no Ronny Prince, but he knows how to write a contract."

The director had pointedly avoided looking at Alvee, so I knew that my earlier suspicion was true. It had been Alvee's bad advice that had rocketed Mikey's promising career to oblivion.

Maury said to Steve, "His contract is ironclad, but iron melts at the application of enough heat." He rubbed his fingers together. "Do you still want him for the part?"

Steve shrugged. "I imagine he'd still come cheaper than anyone else."

"Of course. He's working in Australia, for God's sake."

After talking to this canny agent, Maury had then called Michael McCown personally.

It was another unkind joke between director and screenwriter: Mikey wouldn't have believed that the offer was real, had it come from the former nobody whom he'd ignored so utterly when they'd worked together on *She's A Peach.* What goes around had come around, and there was absolutely no reason why no-longer-a-nobody Steve Shea would be interested in helping out someone whose career had hit a brick wall. Steve was entirely sure that Mikey would've thought it was some kind of mean jest if he'd been the one to make the call.

I considered that perhaps drug-euphoria was making young Master Shea overestimate his own importance. Michael McCown had been quite famous once, and since he'd been *overseas,* maybe he'd missed Steve's successes. Maybe he'd still never heard of him.

On the other hand, it was good to see a little show of ego from my self-doubting friend.

Maury made some calls across the pond, and a good chunk of pounds sterling was converted to Australian dollars, most of which went to line the pockets of Mikey's shrewd agent. Released from his contract, before you could say *Qantas,* he was on the next flight home from Down Under. He was expected within the hour.

A leaf had been scared up for the usually intimate dining room table to allow it to seat the cast, director, and screenwriters. Scripts were set up before each place, but Steve and Mina ignored them, chatting happily with Maury. Alvee idly perused his, not contributing to the conversation.

I really didn't have much to say either, so I sat quietly across the table, just looking at him, thinking about how much I loved him. He was beautiful, clever, affectionate; he was a consummate actor. And I was the luckiest woman on God's green earth.

Alvee felt the weight of my stare, the energy I was sending his way. He glanced up from the script, smiled. His returned energy warmed me to the ends of my fingertips. We were back.

Movement in the doorway behind Alvee took my attention from making eyes at him. A stranger, looking quite lost, was standing there.

Seeing an unfamiliar person in my house was startling. One had to buzz at the gate, and then Kimura usually came in and announced all visitors, like a royal herald. I guess Maury and Alvee were a kind a royalty, after all.

I blinked in confusion at this guy, just wandered in on his own. He was chubby, jowly; his sandy hair was wispy, lank, kinda bunched up on one side, as if he'd recently slept on it. He badly needed a shave. His dark eyes were bewildered. I had absolutely no idea who he was.

Alvee turned around to see what I was looking at. "Hiya, Mikey!" he cried heartily and rose.

OMG, now I saw, now I realized. This fat, lost . . . *wreck* was Michael McCown!

I immediately glanced down the table at my confreres. Mina and Steve were as shocked as I was at Mike's state, but Maury seemed not surprised at all.

Mikey was hugging Alvee, as if he was a long-lost brother, miraculously restored. He practically clung to him. Then he seemed to remember himself. "Christ, I'm so glad to see you, Alvee!" Mike hugged him again.

"I'm glad to see you, too, my friend," Alvee said when he was finally released from Mike's embrace. "How's Australia been treating you?"

"How do I look?" Mike said with low bitterness. "That's how it's been treating me. I'm so glad to see you," he repeated, but restrained himself from hugging Alvee again. It wasn't very macho, after all. "No one would talk to me but you, after I fired –"

"Well, you're back where you belong now," Maury said with atypical kindness.

Mikey turned, and I realized that, until the director spoke, the wretched, forgotten actor hadn't noticed anyone in the room except for Alvee. He hadn't made eye contact with me when he'd wandered in; he hadn't been looking for anyone else. Perhaps he thought it was Alvee who'd suggested him for the part.

Next Mike noticed Mina, and a faint, regretful smile touched his no-longer-adorable mouth. She returned it, and like Maury's, it was full of kindness. She rose and hugged him silently, as one would a friend returned, beaten but not broken, from tragic experiences.

Steve wasn't even in the spotlight at the moment, but he still considered himself to be doing better than Mikey, so I expected to see that self-important expression of schadenfreude on his face again. *Oh, how the mighty have fallen.* Instead, I watched a little of the shine go out of his *I got all polished up for Mina and she likes it* confidence.

Mina had only ever associated with Michael McCown out of ambition, or so Steve had always told himself. By choosing Mikey for this role, he'd intended to demonstrate (especially to her) that he was a success, and therefore, he could charitably throw a hungry dog a bone. As a result of some incredibly bad business decisions, Mike had become a has-been, and far too soon, so Steve had reckoned that Mina wouldn't possibly be interested in him now. Steve thought that she'd appreciate his show of pity, and maybe she did, but I didn't get that she pitied Mikey herself.

I knew something about Mina that apparently Steve didn't know: she was a good person. Although her involvement with the action star hadn't furthered her ambition, she didn't hold it against him, especially not now. They had once been *friends,* at the very least, and she was just glad to see him. It occurred to me that the opposite of pleasure derived from another's misfortune was gratitude that you were doing okay.

And perhaps there had been more genuine affection between them than Steve had allowed himself to admit. I thought that it was dawning on my good friend that his undisguised attempt at humiliation might yet turn around and bite him in the ass. I wondered if a triangle was still one of his favorite shapes.

To make matters worse, when Maury said, "You remember our screenwriter, Steve Shea?" I noticed a return of that confused look to Mikey's face. He most assuredly did not remember Steve Shea.

In Hollywood terms, *She's A Peach* had been a geological epoch ago; Mike had been a somebody then. He'd shared top billing with Alvee, and like Alvee, he hadn't had any scenes with the Third Man. Just as I'd speculated earlier – Mikey didn't recognize his benefactor at all, especially since he'd been introduced as screenwriter.

Kimura materialized in the doorway and announced, "Mr. Armand Hambrick."

Unlike Michael McCown, my once upon a time, self-appointed rival for Alvee's affections knew how to make an entrance. He swept grandly into the room, resplendent in a black suit, brilliant white shirt, and pale green tie that played up his eyes. The shine on his shoes was blinding. Gone was the nonchalance of top-knot, white linen and sandals.

(*The Picture of Dorian Gray* and my first ever glimpse of Franck O'Day, live and in person, crossed my mind simultaneously. From my first journal: *Franck wore a flawlessly tailored, slate gray, double breasted suit. He wore it effortlessly, like he dressed this way every day – one got the impression of a very wealthy, very confident executive.* So it was with Armand. He was *working* that black suit.

He was arrayed as befitted a not-unattractive man in his oh, perhaps late-forties. He certainly wasn't eighty, appearing to be an exceptionally well-preserved fifty (as Franck had been), and that's why the infamous painting also occurred to me: the still-haughty Brit wasn't even quite forty yet. As with the picture hidden away in the attic, Armand's excesses were unmistakably evident on his face. Clothes do make the man, and it would've been pathetically undignified for him to still dress like he was thirty, because he'd ceased to look it some time ago.)

But still, as I say, his entrance was grand. He breezed past Alvee, ignoring him (and me) utterly. He embraced Maury as an old friend and colleague – he didn't thank him for the part. The director introduced him to Mike and Steve, and he shook their hands, a polite look of *So nice to meet you, unknown actor and nobody screenwriter* upon his patrician face. He smiled charmingly at Mina, kissed her hand.

His director and his new colleagues greeted, Armand turned and winked at me, as if just then noticing my presence. They say a picture is worth a thousand words, and so it was with Armand's wink.

I'm sure you've heard of my affection for Alvee by this late date, Screenwriter. There's no need to pretend it doesn't exist anymore, especially not to you. I salute your continued presence here – you must be amusing, indeed. But novelty – variety, as they say – is the spice of life, and now that I'm returned . . .

Armand took a step toward Alvee. He was once more before the object of his desire, and having repeatedly confessed it over the years, he paused. Like Mikey, Armand also wished to embrace his former costar, but unlike Mikey, he wanted to communicate so much more than just the relief of interrupted friendship. *Christ, it's good to see you.*

What Armand wanted to communicate had all been on his part. It had never been interrupted because it had never been returned.

Had it? his green eyes asked Alvee.

Alvee smiled, dismissing this most important of unspoken questions. He opened his arms in welcome, nonetheless, and allowed Armand to embrace him.

Armand clung to Alvee, as Mikey had done. He took his face in both hands, and dared to kiss him on the forehead, lingeringly, as if in slow motion. "How I've dreamt of seeing you again!" he whispered.

Alvee smiled faintly, and that was enough for Armand. His return smile was brilliant.

I glanced at Maury, who rolled his eyes. *The hope that burns eternal, is it not tiresome?*

The fact that Maury harbored the same hope, despite his mystical congruence with Maki, was also present in his expression. He had accepted the status quo between himself and his muse, a lifetime ago, however. Sharing friendship eternal with Alvee was more than enough; Maury's hope had ceased to *burn.* Like the sun rising in the west, what would never be, would simply *never be.*

Yet it was plain that Armand had not accepted this unalterable fact, and I thought that if Maury had pity for any of us, it wasn't for me, the hesitant, self-conscious screenwriter;

or Mina, who'd loved neither wisely nor well. It wasn't for Steve Shea, whose past successes were beginning to be overshadowed by his self-doubt and drunken, drugged self-abuse; nor was it even for lost, washed-up, has-been Michael McCown.

Maury was not big on pity – there was no profit in it in this town – but if he felt sorry for anyone, it was for Armand Hambrick, inextricably enmeshed in his desire to worship an idol that simply wasn't having any.

There was a split-second of silence. Mina was patting Mikey's hand; Steve looked longingly at the liquor decanters across the room. Armand still gazed at Alvee with a different kind of longing; Alvee's expression said, *I know you love me, and it's okay, but please don't make a fool of yourself.*

The director clapped his hands. "Now, my children! Since we are all merrily met once more, shall we commence discussion of this new dog and pony show?"

An Awakening, Rudely Delivered

Despite the opulence of Alvee's digs, it only had four bedrooms, plus a guesthouse (located over the garage, a la Billy Wilder's classic) which Kimura occupied. So while they were friends and colleagues, Mina and Steve, Mikey and Armand, all left after dinner. There would be no sleepover, Californication-stylie, as fans like to imagine occurs when the stars congreet.

Alvee was relieved to see them go. He wasn't interested in witnessing any renewed triangles between the screenwriter and the onetime action star and the now-grown ingénue; and he surely didn't want Armand lying in wait and attempting to corner him, should he get up in the middle of the night for a snack.

"Christ, I thought they'd never leave," he said with uncharacteristic annoyance. "Why do you suddenly want to turn our home into an appendage to the studio? Couldn't all this have waited until the production meeting?"

Maury perused the script, elaborately ignoring him. He murmured, "Guilt doesn't become you, my darling."

Alvee's eyebrows rose. "What do I have to be guilty about?"

Still Maury didn't look at him. "The wages of sin have taken their toll on Armand and the cast of *She's A Peach*, except for charming Mina." He smiled at me, still paying zero attention to his muse. "Isn't she still just adorable?"

I nodded, but was more concerned with Alvee's unexpected resentment than Mina's cuteness.

Finally, Maury addressed him. "Yet you remain eternally beautiful, eternally bankable. Always the star."

"And that's just how you like it. Why should I feel guilty about it?"

Maury looked back at the script and idly waved his hand.

Still angry, Alvee mumbled, "It's past my bedtime," and left the room.

The director and I lingered at the dining room table, giving *Diplomatic Opportunity* one last go-over before retiring for the evening. Mostly I just sat there and watched him as he read it over his half-specs; I was tired after the evening's reunion, and Steve had taken all the Pick-Me-Up-Powder with him. Still, I thought I should be on-hand if the man with the plan had any questions. He paused occasionally, jotted things in the margins, and ignored me as if I wasn't even there. Apparently, he had no questions.

To break the silence, I commented, "Mikey sure is a mess, though."

Maury's eyes flickered up, skewered me. *What are you trying to say, Carol?*

Now I felt uncomfortable. Maybe stating the obvious about Michael McCown's appearance was considered gauche. It was all right for Maurice Claremount to talk about *the wages of sin,* but not me. I learned something new every day.

My director was waiting, so I stammered, "I mean, what do you think he's been *doing* there in Australia, to make him look so . . . so . . . worn out?"

"What do *you* think he's been doing?" When I didn't reply, he continued, unsmiling. "Perhaps he's been doing the same thing that you and Steve have been doing. Killing the pain and calling it living it up."

"I don't have any —"

"No. You don't. Yet you've been wallowing at the feel-better trough, right there beside Mr. I-Can't-Get-Over-That-My-Television-Show-Was-Cancelled."

I was a little taken aback, and leapt to defend Steve. "I think he's gotten over it now —"

"Yet his habits remain. That's why they call them *habits.*" Maury threw the script onto the table and tossed his specs on top of it. He sighed. "Steve's feeling sorry for himself, but doing this picture *should* allow him to step back and see that *Editor* wasn't the be-all and end-all of his career. He's pouting – all that claptrap about taking a vacation from screenwriting, not wanting to act – that's because he's not the whole enchilada – writer-producer-star – at the moment. He should be fine if he doesn't allow himself to sink any further. He needs to build a bridge and *get over it,* for God's sake."

Maury paused. "Maybe you should tell him that, Carol. You're his *best friend,* right?"

Never one to beat around the bush, Maury had laid out plainly what I'd purposely overlooked all along. Maybe it was time for me to actually be Steve's friend, instead of his enabling-him-to-feel-sorry-for-himself-drug-buddy.

"And you're being too hard on poor Mikey. Steve's got you and me. He's got his television chums in New York. He may have Mina again, if he doesn't shoot himself in the foot. But Mikey made a grave error in an unforgiving business. He doesn't have a friend in the world, except for Alvee."

This statement surprised me and it must've shown on my face. "You really must converse with your beloved more, Carol. Seriously. You bask in the warmth of his affection, but you don't pay enough attention to what else he does.

"He was Mikey's mentor, remember? And all this time, Alvee's been talking to him, bucking him up, telling him that doing foreign dogs that'll never get out of their country of origin – that's all okay, because Alvee has faith in him. Alvee's his friend. This lifeline from Alvee is probably the only thing that's kept the kid from taking any irreversible steps to oblivion."

Maury paused, then narrowed his eyes speculatively. "What you have to ask yourself, of course, is – what does Alvee get out of it?"

Maki appeared in the doorway, and said something tenderly to Maury. *It's getting late. I miss you.* Or at least that's what I imagined he said. Maury rose; all work was officially concluded for the evening at this gentle summons from his soulmate. As if I was a somewhat dim pupil (but I was trying), he patted me affectionately on the top of my head. He bid me sweet dreams and glided out of the room.

I remained at the table, and did what he'd suggested, as I always did. I asked myself, *What is Alvee getting out of his friendship with Michael McCown?*

The answer came quickly enough, because it was simple. Alvee was getting surcease of guilt, that's what he was getting. He'd given a young, hot star ruinously bad advice. Yet Mikey still looked up to him, still wanted to be his friend. He'd not asked Alvee for any help with his career – we would've heard about it if he had. Evidently, all the kid wanted was a little encouragement, a kind word, from his good-buddy, big brother Alvee. It was the least Alvee could do to accommodate him.

****

In my bedroom was another one of my favorite pieces of furniture: a lavish dressing table with a lighted vanity. Like the exquisitely lovely credenza in the dining room, it had also once belonged to Jessika Yerdlay. I perched on the mauve, velvet-upholstered bench, but didn't sit facing my reflection; instead I considered Alvee. His back against the ornate headboard of my bed, ankles crossed, he was answering his fan mail on his laptop, waiting for me.

I thought again about how much I loved him. He was incomparable: in dress, in manners, in temperament, in activities behind closed doors – all the things that I admired in a man. Surely, he was egotistical, he was secretive; but that was because he possessed an awesome acting ability, as well as supernatural gifts. He had not been so egotistical nor so secretive as to have not shared them with me.

And who was I? Not beautiful, not educated, not a starlet, not really even a screenwriter. Like a million other women, around the world, I was just someone who loved him, and out of all of them, he had chosen me with whom to share his unusual life.

I again thought of my hidden journal, and of the story idea that Maury had so efficiently and irrevocably *put to the sword: it's been done.* I felt ashamed of myself. Alvee possessed secrets, true, but that didn't make him anything like the mass-murdering monster I'd once ridiculously dreamt him to be. Nor was he anything like the manipulative, lying imposter (with an attorney at his right hand), as I'd cast him in my fortunately aborted screenplay.

He was a good man. He had allowed his almost-stepdaughter to love him (physically) in Japan, and later, while he languished in obscurity after his return to the States. He continued to allow Armand to love him (in his heart), although the fact that Armand had decided to let it show was aggravating him a bit. He had befriended a young, stupid actor, and continued to be his pal, even when Mikey's acquaintance could be of no benefit to him. All these were the outward shows of a good man.

Again, he felt my gaze upon him. He put his laptop on the nightstand, got up and sat on the corner of the bed closest to me. He smiled, and his eyes glowed with affection – I remembered Lori's words: *he's got the bluest eyes.* Alvee Smith-Killem was beautiful, and he was never more beautiful than when he smiled at me.

"Are you and his royal highness finished now? You've been so busy . . . I've missed you, Carol." He reached out and took my hand, and as always, I felt warmed to my very core.

"Yeah, it's done, at least as far as I'm concerned. Once it starts in production, Maury won't need me or Steve, unless he wants rewrites. We don't really need to even be on-set . . ."

But Alvee knew all this. He knew I'd want to be there, anyway, just to watch him act.

His smile turned to amusement, and his silence stretched out until I finally said, "What?"

"Ah, Carolyn!" He squeezed my hand. "My erstwhile biographer, my little girl from River City. Maury's made you over in his own image. You've become his minion. You've become the *Spawn of Claremount.*"

It could've been a compliment, but the way he said it wasn't very nice. It was offensive, in fact. Was this going to start another tiff?

"Maury's always said that you'd like me better if I was part of the team."

"I couldn't like you any better." Alvee wasn't picking a fight. He rose, put his arms around me. I was enveloped in his intoxicating scent, the warmth of his energy. *He couldn't like me any better.*

Then he released me abruptly, sighed. "But you could leave off trying to drink the world under the table, ease up a little bit on trying to snort up Peru. How does that song go? *Lines on the mirror, lines on her face?"* Alvee chuckled at his own wit. "I know Steve's your friend and all, but now that Mikey's here, I'm sure that the two of them will bond over their mutual failures, and you can leave them to the fast lane of self-pity. *If you wanna get down, down on the ground . . .* Let them roll around without you."

Alvee had refreshed his knowledge of popular music, even if he was still several decades out of date. I should've been amused, but I was appalled. Addict's excuses sprung to my mind: *I don't do that much, it's just a means of relaxation, it helps the creativity flow; I can quit at any time.* Excuses they were, but they were true – I had only *wallowed* with Steve out of camaraderie. I didn't need drink or drugs, and the idea that Alvee would even imply that I had been overdoing it –

I laughed nervously. "I surely don't want to end up looking like Mikey. Old before my –"

"When I was a little boy, about ten," Alvee interrupted, "there was a girl that used to come in once a week, to help my mother around the house. Some neighbor's daughter. She was, as the saying goes, as homely as a mud fence. As ugly as homemade sin.

"But she put on airs, according to my grandmother. She thought she was above the other farm girls. 'She flounces around here as if she's the cat's meow,' Grandma said to my mother once. 'I ask you, Louise – ain't they no mirrors in her house?'"

The harsh twang of Alvee's consummately counterfeited Midwestern inflection grated on my ears. I wondered if he had it down so well because he'd actually talked like that when he'd first arrived in Hollywood, nearly seventy years ago. I suddenly wondered if he'd taken voice lessons to get rid of that awful accent, so I missed, at first, the import of his words. Maybe I missed it on purpose. *What're ya trying to say, Alvee?*

He answered my expression. "What I'm saying is this, Carol. Leave the demons of excess to those that have to work for a living. They earn them." Again, he smiled at his own wit. "I know you've enjoyed playing screenwriter with your pal Steve, but misery loves company. Don't let his problems and the way he deals with them become yours. Don't let your friendship with him mark you."

The insult, that I was just *playing screenwriter,* was not the object of Alvee's lesson. When I just sat there, silent in outraged offense, he nodded at the mirror behind me, and without waiting for me to look at myself, he kissed me on the forehead, then serenely left the room.

When he was gone, I whirled, and in dismay, I minutely studied my reflection. Was Alvee right? Like upon that fictional picture, had my unaccustomed intemperance already begun to show on my face? Was that a new line beside my eye? Was that glint in the light a gray hair? Maybe I did look a *little* tired, a bit hollow around the eyes, but Steve and I had worked hard on *Diplomatic Opportunity*, burning the midnight oil, the candle at both ends, as the clichés go. So, yeah, maybe I did look a little run-down, but Alvee couldn't seriously be suggesting that my little foray into the dark side could show so soon . . .

As if summoned by my rationalizations, I seemed to see Dolores Adamson's ghost beside me in the mirror. (Say what you will, no matter the consequences, a little Bolivian

Marching Dust surely did add another layer to my imagination.)

Lori was as she'd been in life, impossibly thin and positively frail-looking, as if the merest Santa Ana wind might blow her away. Her face was lined and sallow, like an ancient parchment that had been folded and unfolded, over and over again, for centuries.

Like the Eye of Age, my own, long-deceased grand-mother's voice said in my head.

I waited to hear Lori's voice, quiet and wavery, and I was not disappointed. But Franck O'Day's almost-stepdaughter, his one-time eager lover, didn't have any Teiresian prophesies from beyond the grave for me. She simply repeated Maury's *Just Say No* admonition: "The wages of sin is death, Carol."

I blinked, and of course, the imaginary apparition was gone.

Maybe Alvee was right about my having fallen nose-first into Steve's seemingly endless supply of cocaine. And even if it was true that I'd done it because it was fun, whereas maybe he did it to escape from his troubles, real and imagined – his *habit,* and his frequent trips to where the liquor lurked, had certainly taken a toll on him. Not only on his looks, but maybe on his already-waning confidence, also. The drug was becoming that oft-cited crutch to Steve: a pick-me-up in the morning, a keep-me-going at noon, a time-to-party at night. Pretty soon, he would *need* it. Maybe there was some truth to that vicious circle they always talk about.

I was still confident, but after too many more conversations like the one I'd just had with Alvee *(ain't they no mirrors in your house?),* maybe I wouldn't be. Not to mention the fact that my hopped-up imagination kept dragging poor, sad, dead Lori into my mind. Maybe Alvee was right. It was time to quit while I was still ahead.

And Maury was also right. It was time that I be a friend to Steve, and try to get him to quit, too, to again live up to all the potential I'd seen that day at the Hilton, when he'd auditioned for *She's a Peach.*

Trouble in Paradise

At the first production meeting for *Diplomatic Opportunity,* it seemed that all the actors had their egos in check: no one arrived late.

Except for Alvee.

I was surprised, but not entirely. The director and his favorite actor had had what could only be described as an *argument* at breakfast. Alvee's attitude – now *there* had been some surprise on my part.

As we were finishing Kimura's hearty farm breakfast (Hollywood style) of eggs and lobster, topped with caviar, Maury said, "I'd like to expand the Wednesday night luau next week. As lead-up to Papa-san's birthday celebration."

Alvee glanced up from his plate. His expression was blank, expectant, but I caught a slight edge of irritation. The beginning of my surprise: What did God's gift to me, to Hollywood, to the world in general, have to be irritated about? Maury, his friend for more than a lifetime, caught the tension, but ignored it.

"We could make a little cast party out of it. Steve and Mina are Carol's friends, and you know how much Maki likes Armand. And poor Mike doesn't know a soul in this town anymore."

Maury shook his head sadly, and I stared at him in frank amazement. I knew he loved a party, but only if someone else was throwing it, and it was anywhere else but our house. And it wasn't like him to associate with his cast, especially not *this* cast: two has-beens, and a starting-over starlet; or with screenwriters like me and *Coke Ennyday.*

It was an odd request, and I watched Maury wait for Alvee's reaction. Alvee said something to Maki in Japanese, and the monk shrugged indifferently, then asked Maury something. Maury nodded without looking at him, his gaze still glued to Alvee.

I waited for a translation, but none was forthcoming. Maury and Alvee continued to stare at each other; it was as if I wasn't even there.

"Why do you want to vex me with these people?" Alvee said at last. "I've agreed to make this . . ."

He seemed to notice me again, and refrained from applying a disparaging appellation to the movie I'd written. More surprise: He didn't like my screenplay?

"Why do you insist on wanting to pal around with them?" he continued. "As if they were —"

"What? As if they were *equals?* Something more than mere fodder for your —"

"My what?"

Your ego, I thought.

Steve and Armand, and especially Mikey – *the old gray mare, she ain't what she used to be.* There was no denying that. But Alvee was still as matchlessly perfect and on point as the day he'd met all of them.

This was an unfortunate but indisputable truth, and now two new questions thumped at my surprise, like fingers flicking a balloon: Why did this fact annoy Alvee so much? It wasn't like his fellow actors' bad life choices had been his fault (except for Mikey's, perhaps). And even then, it hadn't been Alvee who'd led him to take out his frustrations upon himself.

And the second question – seeing that his friends' states of overindulgence *did* annoy Alvee so much, why did Maury want to rub his nose in it?

The director didn't answer Alvee's question, dismissed it with his customary desultory wave. "It's just that Carol never gets out of this mausoleum. She should get to see other people sometimes, instead of perennially being cooped up here with only you —"

"Do you feel cooped up here with me, Carol?"

Alvee was pissed now. I seemed to be seeing that more and more, of late. He wasn't mad at me, but the glower in his blue eyes was *aimed* at me, and that was quite discomforting, so I said quickly, "No, of course not, Alvee. I love –"

"You've made her into a cenobite, just like you," Maury said. "And I don't think that's healthy."

Alvee laughed harshly, threw his arms out. "When do you ever leave this ivory tower?"

I was suddenly confused; what exactly were they talking about? Didn't an ivory tower have something to do with college? Weren't the cenobites the bad guys from the *Hellraiser* movies? What did any of that have to do with me? How did I become the center of this argument, anyway?

I glanced at Maki, and he looked back at me blankly. He had no idea what they were saying, either.

"I'm not suggesting that we all start dining at the Marmont with the hoi polloi."

Maury was referring to the legendary Chateau Marmont, a Tinseltown landmark, frequented by stars and their hangers-on for decades. John Belushi had died there. Franck O'Day had twice lived there: after his wife's tragic murder, when he put the house where it had occurred up for sale; and again, when he'd secretly returned to the States after his sojourn in Japan. Maury's mention of the place was another surprise. He rarely made reference anymore to Alvee's life when he'd been Franck.

"Nor am I suggesting that we start having gigantic parties, and inviting the whole town. Damnable photographers and all." Again that wave of the hand. "I'm just saying it might be enjoyable for Carol to see some *people* for a change –"

"Won't she see these people on-set?"

"It's not the same thing. You've already scheduled the performers for Wednesday –"

"Whatever. *Do what thou wilt.*" Alvee tossed his napkin onto the table in exasperation, just as Kimura materialized and announced that Steve Shea had arrived.

"There ya go, Carol," Alvee said. He didn't look at me, but continued to glare at the director. "Your mid-sized chariot awaits. You'll get to see the real world at last. Maybe you can stop for gas."

Alvee rose, and I watched him turn off his pique like flipping the light switch of legend. He presented a countenance of smiling welcome and friendliness to Steve Shea, bid him good morning, told him he'd see him at the studio. His anger didn't even show in his stride as he left the terrace. He was *such* a good actor.

Steve said good morning to the director, bowed to Maki. I hadn't even had the opportunity to give Maury a *What's wrong with Alvee?* look before he was making small talk with Steve about the upcoming meeting. Then he, too, rose and left us.

Maki resumed reading the Japanese-language newspaper beside his plate. It wasn't like we were going to discuss the weirdness that had just occurred, nor even chat about the weather. Steve said, "Are you ready? I told Mina we'd stop and fetch her."

I nodded, and we bowed goodbye to the old monk and left the house.

When we got into the car, Steve suggested a brief, familiar diversion. Just the way to start the workday, the way we'd started it whilst we were working on the script. Why should the first day of production be any different? Or the first day of shooting? Or the wrap party or the premiere or . . . Maybe it was getting out of hand, and Alvee and Maury's admonitions crossed my mind, but Steve already had his handy mirror out, and it wasn't like anybody could see us, and after the strangeness of the morning (already!), I thought yes, I could indeed use a little pick-me-up.

"We should stop doing this, you know," I said, checking my nose in the rearview mirror.

"At least until the next screenplay." Steve grinned. "But you're right. I sense that your boyfriend doesn't approve, and Mina definitely doesn't approve."

"Things are going well with you guys?"

"So far. This week. We'll see if it continues after shooting starts." That nice-guy smile, sans bitterness for a change. That meant that things really were going well.

Steve made mirror and contraband disappear and started the car.

I peeped at him cautiously. "Has she said anything about Mikey?"

He smiled again as the gate clanked open. "That's why we gotta quit the coke. Mina's convinced that it has to be drugs that've led to Mr. McClown's fat slobitude.

"But it's not the case. Believe it or not, Mr. Unparalleled called me the other day. Had some questions about the script. He even lowered himself to come by my apartment. We got to talking, and – Mikey doesn't do any drugs, Carol. Something about a promise he made to his mother. He won't turn down a bourbon on the rocks or three, or five, but he doesn't do drugs. I figure that maybe the Outback just takes it out of a guy, or maybe they just fed him well down there. Maybe they paid him in food." Steve shook his head at the profundity of it. "But for Mina's sake, we'll quit. This is the last I've got, anyway. As soon as it's gone, we're done. Okay?"

"Sounds good to me."

I was glad. I didn't feel overly inclined to quit otherwise, despite Alvee's obtuse (or not) supposition that my acquaintance with Steve (and his acquainting me with that *high quality* yeyo) was starting to show on my face.

Maury's advice was correct: I should try to convince Steve to lighten up, to stop feeling sorry for himself – what were friends for, but to speak up when their friend was overdoing it? He was right – I shouldn't be *wallowing* with Steve when it appeared that he might be on the brink of developing a problem. He had pointed out that my friend might need a little looking after, but unlike Alvee, Maury had not presumed to be parental. He hadn't suggested that my frequent round-ups aboard the white pony were affecting me in any way.

Call it defiance; Alvee might be quite a bit older than he looked, but still I bristled at his talking to me like he was my daddy. In other words, his tone had not really led me to look around for a wagon upon which to climb.

But he was right, nonetheless, and Maury was also right. I was glad that Steve had decided that we were gonna quit.

****

Mina lived in a beautiful house that would soon be all hers, once her divorce from the pushy producer was final.

"Gotta love a community property state," Steve commented, as she walked down the steps and hopped into the car with us.

****

It really wasn't necessary for the screenwriters to be at the first production meeting; it wasn't necessary for us to be there during the upcoming shoot, either. *Diplomatic Opportunity* was done as far as our roles were concerned, unless Maury wanted something rewritten, and even then, he'd probably just do it himself, on the fly.

Because I was unnecessary, I found that I enjoyed production meetings, however. No one was going to single me out, ask me any questions; I just blended in with the furniture.

I liked to hear Maury's introductory speech to the cast and crew, liked to listen to the initial table read. Steve wanted to hear Mina's first take on our clumsy call-girl-with-a-heart-of-gold, and Mikey's love-sick attaché. I wanted to hear Alvee's rendition of Vaughn.

When the three of us arrived, there were the requisite members of the crew lounging around the room. There was Armand, consulting the script over a pair of half-specs, a la his director.

Mike McCown was seated beside him, and I noted that he'd cleaned up considerably. He'd visited his wizard of a cosmetologist, and his hair was again a blend of myriad highlights and undertones, like a veteran lifeguard. Now he only looked maybe eight or nine years older than he actually was, maybe only twenty pounds overweight, instead of thirty-five.

Armand asked him something; Mikey consulted his own script, then leaned a little closer to the Brit to reply. I was more than satisfied with our casting choices. Regardless of their real-life personalities and peccadilloes, these men were professionals. Outside the studio gate, they had set down any lifestyle-choice difference of opinion that they might've had. *Diplomatic Opportunity* was another chance in the spotlight for both of them, and it wouldn't pay for either of them to do anything other than work excellently together. They already appeared to be the father-son conspirators that they were set to play.

But my darling Alvee wasn't sitting at his accustomed place at his director's right hand. Maury wasn't at the table, either. He was talking to Sylvia, and when he saw my surprise at his lead's absence, he rolled his eyes and dismissed the script girl.

Steve and Mina went to take their seats, and I paused to have a word with the auteur.

"He's having a snit," Maury said in discreet annoyance.

"What exactly is his problem?" My amazement was also quiet. No reason to broadcast the anomaly of Alvee's tardiness; no use shoveling speculation into the on-set gossip mill on the very first day.

"He doesn't like to bear witness to *there but for the grace of God, go I.*" The director nodded over his shoulder at the rest of the cast.

"It's not his fault that they're . . . It's just ridiculous for him to be acting like this."

Maury studied me minutely for a heartbeat; I thought he might hold forth again upon the wages of sin. But now was not the time.

He sighed. "His objections have been duly noted. We'll skip inviting the cast to the luau." When I looked disappointed, he smiled. "Fear not. They're all still coming for Papa-san's birthday celebration. In a war of wills with Alvee, I know which battles to concede. And because I do, he'll show his appreciation by being back to his gracious self for the party. I know him."

"You're the director."

****

I thought that Alvee's grace was a trifle slow in returning.

For the first week and a half of shooting, he again played at being a Method actor, remaining in character between takes. He smiled and chatted with Mina, of course: their characters were siblings. But Vaughn disliked and suspected the diplomat and his son, so Alvee shunned Mike and Armand. They didn't notice; they were actors, too, and they figured that Alvee's ignoring them was all part of the on-set make-believe world.

Alvee and Maury and I dined out, most nights. We had a movie in production, so it was again time for its lead to be seen. He smiled for the photographers outside the restaurants, signed autographs and was kind and patient and chatty to any fans that had the nerve to approach him inside.

Being out before Alvee's public precluded any more discussions of my Maury-proclaimed seclusion and what should be done about it, however. Nor were the wages of sin as they had been earned by Alvee's fellow actors mentioned. The star of *Diplomatic Opportunity* and its director and screenwriter spoke of banalities as we dined: the weather, how the shoot was progressing. For three people who were as close as we were, it struck me as odd, but on the other hand, we couldn't really discuss our personal lives in places where the walls had ears.

At night, at home, Alvee was his normal, loving self. He even complimented my appearance, said my healthy glow was returning, now that I had quit the Coca Express.

"It's love," I told him. "Mine for you, and Steve's for Mina. And we didn't have to attend a single meeting."

"I'm charmed," he replied expressionlessly, then added, "I'm so happy for them."

"You're happy that they're not hanging around here."

Alvee shrugged. "Steve and Mina are tolerable. Like his majesty said, it's good for you to have friends, people who don't want anything from you."

Left unmentioned were Mike and Armand, even though neither of them wanted anything from me. In the hierarchy of the movie business, I was nothing to them, and they spoke not to me, above the most perfunctory of pleasantries. On a personal level, it was similar. Armand still considered me to be his *tiresome* competition, and I doubted that Mikey's misogyny had faded with his career.

The one-time hot property looked at me the same as had the cast and crew of *Kinship*. I was Alvee's squeeze, and it didn't matter if I could write or not. My purpose was simply to keep the star warm at night. Mikey had once attracted a legion of similar sycophants, so because he viewed me this way, his respect was minimal.

Neither he nor Armand wanted anything whatsoever from me, unless it was for me to go away. It was my beautiful and talented Alvee from whom they both wanted something.

Armand wanted what he simply wasn't going to get. Hope was eternal, and never was a long time, in the Brit's worldview. It was unmistakable, therefore, what the formerly commanding British sodomite wanted from Alvee. Maybe I'm being unfair – maybe it wasn't obvious to everyone on-set; Armand was a professional, after all. He didn't exactly fawn over Alvee, but that was mostly because Alvee avoided him. Still, if you looked for it, you could see that his ache consumed Armand, now that he was again in Alvee's presence. All the years of sending unrequited (bad) poetry had done nothing but whet his appetites for Dorian Gray.

Armand still considered himself to be attractive, and he was, enough. Maki continued to be charmed, and the junior make-up assistant was positively besotted with him. But Armand didn't indulge the star-struck young man. Such a thing wouldn't have escaped the micromanaging eye that the director kept on his set, so if anything was going on, I would've heard about it. Once he was at home and had shed the mantel of awesome auteur, Maurice Claremount could be a shameless gossip.

It seemed that Armand was saving himself for Alvee, as if he was sure that Alvee was due for a sea change, any day now. Surely, he had to be bored with me, after all this time? How many, *many* years had passed without Alvee's ever having been even *the tiniest bit curious* about such matters, was of course unknown to Armand.

Michael McCown wanted Alvee's praise, his advice, his friendship, his *time.* And although he had given all these things to the kid, long-distance, via text and email and phone conversations, Mike's wanting the two of them to be buddies again as they had been during the shoot for *She's A Peach* appealed to Alvee not in the least.

The former action star had not gained any depth, any perspective, during his exile overseas. He still said the most outrageously inappropriate and insulting things to anyone his damaged ego felt were beneath him. He was still an actor, was he not? Who cared what the little people thought? It was still okay for him to openly refer to the make-up guy as a *fag;* it was perfectly within his rights to leer appreciatively at Sylvia's niece, an apprentice script girl.

"And he didn't even read his contract," Alvee told me with disgust. "If Maury had wanted to cheat him, Mikey wouldn't have even known about it until he got his first paycheck."

"He figures you'll look out for him, this time."

Confusion showed in the blue eyes. "What do you mean, *this time?"*

"Weren't you the one that told him to fire Ronny Prince?"

Alvee frowned. "Who?"

"Didn't you tell us, once upon a time, that Mike's agent was robbing him blind? That the guy wasn't getting him the parts he deserved? Didn't you advise Mike to fire him?"

Alvee shook his head. "I don't know anything about agents, Carol. I don't even know that much about contracts, but the one Mike had seemed a little lopsided to me. I thought Maury could've asked someone at Title XVII to take a look at it for him, but when that didn't pan out, I told Mike he should find a lawyer or someone to help him renegotiate it. I didn't tell him to fire his agent."

So it hadn't been guilt that had prompted Alvee to keep up his friendship with Mike whilst he was overseas.

Whatever the reason, it seemed that he was regretting it now. Mike's renewed suggestions of hitting the nightspots and attending sporting events exasperated him; Alvee was running out of excuses for declining. Maybe Maury had been correct in his observation: Mike was a used-up also-ran, and maybe Alvee, perennially fresh and at the top of his game, just didn't want to look at him.

Not even two weeks into the shoot for *Diplomatic Opportunity,* and all Alvee wanted was to get away from both Michael McCown and Armand Hambrick. He was still attentive to me, but he was also distracted by these annoyances, so his attention was not what it should've been. Maybe he wanted to get away from me, too . . .

He was positively cold to his director. We'd been the ones that had press-ganged him into making this flick, had we not? We'd chosen the cast. It was our fault that he was being subjected to the attentions of these people.

It was rather small of him, in my estimation. How above it all he was, that it was a nuisance to him to be subjected to the abject love and genuine friendship of his fellow actors. It wasn't that he didn't like Mike and Armand, per se, it was just that he didn't want to be bothered with them. They were of his past.

His attitude made me almost feel sorry for them. But only almost, because I didn't like either of them. I wasn't annoyed at their presence, like Alvee was. Having to work with people you didn't like (and who didn't like you) was all part of the shoot, of the movie business, of Hollywood. Maybe it's a part of *all* businesses. There had been a girl named Steffie, with whom I'd been forced to work in my almost-forgotten, previous life, when I'd been that regular gal, legal secretary. Like the action star and the Brit, Steffie hadn't liked me, and the feeling was mutual. But we smiled and made small talk and pretended to be friendly, because we couldn't escape each other in the office.

You're just gonna have to get over it, Alvee, my love. You're gonna have to find your way clear to muddle through, somehow. Just like it turned out with Steffie and me – it's not like you're gonna have to put up with Mike and Armand forever.

A Short Historical Digression

In the course of my interviews with him, Franck O'Day had revealed how he and Robert Ecksmith had come to make that life-altering trip to Japan. To get away from Jessika Yerdlay, Franck had first fled with Bobby to his estate in England.

"The only tedious part of my English sojourn was Jessika's constant letters and telegrams. She begged, she pleaded, she cajoled. She threatened to get on the next plane. Bobby would read her letters aloud to me, in his best Scarlett O'Hara voice, even though Jessika sounded nothing like a southern belle. I think Bobby just liked imitating one. He was hilarious.

"He took her threats to come to England as seriously as if she'd threatened to board the next plane to come and murder me, however. After one particularly bitter missive, wherein she made vague allusions to airlines and flight schedules, Bobby said to me, 'Let's go to Japan. She'll never find us there.'

"He'd always been fascinated with the Far East – the culture, the languages, the religions. But Japan had always been his favorite, and he was developing a script that would take place there. *Shogun* wouldn't be published for years, but in 1967, he had an idea for a similar kind of story. I never really got all the details – the script was mostly in his mind – but it was basically the saga of a blue-eyed European and the swath he cuts across feudal Japan. Or something like that."

So the two of them even had an excuse to visit the Land of the Rising Sun: they were scouting locations, might even audition some local talent.

Franck said, "I sent Jessika a telegram, basically telling her that I was going where she couldn't find me and I wasn't coming back. And then we went.

"When we traveled in the countryside, Bobby went almost completely native, dressing traditionally, visiting Buddhist shrines. I thought he stuck out like a sore thumb. There was nothing even remotely Japanese about him.

"But he had a knack for languages, and within a few months was conversing fluently with the locals. At least he seemed fluent to me – my knack is for memorizing long passages in English, usually called scripts – and I only ever picked up a few phrases in Japanese.

"The people we met were kind and respectful to the Englishman in their native dress – they invited him into their homes, spoke to him at length, told him their histories and their mythologies. I mostly sat around and nodded a lot. It was beautiful there, and I never missed home once.

"But one cannot escape from one's past, especially when one's past is helmed by an obsessed harpy who woke up one day and realized that she'd been abandoned via telegram, and then decided that she wasn't going to take it lying down."

A studio flunky named Karl Izona found them in Japan. He told them about Jessika's accusations of child molestation.

"The studio would pay for my representation, if it came to that, Izona said. When that beneficence didn't make me immediately start packing, he next rattled his saber vaguely on the studio's behalf, mentioning the little matter of the unfinished, barely even started *Two Green Keys,* by now forgotten by everyone except producers, their accountants, and their lawyers.

"I told Izona conversationally that I would return to the States when I was damn good and ready, and in the meantime, the studio and all its minions (including himself) could just collectively kiss my ass.

"He wasn't offended. He was being paid not to be offended. Dealing with actors and their outrageous whims was his job. He said, 'The longer you stay away, the worse it looks on you, Mr. O'Day. Not only as far as this unfortunate . . . *family matter,* goes. Your prolonged absence reflects badly on your reliability. Your employability, shall we say?'

"I opened my mouth to ask Izona if he knew who he was talking to, if he knew who this skinny guy in the kimono sitting across from us was. But Bobby held up his hand. He recognized a *You'll never work in this town again* threat when he heard it, and he took it seriously.

"I was just a dumb actor; I didn't know anything about, nor could I have possibly cared less about, the powerful studio political machine that had breezed in like the fog and congealed in front of us in the person of Karl Izona. But Bobby knew, and I deferred to his advice."

So, Franck told Izona that he would return to the States, and the studio man left them to make their own arrangements. He already had a round-trip ticket.

"When we arrived at the local airport, there was a lone American photographer sitting at the bar. He recognized me, if not Bobby, and bought us a drink. He told us he'd lost his reporter at the neighborhood whorehouse, and asked if he could hitch a ride with us. We told him that he was more than welcome, but at the last minute, he thought better of leaving his partner behind and changed his mind. He took our picture, wished us good luck, and went back to the bar to wait for his reporter."

The photographer's snap was the last known picture of Franck O'Day and Robert Ecksmith; it had once appeared on *TwoGreenKeys.com.* In it, the 1960s were on full display: it was in color, with that yellow, always-looks-like-it's-a-summer-afternoon quality of pictures from the era – a feel that you can now easily duplicate on modern shots with a few clicks.

Bobby had straight, scraggly, shoulder-length blonde hair, and a full, droopy mustache. Franck's black hair was not as long as his friend's, but shaggier, curlier, covering his ears and reaching to his collar. He sported impressive, mutton-chop sideburns. They both wore Aviator-style shades and heavy coats. They were both smiling widely, evidently not in the least bit concerned with what they were returning to the States to face. The fuselage of a small plane was in the background.

Little did they know that what they were about to face was death. The famous Hollywood duo's last hit would be the side of a Japanese mountain.

But of course, they didn't die in the crash. They were rescued by Russian hikers.

Franck continued. "I woke up in a room in someone's house, dressed in Japanese clothing. Bobby was still unconscious, lying in a bed across from me. He was out for two weeks – I wouldn't call it a coma, because he tossed and turned and talked in his sleep. He called out for me a couple of times."

Bobby at last woke up, and Franck was flooded with relief.

"I was so glad that my friend was awake and alive, but I was also glad that he could communicate with these people. 'Where the hell are we?'

"'We're in a little town called Kumano, in a place called the Kii Peninsula,' Bobby said. 'The best thing is – no one here knows who we are. No one out there . . .' he spread his arms to indicate the world, '. . . knows where we are. I think we should stay here forever.' He grinned at me.

"'We gotta get back, Bobby,' I said. 'Jessika, the studio . . .'

"'You're dead, Franck, my darling. I'm dead. If they knew where to look for us, they would've found us by now.'

"Then, there was a knock on the door. It was a young man in traditional dress.

"'I am Nakano,' he said in a thick accent. 'I come from *Kimpusen-ji.*'

"'You speak English,' I said.

"'A small,' Nakano replied shyly, and bowed a little again. 'I come to take you to *Kimpusen-ji.*'

"Bobby said something to Nakano in Japanese. He smiled in pleased surprise and said something back. They began a regular conversation. I just stood there like an idiot.

"Bobby and Nakano finished their little talk. They bowed to each other, and Nakano left. Bobby clapped his hands and rubbed them together, grinned widely. I was annoyed, still in the dark about where exactly we were, what exactly was going on.

"'Don't frown, my darling, it'll give you wrinkles,' Bobby said. He waited another moment, just to piss me off that much more, because it amused him. Then he said, 'Okay. That was Nakano. He's a monk, of the ancient *Shugendō* religion. It's rather a nature sect, a blending of Buddhist and Shinto. A mountain faith.'

"Bobby started to tell me what they believed. I told him that I didn't care what they believed. But . . . I'd been thinking over his suggestion. Maybe we should stay here, for a little while, anyway. It was beautiful country, and if the world thought we were dead, why not stay dead for a while? I had nothing to go home to, no desire whatsoever to go home. That's why I'd left the country with Bobby in the first place, to get away from all the things I didn't want at home.

"He spoke the language, even if I didn't. It would be fun. We could step out of the wilderness for a big comeback, anytime we wanted to.

"I asked, 'What does Nakano want?'

"'He wants to take us to *Kimpusen-ji.*' Bobby didn't wait for me to glower at him, but instead explained immediately. 'It's a temple.'

"'And why does he want to take us there?' I asked.

"Bobby grinned even wider, shrugged. 'I have no idea, my darling. No idea at all. Perhaps it's kismet.'

"Kismet. Fate." Franck laughed, shrugged. "I never did find out precisely why Nakano had been sent to fetch us. Bobby told me some story once – he said it had to do with a Japanese good luck charm that he'd been wearing when the plane went down. Some symbol that he wore around his neck. When the Russians brought us in – one of the locals had seen it and got in touch with the monks.

"I don't know. Something like that. Bobby makes stuff up a lot, Carol. He's a storyteller, an artiste. He never lets the truth get in the way of a good story.

"We went to *Kimpusen-ji;* we were taken to the head guy. His name was Maki."

He invited them to stay, although their status in the outside world meant nothing to him.

"We worked for them – Hollywood heartthrob Franck O'Day and famous English director Robert Ecksmith performed manual labor for Japanese monks. Bobby was happier than I'd ever known him to be, and I liked it there. The air was clean, the water fresh – and not a single studio sycophant in sight.

"Bobby studied with Maki, and he and Maki developed a . . . *relationship.* I don't know if there was anything physical to it in the beginning. We never discussed the physical relationships that Bobby had. But his tone was soft and awed when he talked about Maki. He spoke of the transcendental oneness of their souls, the complete blending of their energies – as Maki taught him all the steps, as they ascended through the levels of enlightenment together."

Franck paused. "It all sounded like bullshit to me. From all the flowery language, I was convinced that they were lovers." He grinned. "But then Bobby showed me what he'd learned. And the years passed. Maki showed him, and he showed me."

I asked Franck, "What did he show you?"

"I learned *Shugendō.* Spiritual power, the balance between humanity and nature. And I learned *Reiki,* the mysterious atmosphere, the supernatural influence, the universal life energy."

I must've looked skeptical, because at the time, I was. *It all sounded like bullshit to me.*

Franck barked a short laugh. "Ah, it's nothing, Carol. Just a weird Eastern spiritual practice. *Reiki.* It's not even ancient – it's only been around since the '20s. Harnessing the energy of the universe. It keeps me young." Franck looked at me, willing me to say something, expecting me to defend my unbeliever's expression.

"Well," I said and smiled at him, "it certainly seems to work."

The former matinee idol roared laughter, and that was the end of my interviews with Franck O'Day.

The Nipponophile and a Celebration of Love and Gratitude

The concept of weekends as being time off, of their being the two whole days that separate one work-week from the next, is something foreign to Maury. Time is money, and if the sun's up, the clock's ticking, regardless of what the calendar says. He's like some kind of 17th century factory owner in his work ethic: he offers his cast and crew every other Sunday off, with the option to revoke this privilege at his discretion, OSHA be damned.

But no one's ever quit, no one's ever sued, no one's ever really even complained. It isn't like the head of Title XVII Productions is cheap. He pays everyone handsomely for their overtime.

But since Maki's birthday celebration was scheduled to commence that night, Maury let everyone go before lunch on Friday, telling them he'd see them all bright and early Monday morning; the whole weekend off. There was a moment of stunned silence, then a cheer.

Not only was Kimura's dinner scrumptiously presented that evening, it was served by an attractive young Japanese man and woman garbed in *hakama* and *kimono.* To my amazement, Maury and Alvee also were also dressed traditionally, in yellow *sodenashibaori* (a long tunic) and white *suzukake* (a flowing white shirt). Maury explained that to honor Maki, to remind him of their love and gratitude, they had donned this garb of the *yamabushi,* the followers of *Shugendō.* They were entitled to the garments, Maury said, as once upon a time, beside the esteemed monk, they had also practiced the –

what did one call it? The faith? The doctrine? I wasn't really sure.

As Maury had prophesied, Alvee was finally his normal, jovial self once again. As well he should be, I thought. He owed his understanding of the application of the universal energy to the birthday boy. He laughed and joked with Maki in Japanese, revealing that, despite what Franck had always maintained, he knew more of the language than he let on. He smiled at my ignorance, offered no translations. He occasionally squeezed my hand.

Just exactly how old Maki was remained a mystery to me. He was a hundred, beyond a doubt; maybe he was a hundred and twenty-five. It was some major milestone, I was sure, because while Maury always celebrated his partner's birthday, this year he outdid himself.

The lavish dinner was just the beginning. On Saturday afternoon, Maury told us that he had a surprise for his lover, and asked us to take Maki for a ride whilst it was delivered. Alvee summoned a limo. I thought the old monk was thrilled to get out of the house as much as he was in anticipation of Maury's surprise. If anyone was a *cenobite,* it was Maki. (I'd Googled the word and found out that it meant simply *a member of a monastic community.* One should never depend on the depictions of unfamiliar words as they are appear in the movies.)

We returned just as the sun was sinking into the west. The cast of *Diplomatic Opportunity* had arrived, and were sitting around the table on the terrace. Again, the lovely young couple served them Japanese delicacies.

Maury glanced up at us as we came through the French doors, and Alvee made a point to frown at him. He knew that these guests had been invited, but still he wished to communicate his continuing displeasure at Maury's insistence on *palling around* with them.

But when the party turned to greet us, Alvee unleashed his incomparable smile. None of them could've guessed that he was anything other than delighted to see them, every one. I say it all the time, but I'll say it again. He's *such* a good actor.

Steve and Mina, Mike and Armand rose and bowed to the guest of honor. Armand said something in Japanese; Maki replied and also bowed. Armand said something else: apparently Maury had schooled him in a little more of the language.

The beautiful girl offered us small glasses. Alvee drained his in one gulp, and when I hesitated, he also drank mine. *Nihonshu,* he called it. The girl refilled our glasses from a small earthenware bottle. I sipped mine cautiously, and Alvee smiled over the rim of his glass. Whatever his true mood, at least he'd decided to have a little fun.

Maury featured us with a grin of pure, almost childlike joy; he threw out his arm dramatically and said, "Voila!"

Upon the tile at the farthest end of the pool stood a massive object, wrapped in burlap, and tied with a thick, black rope. Once upon a time (it seemed like a million years ago), I'd watched from the window of the late Jessika Yerdlay's bedroom, whilst Kimura pushed lounge chairs out of the way in this area. He'd then stuck tiki torches into hidden holes in the tile.

He had done so again. The giant . . . *thing,* at least seven feet tall, was ringed in flame. Alvee smiled; *he* knew what was under the burlap, and I felt a small slight that I'd been left out again. No one had told me about this. Maury had mentioned only that the birthday surprise had something to do with a movie that we would all be seeing later, one of Maki's favorites. I thought that the limo ride through the hills had actually been just an additional treat.

Alvee put his arm around Maki's shoulders, and we all went down to the pool for the big unveiling. Always the showman, Maury had the rope rigged so that with one brisk tug, the burlap fell away to reveal –

"*Kongō Rikishi!*" Maki exclaimed in wonder.

It was a stone-carved statue of a fierce Japanese warrior or god or demon. Or something. Frowning majestically, he was stunning, fascinating, frightening. *He could be the paymaster for the wages of sin,* I thought with a little inward grin.

Maury was receiving Maki's astonished hugs, so the five of us, equally astonished, looked at Alvee for explanation.

But Alvee was not in an expansive mood. *"Niō,"* he said simply. "They usually come in a pair." He sipped his *nihonshu,* and finding the little glass empty, he signaled the young woman for a refill. "The guardians of Buddha. Now our home is complete."

No one, including me, was sure if Alvee was kidding or not.

Science Fiction Double Feature

The leaf had again been placed in the dining room table, so it was large enough to accommodate the guest of honor, plus a director and an actress, three actors and a couple of screenwriters. Such a crowd of Hollywood insiders often filled the table, I imagined, when Jessika Yerdlay had been queen of the castle. Two of those present had, of course, actually dined with the starlet, lo, those many, *many* years before.

As the second exotic feast drew to a close, Steve asked if he might have a word with me, outside. Everyone was talking shop, so they didn't notice our exit.

The terrace was silent, shot across with fitful moonlight. Steve paused, glanced behind us, then said, "Let's go look at that thing again."

I followed him down the steps and around to the end of the pool. The tiki torches still blazed around the guardian. He held one hand up in a warding-off gesture, as if forbidding us to come any closer.

"Wow," Steve said. "Do you think it's authentic? Like from a temple or something?"

"I'd say it's definitely from the old country. Maury's rather a connoisseur of all things Japanese."

"It must've cost a fortune just to ship it here."

I shrugged. Money was meaningless to Maury. "Nothing's too good for Maki. They've been together for a lot of years."

I waited for Steve to tell me what he had to tell me. I was pretty sure that he hadn't left the party so we could discuss Far Eastern statuary in the moonlight. Maybe he wanted to confide some good news about how his relationship was progressing with Mina. I'd noticed that they were holding hands when we went in to dinner.

But that wasn't it at all. Steve glanced nervously back at the house again. "You wanna smoke a joint, Carol?"

I blinked at him, nonplussed. It seemed that my good buddy Steve Shea would always be saying things that left me dumbfounded, things that I never expected to come out of his mouth. *You're Carolyn Adyon. You wrote the story for Kinship. I consider you my best friend. You wanna smoke a joint?*

"I am one hundred percent cocaine-free," he told me. "But what's a party without at least *some kind* of consciousness-altering? Come on, Carol. Everybody's doing it." He grinned. "First time's free." Steve produced a fattie and a lighter from the seemingly bottomless drug cornucopia that was his jacket pocket.

"It'll enhance this movie we're supposed to see." He put flame to the joint, and glanced up at the house again. Holding his breath, he croaked, "What are we seeing again?"

So Maury had also told the rest of his guests about the movie part of the surprise. But I'd been given no more info than they had: I knew only that the founder of the feast had acquired a copy of one of Maki's favorites, and had caused it to be subtitled in Japanese for the birthday boy's special enjoyment.

I imagined that Maury hadn't clued me to the film's title, because, hell, I might've spoiled the surprise by letting it slip, whilst Maki and I were discussing the weather, or when he was telling me about the latest news reported in one of his Japanese newspapers. *As if.* I frowned. Sometimes Maury treated me like I was that goose.

"It's a surprise," was all I told Steve.

"Whatever it is, this'll make it better."

He offered the joint to me, passing his other hand through the air above it in an ineffectual attempt to disperse the smoke. It was less illegal, less addictive, true – but perhaps more consciousness-altering, at least to me. Unlike the cocaine I'd tried that one time in the past, whatever kind of pot I'd smoked in my youth must've been *good.* The few times I'd indulged – it had always gone directly to work on my imagination.

That evil little voice inside (the one we all have) said, *Oh, what the hell,* and I took a (probably too big) hit. I knew Steve was right about a little marijuana enhancing my movie experience, because I remembered . . .

The last time I'd smoked pot had been with Ruthie. It was before we'd met Franck O'Day; at the time, I still believed him to be long-deceased. She'd talked me into not only watching *High Times in Manhattan,* but also the forgotten dog he'd made with some director I'd never heard of. Some guy named Robert Ecksmith.

The first time I viddied Franck on the screen, I was finally able to understand why Ruthanne was besotted with an actor that had been dead for twenty years before she'd been born. Yeah, he'd been attractive enough in the pictures she'd shown me, but just how attractive he was didn't come alive for me until I heard him speak, watched him perform.

I didn't fall in love with him then, not like Jessika Yerdlay and her daughter, like Uncle Jessie and Patrick Morrison and Robert Ecksmith, none of whom I'd heard about yet. Not even like my friend Ruthanne – I just didn't have her imagination about such things. I couldn't love a dead man.

And since we'd been smoking the demon weed, I could never be sure – was it the drug's influence or Franck's portrayal of Perry Calibri? Was it his amazing voice, his crooked smile, his incredible, dark-blue eyes that made his seem positively luminous? Or was it just because I was stoned?

Once I met him, it became clear. Franck O'Day, old-timey matinee idol, presumed dead for almost forty years, was anything but. He was charming, unique; egotistical. He was, as the saying goes, *something else.*

****

As we walked up the steps to the terrace, Steve offered me a stick of gum, just like we were in high school. I felt light-headed and giggly already; then I remembered why I'd never been much of a pot smoker, even in high school, when *everyone was doing it.*

But the recollection came too late. Sure, there was the amplification of my imagination, which was great. But the adjunct to that was that I sometimes became the quintessential paranoid when I smoked pot. Not every time – watching movies with Ruthanne, just the two of us, had been a lot of fun. But if I was at a party, with lots of people around – it'd happened often enough that I should've known better this time.

The little voice that had said, *Oh, what the hell,* now whispered ominously, *Everyone's gonna know what you've been up to.* I anxiously studied Steve for a second; he didn't look stoned. Did I?

It crossed my mind that my good friend Steven P. Shea was a bad influence, just as Alvee had warned; perhaps the very devil. Since he'd stopped supplying me with cocaine, I hadn't missed it – not much, anyway – but maybe a little consciousness-raising via this more common means hadn't been such a good idea, either.

We peeked into the dining room, and found that the other guests had decamped without us. Kimura and the pretty Japanese couple were clearing the table, and he pointed silently downward, indicating that the festivities had adjourned to the screening room.

Christ, have we really been gone that long?

Alvee and the birthday boy, Maury and his guests were perched upon the midnight-blue, velvet seats, waiting for us. All heads turned when we walked in.

Just what I needed: everyone looking at me when I was stoned. It just stoked the paranoia – *everyone's gonna know* – that had already begun to bubble in my mind.

Why was the first row of seats empty? Maury was seated beside Maki in the second row. He chided, "No one sits in the first row, Carol," as if he'd guessed what I'd been thinking.

Is what I'm thinking that transparent?

Steve's guilty conscience (he'd been doing drugs again) caused him to swipe at his nose, out of habit, as he smiled

221

guilelessly at Mina. She smiled back and welcomed him to a seat beside her. That left the one between him and Maury for me, unless . . .

Armand and Mike flanked Alvee in the third row. They looked at me impassively. *They can tell I'm stoned.* No, that wasn't it. It was that neither of them liked me, and neither of them wanted to give up his place beside Alvee to a mere screenwriter.

Alvee shrugged, offered me a little crooked grin: *When you cruise, you lose.* I noticed he had another drink in his hand, in a larger glass this time. Alvee didn't drink often, but he had decided to do so tonight. That was a good thing. Maybe he wouldn't notice that Steve and I had returned from our tête-à-tête somewhat quieter and more red-eyed than we'd been previously.

I took the seat beside Maury. He pushed buttons on the remote; the lights dimmed and the curtains parted.

I was amazed to see a pair of disembodied crimson lips float forward from the black screen. I didn't have to wait for them to begin singing to know the title of Maki's favorite American movie.

To my dismay, my partner in drug use giggled. *Everyone's gonna know we're stoned.*

"*The Rocky Horror Picture Show?* I haven't seen this since college!" Steve squeezed Mina's hand and she gave him a blank smile.

Not a fan, I thought. *Boy are you in for a surprise.*

Even though I'd known that they we going to be there, I was still amazed to see the Japanese subtitles at the bottom of the screen. It was good that they were indecipherable, because in my distracted state, I might've tried to read them, even though I knew all the words. *Rocky Horror* had been another one of Ruthie's favorites.

"Lick those lips!" Maury shouted at the screen, and giggled as if he was as lit as Steve and me. "Papa-san knows all the lyrics to the songs, Carol," he whispered. "But it's always been phonetic. I've translated for him . . . But now he can read it all himself." He giggled again, kissed Maki on the cheek. Maki returned his kiss in loving amazement.

"Like a . . . x-ray!" Armand shouted. Maury turned and gave him an entirely American high-five. Of course, the commanding British sodomite would be familiar with the flick. I could even imagine him showing up at a few midnight screenings in the London of his youth, dressed as Rocky (gold boots a flashing), what with his being a blondie, and all.

I peeped at Mikey. He frowned. I was sure that he'd never seen the cult classic, but I was just as sure that he'd undoubtedly *heard of it.* His militantly hetero sensibilities were about to mightily offended, and the idea of that made me giggle out loud.

Alvee grinned at my giggle. *Can he tell what I've been up to?* I didn't think so. "Fuck the back row," he said conversationally, and gestured at the screen with his drink.

Mike continued to frown when Steve and I, Maury and Alvee and Armand shouted the requisite responses at the screen. Maki even said a few of them in Japanese. The former action star refused to be amused. This was not entertainment suitable for a red-blooded, all-American homophobe such as himself.

"Lighten up, Mikey," Alvee told him once. "It takes all kinds."

Mina got over her initial surprise and laughed along with the rest of us.

In the middle of the transducer scene, I glanced over at Maury, and was surprised to see his happy smile fade. He felt me looking at him and gazed solemnly back at me for an extended moment, or so it seemed, owing to my *raised consciousness.* He said in a stage whisper, "When Columbia speaks . . . tell me who it reminds you of."

I knew the lines, but I listened again keenly, with all the attention available to my spaced mind. Columbia yells bitterly at the sweet transvestite: *"You chew people up and then you spit them out again. I loved you. Do you hear me? I loved you! And what did it get me? Yeah, I'll tell you: a big nothing.*

You're like a sponge. You take, take, take, and drain others of their love and emotion . . ."

Maury grinned humorlessly and I blinked stupidly. Alvee leaned forward and whispered in my ear, saying the next lines along with Dr. Frank N. Furter, *"It's not easy having a good time. Even smiling makes my face ache."*

My beloved Alvee, always fresh, always on, always *finished*, could not possibly care less (not even in two lifetimes) that Maury was implying that Columbia's words could be describing him. His carefree, indifferent grin dismissed his director's unmistakable innuendo.

But I did not.

Perhaps it was the drug working in my blood, strumming the chords of paranoia, as it always did. When I glanced over my shoulder at Alvee, then at fat Mikey to his right, worn-out; and Armand, old before his time, to his left – once again, Lori Adamson's voice spoke in my head.

When I'd known Franck's almost-stepdaughter, she, too, had been old and worn-out. But it was neither drink nor drugs nor hard living nor even hard work that had sapped Lori of her youth. A child of Hollywood wealth and privilege, she'd never worked a day in her life. According to her, it was her devotion to Franck O'Day – and what he'd made of it – that had turned her into a little old lady, years before nature's natural course.

Coupled with my dream of the fire and its horrendous revelations, it had been Lori's tales of loving Franck that had caused distrust and apprehension to blacken my first days with Alvee, as a matter of fact. And now it all came back.

In prologue, she'd told me that, when Franck first summoned her to Japan, the years hadn't been kind to the former star.

"He looked as though crows had barn-danced around his eyes – the black sheen of his hair had gone to salt and pepper. Franck O'Day, idol to millions, was not aging well. Not well at all. He was going to be forty-three, but he looked fifty, already, if he looked a day."

Lori told me that his change in appearance hadn't mattered to her – he was still her beloved Franck, and after she cornered him in her hotel room, on that first visit to Japan –

"He stayed with me for the entire night, and it was glorious. In the morning, he looked five years younger. An outdoorsy forty-five, still older than he actually was."

Lori paused and looked pointedly at me. "It was the energy, you see, Carolyn. All my love and adoration, all my longing – it just detonated, the moment we were together, like an atom bomb. All that energy, all my love – the good people there in Japan had taught Franck how to utilize it, to absorb it. They taught him the life-giving power of it. The love and adoration of others. It was like a nutritional sustenance for him. He'd told me that he'd summoned me to Japan because he needed some of the money that he'd willed to me. But that wasn't it at all. He didn't need money. He needed *me*.

"I stayed for a week. Then, he put me on a plane and sent me back to my mother. He promised to write, and he did. I begged and pleaded to be allowed to return to Japan to see him again. And about every five years or so, he granted me permission.

"Franck always looked the same – a rode-hard-and-put-away-wet fifty. But he always looked five years younger when he put me back on the plane.

"This went on for *thirty years,* Carolyn. Every five years or so, Franck would permit me to visit him in Japan, to shower him with my undying adoration. He would allow me to give him the energy of my love.

"As time went on, my health began to fail. Not long after I returned from seeing Franck in 1996, I was diagnosed with a heart murmur at the ripe old age of forty-five. The doctor was concerned – I told him blithely that I was in love, that it was simply the rejoicing of my heart that he heard through his stethoscope. I always felt lighter than air, poetic and free when I returned from visiting Franck. Emotionally, anyway. Physically, I usually felt like crap, which is why I'd paid a visit to the doctor in the first place.

"The doctor was not poetic. He recommended against any exertion; he recommended against travel. I told him that I wouldn't be traveling again for another five years.

"When I returned from visiting Franck in 2001, I almost died from congestive heart failure. Collapsed right there at LAX. I spent nearly a month in the hospital. The doctors debated whether I should have a pacemaker implanted – in the end they decided against it. I was only fifty – far too young for such a procedure, surely. They were convinced that a little more exercise, a little better diet, and I should be all right. One doctor told me to quit smoking. I didn't smoke. It seemed that my poor heart, which so loved and longed and pined for Franck – was just not up to his actual physical ministrations.

"I glossed over my health problems in my letters to him. But Franck knew. I had read the look on his face when I'd stepped off the plane in 2001, even before I came back and collapsed. Even in 2001 – he still looked like he was fifty. Sure, maybe a little tired, a little worn – but it was a little tired and worn *fifty,* not the sixty-eight I knew him to be. I was fifty – but I was an *old* fifty. I looked older than him. My face was lined. I'd gone gray at thirty-five, then white.

"I'd dyed my hair blonde when I went to visit him in 2001, but it looked bad on me, unnatural. A little old lady with Marilyn Monroe's hair. I saw the look of disappointment on Franck's face, the minute I got off the plane. But still, he entertained me like he always had, and if there was a little distance, a little pulling away, a fleeting look of disgust on his face, I tried to tell myself that I was imagining it. He still loved me. He told me that every time I boarded the plane to come home. And I certainly loved him.

"When the time rolled around for me to visit him again in 2006, there was a surprise. Franck had decided to return to the States. I picked him up at the airport, drove him to a hotel, where he already had reservations. I tried to show him how glad I was to see him, in my most favorite manner. Franck took me by the shoulders and gently told me no. He was concerned for my health, he said. Such activities were not good for people with heart problems. His concern seemed genuine – the idea that I was a shriveled-up old bag, and that he was disgusted by the very suggestion, hardly showed in his eyes at all. He still looked an outdoorsy fifty or fifty-two."

A few months after Franck's return to California, The Egyptian Theatre in LA showed a weekend marathon of all of Robert Ecksmith's movies. Lori said, "Bobby did some great work, almost all of which is still respected and discussed – if not, The Egyptian wouldn't have undertaken a retrospective of his films. But the film in which Franck O'Day appeared is neither respected nor discussed too much anymore, unless it's to deride Bobby's misstep, to ask, *What was he thinking?* But once the derision is delivered, everyone, universally, recognizes Franck's stellar contribution to an otherwise utterly forgettable film. The small crowd that sat through it in its dismal three am time slot were not there to experience its director's genius, therefore. They were there to see Franck.

"Without a shadow of a doubt, the thirty or so people who were there to see it – young women like your friend, old women like me – a cadre of drunken homosexuals – they were all dyed-in-the wool Franck O'Day fans. No one else would have bothered with such a terrible film at such a terrible time, even for the purpose of making fun of it. Franck sat in the back of the theater and basked in all the adoration that was aimed at his image on the screen.

"He looked ten years younger when I saw him the next day. And *Manhattan* is screened all the time at one or another of the little theaters downtown. It was even shown with the *Oscar Contenders of The 1960's Film Festival,* even though it wasn't even nominated. I didn't see him for the whole two months that one ran. I think he was probably at the *Marmont,* reliving the glory days, when he wasn't in the crowd, incognito, absorbing the adulation.

"When he came back, he looked like he does now, except for a little puffiness, which I put down to attending all those late show times. The film wasn't really nominated, after all, so it still played late. He was again a well-preserved forty or forty-five, like you see him now. And it was all a result of the energy he gathered from all the fans watching *Manhattan.*"

Then Lori had sighed, again mentioned Ruthanne. "Franck has the reflected love of his fans, and since he's met your friend, well . . . I think my time with him has passed once and for all. I can't say it wasn't a good run, though."

I did not believe for a second that this woman would give up the one love of her life that easily. But if Franck wasn't having any, then he wasn't having any. What could she do about it?

Yep, Lori's sad tale of the movie star that got tired of her, coupled with my dream of him murdering her and Ruthie and all those other people at the VFW Hall in order to recover his youth, had served to make me afraid of Alvee and his gift for a long time.

And now, looking at Mikey and Armand, I feared again. I glanced helplessly at Maury, but he was enjoying the floor show on the screen. *It was great when it all began, I was a regular Frankie fan . . .*

I remembered his words, when he'd spoken of Alvee's unlikely friendship with Michael McCown: *What you have to ask yourself, of course, is – what does Alvee get out of it?*

I peeped over my shoulder at him. Flawless, gorgeous Alvee Smith-Killem, looking not a day over a delectably healthy thirty-five, sat between two old men.

Maury's words again: *Admiration, to those of us who know how to assimilate it, is like a drug, my darling. It doesn't have to be returned to be useful.*

Was Maury trying to subtly make the same point to me that Lori had proclaimed? That loving Alvee was dangerous to one's health, if he didn't love you back?

(The director should've known better than to use subtlety with me – it had never been one of my strengths.)

Steve nudged me, smiled, whispered, "Is this pot great or what?"

Another fear gripped me. "It's not – there's nothing mixed –"

He shook his head. "Nah. Just regular cannabis. But I know the right people."

He turned his attention back to the screen, and I realized that he was right: I still had a powerful buzz going on. It wasn't helping me to sort out all the crazy ideas that had popped into my mind.

But I tried to think it all out. My life was awesome, perfect, a dream come true. I had not a care, not a doubt in the world. It was just this common drug that was bringing back all the old suspicions. I couldn't again question Alvee's gifts. I couldn't go back to distrusting him. I loved him.

Maury loved Alvee, too. In Japan, he'd taught his muse the ancient secrets, for no other reason than that he *did* love him. But if any of this was true, even slightly – perhaps Maury was telling me that he lamented the uses Alvee'd put them to.

Alvee's devotees . . . Mike, Armand, *Lori*. I recalled that the director hadn't cared for Jessika's daughter, however, any more than he'd cared for Jessika.

"And then there was Lori and her tedious yearnings, finally fulfilled after entirely too long. Lori didn't love Franck either, any more than her mother did. Jessika never really loved anyone but herself, and Lori had simply *wanted* him for too long to ever really love him. She stewed, *fermented* in that desire, and it twisted her inside, Carol, like a deforming disease. Lori believed that her desire for Franck – her physical need for him – she believed that was love.

"You should've seen her when she'd to come to visit him, when she'd to come to Japan. The look on her face – ravenous. Frightening." Maury shuddered theatrically. "Like a sailor on shore leave, after way too long at sea. Oh, how Lori wanted Franck, how she needed him!" He rolled his eyes. "Between the sheets, anyway. Other than that, Lori didn't need or want much of anything. She was always a tough, self-sufficient little girl. Just like her mother – her only weakness was Franck O'Day.

"But want and need are not the same as love, are they? Love is ethereal, eternal, air and fire. Want and need are like earth and water – too easily stymied and frustrated and turned aside by physical roadblocks. Want and need are like hunger, thirst. They demand to be satisfied, slaked.

"Not tonight dear, I've got a headache. No thanks, Bobby, I don't swing that way – these answers enrage want and need.

"But love understands. Love accepts that he has his own wants and needs. Love is just happy in his company. Love is happy to just look, doesn't always need to touch. To *squeeze.* Love is more than satisfied to have his lifelong friendship."

Maury smiled, paused. "But Lori wanted Franck for too long. She'd longed for him – and only him – for so long that the ache turned to selfishness. She thought she loved Alvee, but she really just loved what he'd finally, after so many years of impatient waiting, blah, blah, blah . . ." Maury rolled his eyes again. "Lori really just loved what he finally decided to do for her, *to her."*

No, Maury hadn't cared for Lori. But the director liked Armand Hambrick; his countryman's yen for Alvee was not unlike Maury's own. The only difference, really, was that Maury had his in check.

And inexplicably, Maury pitied Michael McCown. Even if he was a tiresome boor, at heart, he was just a dumb kid with a little bit of talent, who'd made bad career decisions. Hollywood had shunned him, but his good pal Alvee had been his lifeline . . .

Perhaps Maury didn't think either of them deserved the price Alvee charged for the privilege of loving him.

On the other hand, ya pays your money and ya takes your chances. If it was true that Alvee took what was offered and gave nothing back . . . Was he in any way to blame for their devotion? *Don't hate me because I'm beautiful.*

Steve giggled again and the thought crossed my handicapped mind that *he* certainly possessed no great love for Alvee. They were simply colleagues; any more, they were really just acquaintances. Maybe they'd been better friends when they'd done *Editor,* when they'd roomied together in New York, but Steve still harbored a childish resentment that his show had bombed after Alvee left. The fact that he felt a kind of dazed, jealous amazement at Alvee's effortless successes was unmistakable. Yet Steve was a mess, too.

Armand, no longer in the spotlight, again doing theater; Mikey, making movies that no American would ever see; Steve, hesitant to even step in front of an audience. Maybe it was stress and self-doubt that had wrecked the Englishman and the action star, just as much as they were wrecking the writer-producer-actor, he who was unwilling to act. Maybe Alvee didn't have anything to do with it in the least.

Maybe Maury wasn't trying to tell me anything. Maybe it was all just a product of my drugged, paranoid imagination, once again casting doubts where none should exist.

But on the other, *other* hand, Maurice Claremount had always been like the Delphic Oracle to me: he knew all. If he was trying to communicate to me that Mike and Armand's slide was the result of loving his muse, then I figured he knew what he was talking about.

But was he truly trying to tell me anything of the kind? Or was it just my imagination, recalling that old dream of death in Sin City, and sad, jilted Lori's words?

My mind went back and forth . . .

It was all ridiculous. Alvee had indeed been transformed by the energy of his fans' love in Las Vegas, but he hadn't killed them for it. It had just been a tragic accident, the result of the awesome power of too much love and admiration compacted into a tiny space, of Alvee's inability to assimilate all its electrical magnitude at once. It had made him young again, true, but the excess that he couldn't control had set the building ablaze.

Nor had he drained Lori of her youth and vitality by allowing her to exercise the sum of her teenaged fantasies upon him for decades.

It just didn't work that way. If someone loved Alvee, sure, he was able to absorb the energy of their love, to his benefit. But giving and taking are not hardly the same thing. Just because Armand and Mikey (and Lori) showered affection on him, that which he didn't return . . . Whose folly was that? It didn't mean that he *took* anything from them.

Some people just age better than others.

I remembered a report I'd been assigned in high school: tell the class about a famous writer. Wanting to be a writer myself, wanting to be hip and controversial, wanting to be *outré,* I hadn't chosen Kipling or Hawthorne or Mark Twain. I'd chosen Beat icon Williams S. Burroughs.

I learned that he'd lived a helluva life: homosexual, heroin addict, accidental murderer. And individually, not to mention congruently, these unimaginable excesses hadn't ended him before his time. For Burroughs, all the things that are supposed to put you in the ground young had not; he'd lived to the incredible, ripe old age of eighty-three.

Yet you've got your high school athletes, dropping dead at seventeen after football or basketball practice. Some people are just healthier than others; some are simply more resilient.

When she was in her sixties, Lori had looked it. And Armand and Mikey, well . . . in the crap game we all play with Father Time, they were just coming up snake-eyes a little sooner than most. My beloved had no influence whatsoever upon these facts of nature.

Perhaps I was reading more into Maury's insinuation than was there. Maybe the director was just peckish and spiteful because it annoyed him that Alvee didn't want to hang around with the has-beens we'd cast opposite him in *Diplomatic Opportunity.* Auteur and star undeniably had a difference of opinion about the flick – Maury thought it was *good,* or he wouldn't be making it. Alvee, I suspected again, had never liked it, and maybe he thought that appearing beside washed-up actors would limit his appeal. Maybe Maury wasn't referring to the physical transformation of Alvee's admirers at all. *I loved you! And what did it get me? Yeah, I'll tell you: a big nothing.* Perhaps he was only referring to Alvee's boredom with Armand's love, with Mike's friendship.

And maybe it was just another drug that had again dragged Lori Adamson back into my mind, with her ridiculous accusations that Franck O'Day had drained her life force from her, made her old before her time. The fact was, he'd simply grown tired of her devotion, *years* before I'd even met them.

But still, her story had painted a vivid picture. There she was, twenty-five, so thrilled to see her fantasy at last made reality. After I believed that he'd died in the fire, I had not pined for Franck as Lori had after the plane crash, but almost from the moment I saw him young again . . . Alvee Smith-Killem was like no other, exactly as he must've been when Lori had been a love-struck fourteen. I could understand her yearnings.

His rejuvenation was a supernatural miracle, but because of my dream of the fire, Lori's cautionary tale had stuck in my mind. She'd visited Franck every five years, and he'd never seemed to get any older, whilst she withered away, became a crone. Finally, he'd spurned her undying love.

Then Ruthanne appeared – as devoted as Lori had ever been, but *so much younger* – and overnight, Franck seemed to drop another five years, his hair returning from the gray of fifty (though he was eighty) to its youthful black . . .

But none of Lori's crazy allegations about his powers could've been true. They were merely the resentful products of jealousy. Maury had spelled that out to me once: "After Ruthie arrived on the scene . . . how Lori must have hated Franck then. Just like her mother did – she must've hated him and still wanted him in equal measure."

In all honesty, Columbia's complaint was indeed reminiscent of the youthful actor seated behind me, without any dark overtones whatsoever. Frank N. Furter didn't care that the redhead was devoted to him; despite her love, he'd quite purposefully moved on to other adventures. Similarly, Franck had broken it off with Lori years previous to his meeting Ruthanne; so he saw no betrayal in taking up with my friend. Like Aladdin's genie, it had never been possible for Lori to *make* Franck fall in love with her, and since he was bored and the opportunity to entertain someone new had presented itself, he'd acted upon it.

And Alvee could not possibly care less about Armand's burning desire to possess him, nor Mikey's smothering wish to be his buddy. Their very *presence* bored him.

All that was perfectly true, but this encyclopedia of dire meaning that I was cramming into Maury's bitchy comparison was simply not there. The sudden return of all the old fears was just the result of Steve's pusher's insistence on a little consciousness-altering, this time with a substance that brought the paranoid out in me.

I relaxed. My beloved did not *take, take, take, and drain others of their love and emotion.* He did not cause anyone to age prematurely, and the person amongst us that had loved him the longest (perhaps the most), had not been insinuating any such thing. I was just stoned.

I looked over my shoulder and smiled at Alvee. He winked at me, and I thought about the glorious confluence of love and youth-giving energy that would flow between us later, after the has-beens and the self-doubters left.

But because I was stoned, I let my imagination swirl forth in its eddying course. For the sake of amusing the stoned-but-no-longer-paranoid half of my brain, I supposed, just for a moment – what if it was all true?

I'd believed it once. After my dream, I'd recalled Lori's bitter story, and had allowed myself to suspect for a time that perhaps Alvee *could* take more than he gave. I'd given all that tiresome fear voice in my first journal. But then I'd ceased to consider it, because our years together have demonstrated the lie to it. Like Alvee, I haven't aged a day. The give and take of our energy, like Maury and Maki, is mutual. He takes nothing extra from me.

But still – what if it was true? Alvee loves me, but what if the adoration of those for which he does not care is like the sands of an hourglass to him? What if he stands there in the bottom, letting it rain down upon him – *take what you can, give nothing back?* What if, like an hourglass through which time has run out, the person that loves him is eventually left drained of youth?

If it's true – so what?

Surely, I love Alvee, just like a million women in a million theaters once loved Franck O'Day. How could anyone do anything *other* than love Alvee? He's a great actor; he's impeccable. Like Maury has said himself, "Have you ever seen anyone as stunningly beautiful as Alvee?"

Just like those millions of fans, like the director himself, I must say that I have not.

But's there a difference between me and Alvee's legions of fans, as well as between me and mentee Mike, and besotted Armand, and even decades-desirous-and-finally-rewarded Lori. The difference is, *he loves me back.*

Consummate fantasy to women (and men, too) Alvee Smith-Killem could've had anyone he wanted. Yet there was something he liked especially about little ol' me.

Maury's take on it: "Alvee knows that you don't harbor that abject, unshakeable awe of him, like a fan. You know he can do wrong. It's refreshing. All that glassy-eyed, speechless adoration gets old after a while. He needs someone who doesn't expect him to be on all the time."

(Maybe the shrewd director is correct: I'd never been a big fan of movie stars, like Ruthanne was, and I don't worship Alvee like one. I've never really been the worshipful type. Like Eminem says in that song Alvee likes, He's *just plain old Marshall to me.* Maybe that's why he loves me. Maury usually knows wherein he speaks

Whatever it is . . . Even though it might be demonstrable that I'm not the sharpest tool in the shed, I'm smart enough to know better than to ask Alvee why he loves me. As the old fable teaches, there's nothing whatsoever to be gained by dissecting the goose that lays the golden eggs.)

By Alvee's choice, all my dreams have been made reality.

In Japan, he learned to assimilate the energy produced by love and admiration, regardless of its source. But the energy that we share between us – it's like a joint bank account. The dividends of our love keep *both of us* young. Our assets are stable; we haven't aged a day. So why would I possibly care if he spends (on himself) the deposits that others make voluntarily? You could call that one of the multiple definitions of *interest.*

Alvee's not holding a pistol to Mike and Armand's heads, saying, "You *will* love me." If their devotion to him really has made them old before their time, seriously, why would I possibly care? I don't like either of them and neither of them like me. So why should I care about the fate of has-beens, also-rans, and ones *that love not wisely but too well?*

(I'm going to give up drugs, I swear, but damn, don't they make me clever?)

Even if it's true that affection for Alvee Smith-Killem is dangerous to your health when he doesn't return it, I have nothing to fear there. I am unique in the universe. I am a powerful, ageless creature's one and only, and he's mine. What more could a nobody from Riverside ask for than that?

There's no cause to go looking a gift-horse of such incredible value in its philosophical teeth. The magic of our shared love keeps us young. What may or may not happen to anybody else that also loves Alvee, well . . .

(God, I'm about to sound like Maury, because at the moment, I feel his haughty, jaded, worldly indifference. But sounding like the greatest director that I know personally is never a bad thing.)

What may or may not happen to others that love Alvee, well . . . that's why they call 'em *their problems,* is it not?

****

Maybe I should put this journal away in the same safe deposit box with the first one.

Since he balked at my idea about the nosy Vegas cop – since he doesn't want his story told, I'd put a different instruction on the envelope containing the key, however: *To be read along with the Last Will and Testament of Alvee Smith-Killem.*

Because we've all gotta go sometime, even him.

Maybe.

After the both of us have passed on, some aspiring screenwriter could use my journals as a treatment for a screenplay. Surely, they're a little wordy (maybe it could be a miniseries!) but real screenwriters (like Maury and Steve) know how to cut through too much description, how to get to the gist of things – they excel at *The Two Minute Drill*.

Somebody should tell Alvee's true Hollywood story. It has all the makings of a great movie: love fulfilled, as well as unrequited; tragedy, mystery, dark suspicions; the fickleness of fame. The ticket-buying populace would love it, just like they've always loved him.

Also by LM Foster

A Passing Resemblance
Contrariwise – A Tale of Twins
Corvino
Crypsis
Duck Feet
Peter's Sisters

Two Green Keys
Two Green Keys
Adapted for the Screen

One Wilde Ride Trilogy:
Part One: It Might Have Been
Part Two: An Exceptional Boy
Part Three: What Should Never Be

Stars and Guitars:
Talk To a Movie Star
Where The Guitars Play

Tom and Wiley:
This Carnival of Strange
Wiley Royce
Generally Recognized as Safe
Wiley Royce Versus The Martians

www.ingramcontent.com/pod-product-compliance
Lightning Source LLC
Chambersburg PA
CBHW070603130626
46556CB00001B/255